WEY BACK WHEN

(Wey Back in Time 1)

S. J. Blackwell

Welcome to the world
of the Weys ...

... and as a thank you, I'd like you to have a free copy of my standalone prequel short story, **The Wey We Were.**

All you have to do is click on the link at the end of the story, and let me know where to send it.

You can also find me pretty much anywhere you might want me here on Linktree.

I've written stories since way back when, so my husband, who loves creating and recycling, decided to build me a den at the bottom of our garden – a quiet, magical space where I could escape to write. If it wasn't for his hard work, I don't think I would have gone back to this idea and started writing again. So this one's for him.

To my wonderful David - Thank you for my tiny house.

FOREWORD

You might notice something special about the chapter headings in this book. Head over to Spotify, search for *Wey Back When* and immerse yourself in the music while you're reading the story.

CONTENTS

My Fam

(plus a few olds)

<u>2019</u>

Maisie Wharton - me. Nothing to see here.

Jasper Lau - my blud, bestie, BFF. Hates cramped spaces, likes designer labels.

Ani Chowdhury - my other BFF. More brains than a *University Challenge* reunion party. Weird, but in a good way.

Elizabeth Wharton - my mother. Works at my school, Drake's.

<u>1987</u>

Lizzy Brookes - Little Miss Reckless. My mother, in about fifteen years.

Scott Kelly aka Patchouli - Lizzy's buff older man.

Glenda and Henry - Lizzy's rents. My nan and granddad.

Paul - Lizzy's biker big brother. My uncle.

Dave - his biker 'mate'.

Rowena - Paul's latest crush.

Rob Simmons - hottest boy in the second millennium.

Valerie - his mother.

Kim Fox - Little Miss Runaway. Lizzy's BFF and part of her squad.

Nigel - her dad.

Mary - her step-monster.

Tracy Rutherford - Little Miss Sorted. Lizzy's squad.

Elaine Longhurst - Little Miss Flirty. Lizzy's squad.

Claire Cook - Little Miss Serious. Lizzy's squad.

Ian Hills - Mr Cool. Lizzy's squad.

Brian Walker - Rob's best bro. Lizzy's squad.

Will - his brother.

Neil Thorpe - Elaine's latest crush.

Marguerite Copperfield - Headteacher of Drake's School for Girls.

David Tyler - Lizzy's form tutor.

Frank Bennett - caretaker of Drake's School for Girls.

Chapter One – I Don't Care (Ed Sheeran, Justin Bieber, 2019)

'You are on the cliff edges of time and space, Maisie Wharton, and you have no one but yourself to blame for it.'

I recognise the voice instantly. There is cold stone beneath me, and I know who I am going to see before I open my eyes. I can hear birds twittering, and smell the grass. I'm not at home. I'm outside.

'Am I dying?' I ask the silence.

There is no reply for some time.

'That is not possible just now.'

Say what? a tiny voice in my head says, so quiet I can hardly hear it. 'I can't die?'

'Open your eyes.'

The light hurts, but I do as I'm told and I turn my head. I see the women then: one in black; one in grey; one in white, standing in a line beside me. Their skeletal hands are outstretched over my body, which feels like it's lying on some kind of altar. Like a sacrifice.

Shit!

'If I'm not dying, why am I here?'

'Such a simple question,' one says.

'Such a complicated answer,' another says.

A few months earlier. 24th May, 2019

Legends. Some schools have poltergeists in the canteen that throw juice boxes at virgins every January the 17th. Other schools have gym equipment haunted by demon PE teachers, or apparitions that appear on the tennis courts in baggy white knee-length shorts, hitting green and rotting practice balls at Year Seven chests. Here at Drake's, we have the Old Library. People say there are ghosts. Some say there is worse.

Usually, I don't believe any of the stupid rumours I hear, but when the heavy wooden door creaks open behind me, I miss a few heartbeats. When something touches my shoulder, I almost scream my Skechers off.

'Maisie, it's only us!'

Hands shaking on my thighs, eyes closed, I take a moment or two getting my breathing back under control. 'I knew this.'

'You'll never guess what we found in there. You have to come look!' The squeaky excitement in my BFF Ani's voice is a worry.

Standing a little taller, I shake my head and look at her, acting all extra with her long, shiny dark hair waving about. 'I told you before. I'm not going in there with you. It stinks of pee.'

'There's no pee,' Jasper says, appearing behind Ani. 'Bits of old paper. Tick. Dust, tick. There could even be a few dead rats, but I can't smell pee.' He leans into me and nudges. 'Come and have a look at what we found.'

'You think there are dead rats in there? You're really selling it to me. Seen any ghosts yet?'

I'm not a fan of old things. I like trending things. I'm looking to the future; I'm not fussed about the past. I want to get my exams over and move on from this dump of a town. So you may well ask — if I'm not a fan of old things, why am I standing here keeping watch tonight by the door to the Old Library? Because I have two best friends who are total tools, that's why.

'We're not looking for ghosts,' Ani scolds me.

'Don't go in there alone,' I warble at them, with full jazz hands. 'Watch out for the Grey Lady! Books will fly off the shelves! Give the first floor a miss.'

Ani sighs. 'There is no first floor in the Old Library. You can be a real tard, Maisie. Just come and see what we found. Please?'

'Actually, you're right; it does stink in there. Have I got rat poo on my Vans?' Jasper says, leaning down to pick up a stick and poking gingerly at his shoe with it.

'Rats poo pellets,' Ani says impatiently. 'It's not like dogs' muck.'

'Smells a lot like it,' I say, my nostrils pulsing.

'Maisie, please come in here and see what we found,' Ani says, turning her back on the poo analysis. She's beginning to sound a bit whiney. This is never a good sign.

'Just tell her already, Ani,' Jasper says.

'What exactly do you want me to look at in there?' I shake my long dark hair at my squad in despair. 'The books? I've seen those books. The books in there smell of ancient and they make me want to vom.' I know this entire vintage retro is a thing, but it's so not my thing. Endless wet Wednesday afternoons in double History wrecked any interest I ever had in the past. I only took it for GCSE because my mother would have literally crucified me if I hadn't. Don't think I'm joking. You don't know her and you're the lucky one.

'It's a surprise,' Ani says, beaming. 'You have to come and see it,' she goes on. 'You won't believe us until you see it. And she said we had to watch it on the night of the Fundraiser.'

Here we go. 'Right. Who told you all this again?'

'This girl Orla I talk to in 13D.'

I shake my head. 'I can't believe you listen to her.'

'I had no reason not to.' Ani brushes a stray hair away from her face. 'She's in my set. She's been researching some background on the History of the school, and she told me that … What's the matter with you now?'

I'm shaking my head again slowly. 'Listen to yourself. You honestly believe Orla was telling the truth when she told you this place was haunted.'

'Not haunted!' Ani snaps. I wouldn't be surprised if she stamps her foot. 'I told you this so many times, Maisie. It's the stupid school legend that goes on about The Ghosts of the Old Library. That's just Year Seven stuff. Orla says the book talked about a pathway to other ages. And if you come and look — '

'Oh, other *ages*,' I say before she can get going again. I cover my cheeks with my hands and breathe. 'What are we talking about here then if not an episode of Hill House? Time travel?'

'Yes, I believe so,' she replies, her lovely elfin face still and solemn.

I sigh. 'You just sound like you need therapy, Ani,' I tell her, but I'm getting the feeling I'm losing this battle.

'There was a book in your Mum's office,' Jasper said. 'Ani said Orla read some of it.'

'And she was there reading this book because …'

'She got lippy with your Mum during class and then when she had to go up and explain herself, your Mum got called to some emergency in the canteen,' Jasper says. 'Orla saw the book on the shelf, thought it looked interesting. She picked it up and had a read. It talked about a passage through Time located in the Old Library.'

'You do need to come in and see this right away, Maisie,' Ani is pleading with me now, her hands tugging at the sleeve of my hoodie.

'I don't. Whatever you can see, it has nothing to do with an old book or a hidden passage. It's just garbage. My mother told me the staff made stories up years ago, to stop people trying to get in because the whole bloody building is collapsing,' I say the last two words as meaningfully as I can.

The Drake's School has been around forever, since some time in seventeen hundred and who cares. Every year we get the anniversary assembly, telling us the story of how the whole school got bombed out during the Second World War, and how it was all rebuilt in floor to ceiling glass, with coloured panels and chrome and the landscaped gardens we have nowadays. Everything was blown to bits, apart from the Old Library. That was untouched, apart from one little stone turret on its roof, which was broken by the blast. It's the oldest part of the school, with its solid grey stone walls and high windows; the turrets make it look like a tiny castle or even a church. We're not even allowed in the Old Library with supervision these days. My mother used to let the 'A' Level historians in there with hard hats and harder adults (usually her), but they weren't allowed more than three strides from the exit in case of emergency.

'It's a listed building, which means they don't want to let it collapse,' Ani persists. 'Your Mum's trying to get a grant to restore it. She's even putting the proceeds of this Fundraiser towards its restoration.'

The New Library is in the main block on the second floor. There are a few books in there, I think, but I don't do books if I can get away with it. The Old Library has nothing in it except books.

My mother took me inside once. There are books on dark wooden shelves painted with thick flaking varnish reaching up to the ceiling and right to the back of the room, more books in pokey little alcoves filled with wooden chairs and even more books on tables. I don't know why she bothered showing me, and I told her so. That went down like a sack of sick. As most things do, when the two of us are in the same room.

'It's going to take more than fundraiser money to keep this building upright,' I say, picking out a piece of loose cement between the grey stone bricks.

Ani looks back over her shoulder at the heavy wooden door as if she can hear something inside. 'Why would Orla make something like that up?' she asks, her face crinkled in confusion.

'Because maybe she's not a friend, Ani; maybe she's just a tool who wanted to mess with your head.' I draw her into a hug. 'Jasper and me love you, but you do get all high key about this sort of stuff, everyone knows it. Where is Orla tonight if she's so keen on solving this ancient mystery?'

'She's grounded.' Ani drew a little circle into the gravel path with the toe of her Skechers. 'Her dad said she couldn't come out because of the thing with your Mum, but all the old stories say that people come through on Fundraiser nights. Orla said we should come watch to see if the portal opens up.'

'You. Orla said you should come watch,' I say, feeling exhausted suddenly because, let's face facts, this is all getting a bit dumb. I nicked my mother's keys from the cabinet in her office because they wanted to go into the Old Library, I stood here mainly because I didn't want to go in there and also to make sure no one saw them; I got them in so they could have a proper look around. I love my squad so I did my bit, but enough already. 'I bet she's sitting at home on *WhatsApp* laughing her tits off. Let's cancel, Ani. We're hanging around this old shack on the strength of a few urban myths and a book that's probably non-existent. Let's go back to the bad DJ in the Hall and find who's carrying the contraband.'

'No.' Ani's mouth is set in a thin, determined line. 'I want to go back and watch to see if the lights come back on.' She then puts her hands on hips and pouts. 'Biatch! You made me spoil your surprise.'

I'm already walking away, and I stop mid-step. 'What lights?'

Jasper sighs dramatically. 'Finally, she gets to the point. She swore me not to say because she wanted to tell you first.'

'There was a light — right at the back of the alcoves,' Ani chatters quickly. That's what we've been trying to tell you. We didn't see it until we went right to the back of the library. We were looking around, and this light was pulsing around the edges of one of the bookcases, as if there was a room behind a door in the dark, with someone switching the light on and off. Then it just stopped.'

Jasper walks the few steps to catch me up and nudges my arm. 'Honestly, Maisie, you know I wouldn't mess with you. It was crazy weird. I thought it was the cider, but Ani saw it too.'

'Ani sees omens in the foam on a Costa skinny latte.'

'You're too mean to me,' Ani says petulantly. 'It was only that one time, and the froth looked just like a lightning bolt … Ow! Hey!'

Thinking back, she seemed to appear from nowhere, the girl running hard up the path from the Main Hall towards the Old Library and barging past Ani and Jasper.

In the fading light of the day and the dim light bulb over the doorway, I can make out the long, bushy red hair falling to the middle of her back, reflecting a zigzag pattern in the strands as they move around. She's wearing faded blue denim jeans, and a black T-shirt with Def Leppard emblazoned across her chest above what looks like a burning building with a sniper target. She has black Converse All-Stars on her feet, but she has black eyeliner and mascara that make her eyes seem unrealistically dark and the most high-key pearly, shiny pink lipstick I've ever seen on lips that are curved in an almost perfect 'O' of surprise.

She skids to a halt on the gravel, first looking up towards the Old Library, then back at us.

'Soz,' she says, her voice high. 'I mean, sorry about that. You okay? Can't stop,' she says brightly, her voice unnaturally high. Suddenly she looks embarrassed, and then she turns away and walks straight into the Old Library.

There are a few moments of silence. My brain is screaming silently.

'Sorry, but did I just see …' Jasper begins faintly.

'I saw her. I saw!' Ani bounces up and down and shakes my arms like she's waking me. 'I told you! There's a pathway to other ages in the Old Library! You saw her, Maisie. You can't tell me you didn't see her. That was no ghost. She bumped into me!'

I can feel them staring at me, but I have nothing to say. There doesn't seem to be words available other than to agree with them, and that way is the path to rehab.

So here's the thing. My mother is probably up in her office right now, like she always is at Fundraiser Discos. Doing her paperwork, making phone calls, being Elizabeth Wharton, the headteacher she's been here at Drake's for the past seven years. She was 50 yesterday. She looks like she had a bad night on the wine most mornings - but then most of the time she has had a bad night on the wine. She tells me I'm lucky she doesn't bathe in the stuff.

I had to bake her a big birthday cake, but as my cooking skills are sketchy at best, Uncle Paul had to help, and all the family, including my older brothers, are coming down for a massive party tomorrow. I can't imagine my mother at a party. She's so serious about everything. Her hair is cropped close to her head because she says she hasn't got time to do anything with it. It has big streaks of grey through it nowadays, and she's never dyed them out. I've never seen her wear tight anything, and she doesn't do makeup.

She ran into the Old Library just now, but she is different to the person who made our breakfast this morning, different to the one who shouted at me about my 'lack of commitment' to her revision timetable and the fact that I had no idea of 'responsibility' and it was about time I 'bucked up my ideas'.

As I stare after her, the girl reappears in the doorway of the Old Library. This is no ghost. This is a teenage version of Elizabeth Wharton.

My mother.

'Hey there,' she says awkwardly, 'I don't suppose you've seen my mates?

Chapter Two – Sweet But Psycho (Ava Max, 2019)

Mates?

'We've seen no one,' Ani says, a little breathlessly.

I'm leaning against the cold uneven stone of the exterior wall of the Old Library and from where I'm standing, I can see down the gravel path to where it splits into three: one way leading to the rear of the Main School Hall; the second leading left to the Social Sciences block and the third leading right over to the Performing Arts block. Even with the bass notes thundering out of the Main Hall, I can hear music coming from inside the Performing Arts Block. It seems like someone else decided not to spend the evening busting out moves on the dance floor.

As I'm deciding what to say in reply to this strange yet familiar image in front of me, I spot another girl coming up the path towards us. She stops and puts her hands firmly on her hips.

I'm struck dumb; I can't even. Her top looks like it shrank in the hot wash. She's wearing a jacket with pink pinstripes that looks like she's left a coat hanger stuck in the shoulders and a pair of trousers with massive baggy pleats at the waist that go down tight at her ankles. On her feet are a pair of bright red shiny stilettos with the skinniest heels I've ever seen.

'Brookes? Where the hell did you get to?'

The younger version of my mother breathes out heavily. 'Where've you been? I was looking all over for you, you prat!'

'We were only in the Hall. Have you heard that row?' Red Stilettos looks at me and then at Jasper and Ani. 'And who's this?' she asks, her eyes widening like side plates as she looks us up, down and up again. 'Future people? Past people?'

Younger Mother opens her mouth, looks us up and down, looks her up and down, closes her eyes, opens them again, shrugs and closes her mouth again. One day back in Year Ten History, some chode spotted her in an old school photograph on a wall on the third floor by the Computing Centre, and then that same chode asked her what Drake's was like when she was here as a student. By the time I took my GCSE, I knew more about the 1980s than I did about post-World War One Germany: Morrissey, Madonna and Michael J Fox; Rubik's cubes, rah-rah skirts and rave parties; new waves of British heavy metal, Bon Jovi and the Bangles; Spitting Image, Simple Minds, silk scarves and slam top wooden desks that still had stained inkwells in them.

I guess none of us has any immediate answer to Red Stilettos' question. Ani is just struck speechless. Jasper is still gawping at the new arrival's outfit; Red Stilettos looks like she's just walked out of a Michael Jackson video.

'Future people?' Younger Mother finally repeats through a snort, as if it's the most ridiculous thing she's ever heard anyone say. To be fair, it does sound pretty stupid. 'They're called bystanders,' she says as if that somehow answers a question.

'Okay, okay.' Red Stilettos looks at us, shrugs and turns back to her. 'You could've told us where you were, you skank,' she snaps. 'You bring us through Time, and then you piss off. We've lost Rob, and now Elaine's having another pink fit about Neil. She always listens to you Lizzy, so you have to come pronto. You know what she's like, she's a right -'

'Prima Donna?' Younger Mother finishes for her, and just for a second, there's a hint of the salty voice that she uses with me daily.

'You said it'd be like *Back to the Future* and it's nothing like. Have you heard the music in there? Sounds like someone's garrotting my cat. Even those blokes from Spurs sing better than that. And my granny dresses better than these people. They've got the bloody biggest telly I've ever seen by the reception desk, and it's completely flat! Why would they even have a telly in reception? Do people sit in the Entrance Hall and watch *The Sullivans* while they're eating their cheese sarnies at lunch? When exactly are we? Are we forward or backwards?'

Patting the girl on the shoulder with over-enthusiasm and laughing apparently to herself while glancing nervously at us, Younger Mother says, 'Don't get on my case in front of the new kids, sweetness. Where's Brian? Is Elaine out the front with Claire? Let's go find them.'

Red Stilettos steps back and gives me a critical once-over. 'Does everyone dress like you nowadays?'

Younger Mother thumps her on the arm. 'I told you. Don't talk to them.'

'What were you doing here talking to them then?' Red Stilettos thumps her back. So Younger Mother laughs, and then they're both laughing, and a voice in the back of my head suggests they sound a lot like Ani, and they may not be on medication, but hell do I need some right now.

'We have to go now,' Younger Mother turns back to face us

and speaks slowly as if she thinks I'm stupid.

'That's just … peachy,' I hear myself saying, my voice sing-songing away. Peachy? Where did that come from?

'Sweet,' she says, and the bright smile through her teeth is anything but genuine. She clearly thinks I am the biggest tool in the village. I feel like it right this instant.

Red Stilettos totters off. Younger Mother gives me another untranslatable look, and then they're both headed back towards the Main Hall, to the crowds of people who will take one look at them and wonder where all that hair came from.

'Why did you just say you felt like a peach?' Ani says.

'Why did she call your mum Brookes?' Jasper says.

'What's a pink fit?' Ani asks.

'I'm experiencing catastrophic mental health issues,' I tell them, groaning.

Ani claps her hands like a little kid in a play park. 'This is lit! Can't you guess what's going on?'

'Explain it like I'm five?' I suggest.

'The pathway to the other ages opened, and your mum and her friends came forward from the past,' Ani says as if it's obvious to everyone except me. 'I told you; it isn't ghosts that people see! It's time travellers! That girl in the red shoes said they'd come through Time! I bet your mum's name was Brookes before she got married, wasn't it?'

'You're a total tool,' I say.

She looks at me, folds her arms and waits.

'I don't think I'm well. It's the stress of the exams, making me hallucinate. I need water.' Something stronger, if I could get my hands on it.

Ani continues to look at me, but now she's tapping a foot

on the gravel.

Reluctantly, I decide to temporarily accept the flawed evidence of my eyes and buy a return ticket for the madness train. 'Forward from the past,' I repeat. 'From where exactly?'

'From wherever they were when your mum looked like that, at a guess,' Jasper says. We all look at each other.

'Is this a good thing?' I ask.

Jasper says thoughtfully, 'In all the films I've seen, it's never good to meet your other self.'

'You mean like Mrs Wharton bumping into her younger self as she comes down to the Main Hall to interrupt the DJ, and give her uplifting speech about raising funds for the restoration of the Old Library?' Ani asks.

As we arrive panting at the back door to the Main Hall, I realise our immediate concern about my mother being recognised isn't such a big issue as in the lack of lighting even I couldn't spot her - but because I can't see her, I can't know whether she's still in the Main Hall.

'No one will recognise anyone in here,' I say out loud, 'it's too dark.' Jasper pulls a face. We push our way through the dancers and the hangers-around-the-doorways and find our way into the entrance hall. There's no sign of Younger Mother or her friends out the front of the school. We come back into the entrance hall, just as my real mother appears at the foot of the Main Block staircase.

'Mrs Wharton?' Ani blurts out. 'Yes! Yay! Mrs Wharton.'

Because it is my mother, that is, this is the actual Elizabeth Wharton I know, the woman who has helped to raise me for nearly 18 years. Two of them on her own, although she's not got around to changing her name back; the divorce hasn't come through yet, and she says she's too old to be Lizzy Brookes these days. She's coming down the stairs, complete with her iron-greying hair and under-chin bristles. Okay, I'm mean, but she's my mother, she doesn't have to look good. In fact, I'm a lot happier with this hairier version than the one that just ran out of the Old Library. That version of her was even scarier than usual.

She makes her way over to us, sensible heels clipping on the floor tiles, just audible over the muffled music from behind the Main Hall doors. She's wearing smart black trousers, a white floaty blouse, a yellow fitted jacket with a brooch in the style of a purple rose, a pink and purple scarf at her neck and glasses on a chain hanging down over her chest. Her outfit screams headteacher to anyone who isn't sure who she is, and to me, she screams retro. I swear there are still shoulder pads in that jacket. So embarrassing.

'Hello, Ani. Jasper.' She looks me up and down, disapproving as ever. 'Maisie, I've just messaged Paul on *WhatsApp* to confirm — he's happy for you to go over after half term to study.'

'Mum, I don't need to go to Uncle Paul's to study. I told you this before,' I mutter. Much as I like Uncle Paul, I've got plans that don't involve me being minded by a lawyer who's even older than she is. That way lies no respite from revision for weeks.

She puts her glasses on and peers at me over the top. I hate it when she does this. I swear she only needs them for reading anyway, but she wears them all the time. 'Yes, you do,' she snaps, 'or you'll just spend the week on your phone *Facebook*ing or something.'

'I don't use *Facebook*,' I mutter.

'You won't get into Exeter if you don't get your grades, Maisie.'

'I don't have to go to Exeter, Mother. Just because Lucas and Blake are both there. Just because *you* went there. I told you I liked Brunel.'

'We'll discuss this after the party.' She cuts me dead with a wave of her arm. 'You're coming in to hear my speech, I hope?'

Jasper is looking anti-, but I figure this is more down to the fact that he knows his breath stinks of booze. Ani wants to hunt the weird people. I'm with both of them on this one, but you don't say no to my mother.

'Sure,' I say brightly. 'Just need to pee first.'

She gives me a hard look and gives Jasper a roll of the eyes. 'There had better not be any alcohol on these premises,' she snarls, shakes her head and walks off into the Main Hall.

As the doors slam behind her and the noise levels return to bearable, we look at each other.

'Hard as nails, your mother,' Jasper says.

He has no idea. Well, maybe some. 'So where to look now for the intruders?' I ask. 'They aren't out the front where they said they were going.'

'Your real mum's safe on the stage. For now,' Ani says.

'We should split up and try and find your other mum and her mate,' Jasper says. 'I'll take Social Sciences.'

'I'll stay here and keep watch on her in the Main Hall,' Ani says. 'I quite enjoy the Fundraiser speeches.'

As I said before, Ani is cray. 'So I'll take the PA Block then,' I say, and we split up, without checking what we do if we find

Younger Mother and Red Stilettos again.

As I walk further away from the disco towards the building, I realise there's more music I can hear. No, not music as such. Drumming.

The door to the Performing Arts Block is closed but not locked, and the drumming is louder as I open the door and walk in: someone's snuck in for a bash on the school drum kit.

I step into the tiny entrance hall. There are only two classrooms on this floor, and the drummer is in the one on the right: the Music room. The only light is coming from the floodlights outside.

As I walk further in, the drummer stops briefly, sticks held up. A head turns, short dark hair on top sticking up with the ends all white; I catch the flash of teeth in a smile, and after no more than a couple of seconds, the arms drop and play on.

After a few minutes, the drummer says, 'Most people can't be arsed listening to me practise.' Male, by the deepness of the voice.

'I was looking for someone,' I say.

'Don't spoil it,' he replies, looking down, but I can hear the smile in his voice this time.

'Are you at Drake's?' I ask.

There are boys here, like Jasper, in Year Twelve and Thirteen. It's not easy to tell in this light, but this one looks old enough to be at Drake's. I take a few steps closer to the drum kit, and I can make out faded denim jeans, and a pale grey AC/DC tour T-shirt.

He laughs. 'I'm guessing you must be. I'm at FCAB,' he says. 'I'm Rob.'

'Maisie.'

His nose twitches a little, and it's hot. 'Like in the *Dukes of Hazzard*? No, that was a Daisy, wasn't it?'

'I don't know what you're talking about.'

'No, I don't suppose you do,' he says. I'm not sure how to reply, so I don't. He nods in the direction of the Hall. 'I'm not really into that music. Do people really listen to that kind of thing these days?'

He's smiling at me, and I can just make out the cutest dimple in his left cheek; even with the strange bleached ends to the spiky hair he's hot, but he's not my mother, and I reluctantly admit to myself that I'm supposed to be looking for her. 'Everyone has their own thing, I guess. Look, I really should go back.'

'Why?' he asks.

'Neither of us should be in here,' I say. 'We should be in the Main Hall. We'll get shot if one of Drake's staff catches us over here.'

'No one's come to check on me so far. Apart from you.'

'I've got to get back to my squad.'

He shrugs. 'Okay. Mind if I —?' He nods down at the drum kit.

'Oh no, 'course not. You want me to — ?' I nod my head at the door and close my eyes. You are a tool, Maisie Wharton. Now you're finishing sentences with your head instead of your mouth.

He looks down at the drums. 'It was just cool to have a different audience for a change.'

'Oh,' I can hear in his voice he thinks I think he's crap, and somehow it matters to me that he knows I don't. 'No, I'd like to stay and listen, honestly. It's not that. It's just I need to find my friends.'

'We can go find them together if you like. I've lost my mates too. Let me just tap out one more song. I can't walk past a kit like this.' He gives me an apologetic grin. 'Stay a little bit longer?' he adds, and his eyes twinkle at me, green like glass.

It can't hurt to listen to him play a little longer, can it? Everyone else will be in the Main Hall listening to my mother's speech, and so I smile, sit on a nearby speaker and check my smartphone as he starts to attack the drums again. There's a low signal, new notifications and messages but nothing unusual. I glance at the time — a quarter to nine. Before I've even registered that he's stopped playing, I can hear an unexpected squeaking coming from the back of the room.

I look up into large high windows that face out over the back of the school tennis courts, over the playing fields and beyond to Fletcher Clark's Academy and jump out of my skin. 'Crap,' I say, pointing up at the face at the window. It puts two fingers into its mouth, pulls each corner in the opposite direction, and pokes its tongue out at us. 'Who the hell is that?'

'Oh, that's just a mate of mine, licking the windows,' he says, carelessly, 'but what is that?' He's left the drum kit, and he's beside me, not looking at the window: he's pointing at my smartphone, looking confused.

'What is it?' I ask. 'Jesus, you look like you've just seen a ghost.' I shake my head. Everything is becoming v weird again. 'It's a *Ten R* two fifty-six gig. Early birthday present. Only got it today. Sorry, did you say he was *licking the windows*?'

As I watch, the boy licks the window with a vertical swoop of his tongue, and as suddenly as he appeared, he's gone.

Rob, the drummer, seems more bothered by my phone

than by the window-licker, and it doesn't look like my description helps in any way. He looks like he's about to ask something else but, in the next instant, Jasper and Ani are falling in through the door, looking like they've just run a half-marathon.

'They've gone back into the Old Library,' Ani pants. 'We're going to miss it. You've got to come. Now.' She takes a beat as she sees I'm not alone. 'Who's this?'

'Rob,' I say unhelpfully. 'Likes AC/DC and has a bro who licks windows?'

'Don't say that; Ani will want one,' Jasper says, with a grin more at Ani than me.

'These people in your Old Library — is one of them a red-head in a Def Leppard T-shirt?' Rob asks.

'How did you know that?' I ask sharply.

He looks uncomfortable. 'Not sure you'd believe me if I told you.'

Oh no. Not him as well. This is not happening to me.

Ani pulls a face. 'Are you coming with us or not?' she shouts at me from the doorway, and this time, I'm sure she does stamp her feet before she disappears.

Before I can reply, Rob has run past me through the door, and Jasper has followed him out. 'Looks like we're all coming then,' I mutter to myself, following them.

Like I said before, there's a lot of wood and dust in the Old Library. And okay, it may not be the stench of pee exactly, but it's not a smell you'd buy as a room freshener either. It's all books, and brown shelves up to the windows that sit right at the very tops of the walls covered in grime and cobwebs, with high ceilings that disappear into the darkness above. The red and brown patterned rugs on the floor curl up at the corners, and there's a clock above the doorway, the type that clunks with every minute that passes. At least it would have done if it was working, but it broke decades ago; my mother told us about it in one of her embarrassing road trips through History. Light, and faint sounds of voices and music from the outside are coming in through the high windows. No one can see in from out there.

I can just about see Jasper and Ani halfway down the dim room, peering around the edge of one of the window-height bookcases. I can hear conversation further down towards the darkness at the back of the room.

'No, we need to get back, Elaine, then you can sort it all out.' A female voice. Younger Mother?

'You can't sort it out! No one can!' Someone gives a high-pitched snotty sob.

'Why do we need to go back so soon, Lizzy?' A different voice. Male.

A pause. 'We made contact with too many people. I got a bad vibe about it.' Another pause. 'I only found out about all this today! I don't know what I'm doing.'

'All right, keep your hair on.' Definitely Red Stilettos.

Another male voice. 'He's probably just busy with the band, Elaine.'

Another sob. 'I told you! He doesn't want to know!'

'Why was Brian licking windows again?'

'Search me. I tried to play it down. She was cute.'

'Oh please. We have no idea where we are. She could be a hundred and seven.'

'Or not even born yet.'

Another sob and a cough. I can't work out how many of them are here.

'How exactly does this all work again, Lizzy?' Another female, less hysterical. 'Your mum told you it was to do with temporal shifts?'

'Pretty, isn't it?' Again a female voice, quieter. 'The door. What did you call it?'

'Let's go back, okay? We all need to relax. It's been a bit of a rollercoaster.'

'This place is Nutsville. Did you see what they were wearing it was all so *dowdy*.'

'Just hold hands already.'

'Lizzy? Where is Brian?'

'He's here, isn't he?'

There's a sudden flash of purple light, which makes me turn away, then deafening silence which makes me peer back around my bookcase.

'Maisie!' Jasper hisses. 'Get down here!'

I'm next to them in an instant, and we all move forward until we're standing at the back of the Old Library.

Hidden around the end of the last bookcase is a rectangular frame of purple light pulsing around what appears to be a doorframe, set into the wall. It's partly disguised by the fact that it is mainly shelves of books, but it looks like a passageway through to a lighted room. This light is what Jasper was talking about earlier, and he's right. You wouldn't be able to see it from the main door into the Old Library, and it is beyond weird.

'They've gone,' I say.

'This is totally lit,' Ani exclaims.

'Where did they go?' I ask.

'We need to go through while the light is still there,' Ani is literally jogging on the spot next to me. 'Come on!'

'Go through what to where?'

'We won't know unless we follow them,' Ani says. 'They must've gone through there.' She points at the glowing purple light in front of us.

'Through there?' I ask faintly. She nods. 'That is totally nuts,' I say. 'I'm not following anyone. Especially not into a freaking bookcase.'

Ani sighs as if I'm the one with the problem. 'It's not a bookcase.'

'I'm not following those tools into a freaking whatever.'

'One of those tools is your mum,' Jasper points out.

'My mother before she was a mother,' I point back.

'It's a portal,' Ani says calmly. 'It'll take us through Time.'

'I don't want to be going through Time!' I drag my fingers down the sides of my face in frustration. 'Listen to me! You've got me talking your crap now! There is a perfectly sound explanation for this.'

'So where are they then?' Jasper mutters.

'Shut up!' I snap at him and sigh. 'Okay, say you're right, and it is a portal? We've got no way of knowing where it goes, or if we can get back again! You must be a complete tard if you think I'm jumping into a purple bookcase!'

Suddenly, there's a rush of air behind us. I turn and see the boy who licked the windows in the Music Room sprinting down the centre of the Old Library like a gazelle.

'You joining us for the big bang?' he asks, grinning like a mad clown, and he pushes past me and just seems to be absorbed by the bookshelves and the purple light, and I'm so shocked as I watch him disappear that I stumble and lose my footing, and I grab onto Jasper's hand to steady myself, and I guess he yells and grabs onto Ani to try to stop us all falling, but it doesn't work. I'm lurching forward, and the next thing I know is we're tumbling against the bookshelves, and incredibly, my arm *sinks* into the books as if it's simply a projection of the real thing, and suddenly, there's white heat, purple light, black — nothing.

Chapter Three – Down To Earth (Curiosity Killed The Cat, 1987)

I'm lying on my back when I open my eyes. I move my hands, and I wriggle my feet. It takes a few moments to check that everything is still working and that I don't seem to be bleeding or broken the way I think I might be.

I look around the Old Library. Jasper is lying beside me. He looks peaceful. He doesn't look ill or hurt, but something here is definitely different. Ani is slumped up against another bookcase, but the one with the glowing purple frame is still there behind us. The window-licker has vanished. It's just us.

I sit up straighter. There's the long wooden table in the middle of the room, and there's the same smell of age. Daylight filters in through the high windows. A few more textbooks are scattered across the peeling varnish of the table.

A cold finger strokes the line of my spine. Did I say daylight?

My stomach starts churning, and I'm not entirely sure I won't hurl. The room hasn't changed, but it is different in a way I can't immediately place and there is sunlight outside.

Jasper stirs. He rolls over, and I shake him gently. He groans.

Ani starts and sits bolt upright. 'Did we fall asleep?' She looks around the room. 'Did we fall over?' She points at the bookcase behind me, framed in its strange purple light. 'Look, the light's still there!' She's right. The purple light is faint now with the sunlight streaming down through the windows; you can hardly see it, but it's there.

I'm not convinced I'm not dreaming.

Jasper's sitting up now, stretching, then rubbing his hands over his face. 'How come it's morning?' he whines, pointing at the lightened windows. 'Did we crash here all night? How come no one found us out?'

I shrug. 'Maybe we hit our heads when we fell against the bookshelf.'

Ani pulls a face. 'If we fell against the bookcase, why did we only hit our heads?' she asks. 'Why didn't we go through like they did?'

'Look at that calendar on the wall. 1971? That's well old,' Jasper gets unsteadily to his feet and walks across to a page of dates pinned to the wall nearby. 'And look at those posters on the ends of the bookcases! Why put posters in a room nobody uses any more? How come I never noticed those posters when we came in?'

'It was dark,' I say.

He walks across the room and runs his fingers over the shiny paper. 'These feel like new.' He turns to face me. 'They're not new, though. The closing date of this writing competition is back in the 1960s.'

'We found the portal, your mother and her friends turned up, and they went back through that.' Ani sighs like a steam train arriving at its destination, gazing dreamily at the faint purple frame. 'I guess we can still go through it. If the light's on, it probably means it's still active.'

I rub my fingers against my temples. 'I'm completely over

your investigations, Ani. 'I just want to go home and have a shower,' and, as she huffs at me, Jasper's back flat down on the floor again, pulling me down with him and Ani pushes herself against a wall.

Hearing the footsteps makes us all freeze. I hold my breath until the steps pass the door and fade into the distance. The clock on the wall above the door clunks on another minute.

'Must be the caretaker,' Jasper whispers. 'We should get out of here.' He pulls the smartphone out of his pocket. 'I'll be grounded until I'm 20 for this. I bet Mum's been calling for ...' He stares at the screen and taps it a couple of times. 'Crap. Dead battery. That's not going to help. I need to get home. I'll be in so much trouble.'

I pull my smartphone from my pocket. No signal. I'm on my feet as Jasper's still trying to will enough juice into his phone to send his rents a grovelly text. I'm looking around the room. I see different posters and timetables. There are names of clubs on the wall, lists and dates of musical concerts. There are dates for discos from decades ago, posters for events long before I was born and requests for volunteers to pick up litter. Maybe we didn't see them before because it was dark. Maybe we didn't see them before because they weren't here before.

I still remember some of my mother's History lessons about her school days. As I read the headlines on some of the posters, it's like watching a familiar film through a dense mist that's beginning to clear; Chess Club 1967, a short-story writing competition run by a local radio station in 1975 and a newspaper cutting of girls who won prizes for various subjects in 1980. Now I can hear voices, faintly in the distance. Coming closer.

A bell rings violently in the corner of the room.

Jasper and Ani both turn to look at me as if they are puppets controlled by the same string.

'What in the name of hell?' Jasper says. 'It's Saturday, isn't it?'

'We better get out of here. Now!' I hiss.

'Why?' Ani asks.

'I don't know,' I tell her. I think I do, but I know we have to leave.

The Main Door is unlocked, and we manage to get away from the Old Library and onto the grassy slopes that spread out from behind the main school buildings up to the playing fields we share with FCA, where we watch a group of girls in uniform walk up the path from the main buildings.

Me, Jasper and Ani watch them, and then we stare out over the playing fields we share with Fletcher-Clark Academy. It used to be Fletcher-Clark's Academy for Boys back in my mother's time, and this was Drake's School for Girls. Nowadays both schools have boys and girls in the final two years, so it's just FCA and Drake's.

'Since when did Drake's run lessons on a Saturday?' Jasper says. 'I didn't know we did that. No one told me about that. I don't remember reading about it in any e-bulletins. Are they doing catch-up lessons this weekend? Why didn't anyone tell me to sign up?'

I look across at him, my confused thoughts not ready to issue a statement to my mouth yet, and before I can speak, he laughs, a bit hysterically. 'We really did sleep there all night, didn't we?' he says again. 'The caretaker's so crap here. He probably never thought to check the whole site over before he locked up last night.'

I can hear a few birds singing over in the Park. The flesh at the base of the back of my neck creeps a little under the warm sun.

Ani giggles and claps her hands together. 'First, we were scared because we saw the light, and next we saw them,' she squeals, 'and your Mum was young, and then they got away, and now it's day time and the disco has gone, and there are lessons on a Saturday and there's a poster about the Fundraiser in 1986! We didn't hit our heads! We've come through the portal!'

In the following silence, I can hear voices; girls are starting to sing an Irish folk tune in the Block behind us.

Jasper is looking at me. 'Is she stoned?' he asks, pulling his hands over his forehead and down over his cheeks.

I pull a face. A vein in the side of my head is starting to throb. 'I think we just took a taxi to Crazy Town.'

'We're in the past!' Ani dances on the spot like she needs facilities.

'Oh, get a grip, Ani,' Jasper's brown eyes are bright and unnerving. 'I went along with this fantasy of yours last night because that was bloody strong cider, but right now I need to get home and hope my parents let me go out again before Uni starts.'

'If we're not in the past, which teacher is that then?' Ani asks.

I turn around, and she's pointing at the tall, slim man striding across the grass towards us. He can obviously see us, so I can't see any point in running and making matters worse. The others seem to agree, as they're not moving either.

'What are you all doing out here during Fourth Period?' he snaps.

'Sorry, Sir. We're new here,' I say, looking at him closely.

'So. New girls should be in their *new* form rooms with their *new* teachers having their *new* lessons during Fourth Period,' he says patronisingly. His words snag on my brain; there is something I've forgotten, and something I've noticed at the same time. 'What're you doing here during school hours, boy?'

As out-of-focus memories of photographs sharpen in my head, I feel goosebumps on my arms like the sun's gone in when it hasn't. I've seen this man before. On a photo on the third floor near the Computing Centre. This man is David Tyler, and he's...

No. No, this isn't possible. Except it is possible, and it's a pretty reasonable explanation, considering the chaos.

'I'm new too, Sir,' Jasper gets to his feet, catching on quick.

'You're trespassing, young man.'

'Trespassing? No, Sir, I'm starting in Year Thirteen here.'

Tyler's eyes dim to the colour of thunderclouds. 'What kind of American rubbish is that? Don't get smart with me, lad. This is a girls' school, and unless you're hiding breasts under that top of yours, you don't qualify. And since Fletcher Clark wouldn't let you through the doors in what you're wearing today, I suggest you vanish sharpish before I inform the police.'

I believe it's suddenly crucial that we can't become separated. The posters in the Old Library? Night suddenly day? A single-sex Year Thirteen? David Tyler talking to a male student about having breasts? I can't believe it's taken me so long to nail this down. Toto, we're not in Kansas anymore.

'Sir?' Jasper's face is screwed up in confusion.

Ani, in her pure genius, is pink with joy as the truth dawns for her. 'Bugger me backwards,' she says. 'I told you. We really have come back.'

'Any more of that language and you're in detention, Missy!' he snarls.

David Tyler looked quite fit in the photo on the third floor, for an older guy anyway. This guy is more like some kind of Victorian teacher dinosaur. 'The receptionist lady,' I say frantically, pulling everything my Mother ever taught me about her school days out of the depths of my brain, 'I can't remember her name – she told us to go to the ... Upper Sixth Common Room?' The words feel like Mandarin on my tongue. 'She said ... the Head had asked Lizzy Wharton to show us around.'

'Lizzy Wharton?' he repeats disagreeably. 'We don't have a Lizzy Wharton at this school.'

'She's in your class, isn't she? Sir?'

His eyes narrow and darken to the point that I can't see what colour they are anymore. 'There is no Lizzy Wharton in my form.' He swivels back to Jasper. 'Do you know that trespass on school property is a criminal offence, lad?'

'Brookes!' Ani drops the word like it's the F-bomb.

Tyler looks around slowly, scowling. 'It would appear that your friend requires a Remedial Department,' he says, in a tight little voice, 'and we don't have one of those here at Drake's.'

Ani has come good, and I guess now isn't the time to argue about unacceptable labels with this asscloth. 'Lizzy Brookes,' I correct myself. Of course, my mother would still have her maiden name. I'm such a tool. 'Not Wharton. Brookes. We were told to find Lizzy Brookes.'

'And you thought you would find her up here because you

thought our Sixth Form Common Room was on the playing fields?' He raises both bushy eyebrows expectantly.

'I guess we got lost,' I say limply. I look at Jasper. 'This is my - brother,' I say hesitantly, with words and ideas forming as I speak them. 'He's just come to accompany us to school?'

Tyler's tight face loosens a fraction. 'I see,' he says, clearly seeing nothing. 'This is very irregular, but Lizzy will likely be in the Sixth Form Common Room. Which is in the Main Block. Third Floor. Back there. Not out here!' I storm back onto the path that leads down towards the Main Hall, Jasper and Ani scuttling after me. 'You're lucky it's the end of term!' Tyler yells after us. 'I'm watching you!'

I don't know why that's lucky, or even what term it's the end of, but I'm thankful that he doesn't seem to be all that bothered about watching us; he seems more bothered about lighting the cigarette he's just thrust into his mouth.

'What's going on?' Jasper asks as we walk quickly down the path towards the Main Hall. 'Who was that teacher? I didn't recognise him. Why did he say it was the end of term? Why did he tell me I was trespassing, and why was he going on about bloody America? Is Ani right? Have we travelled back in Time? Tell me she's not right.'

I'm still moving so quickly they can barely keep up. 'Look, can we just get inside, so we don't draw too much attention to ourselves?' I ask. Some hope.

'O.M.G. You do think she's right,' he wails.

Once we're out of sight of David Tyler, I take off my hoodie and pass it to Jasper. 'Put this on, and keep the hood on. Keep your head down and stay under the radar.'

There must be something in my voice that tells him it's

dangerous because he does as he's told. Or maybe my mother's authoritative bark is hereditary.

There's one more thing I have to check with the helpful lady behind the Reception Desk. She's tucked away in a room little bigger than a caretaker's closet where you can actually go in there with her and close the door. Afterwards, we're climbing up the two flights of the stairs that lead from the far end of the Entrance Hall, trying to keep our heads down, trying to ignore the giggles from the girls who pass us as we go up to the third floor and off to the left. I feel strangely calm, even if it sounds like someone is screaming inside my head.

Through tiny windows crosshatched with thin black lines in the classroom doors, I can see the wooden flip-top desks, lined up in front of the scratchy rolling chalkboards that my mother told us she was expected to scribble notes from before the teacher wiped the lot off and filled another board for them to copy. She told us she only decided to study History at Uni because her teacher used something futuristic called a Banda machine that was like an old photocopier. The class got notes handed to them at the beginning of each lesson so they didn't have to write anything much down, and the Banda sheets smelt like vodka so she reckoned they were high by the end of each lesson and convinced that they enjoyed History.

And now I think I'm up to my neck in it - her history.

I turn and face Jasper and Ani. 'That teacher was called David Tyler. He was my mother's form tutor when she was at Drake's. He's in the photo of her class here on the third-floor staircase. In 2019.' I stand outside the plain blue double doors, take a deep breath, and push into the Common Room. We walk inside. As the doors bang together a few times behind us, I stand still and take in the scene in front of me.

'Oh. My. God,' Jasper says weakly.

'We don't go to this school anymore, do we?' Ani says, her eyes wide and excited.

The calmness I was feeling vanishes. I'm freaked out by everything that's in front of me. FML. 'No,' I say. 'My mother does.'

Chapter Four – Back And Forth (Cameo, 1987)

I close the doors quietly behind us. We don't have Common Rooms at our version of Drake's. We have a big area we can chill in; it looks nothing like this. I can't see any tablets or laptops here, neither even a single PC nor an IWB. This is the Upper Sixth Common Room, and the people here are different from the ones who would've been here when it was the Computing Centre yesterday.

The place is pretty empty, except for maybe 20 girls. There are no boys. One girl is sitting in one of the workstations at the back, her head bent over a pile of textbooks. She looks around at us with a scowl as the doors finally thud shut, and then she starts scribbling on a large notepad.

One of the girls is Red Stilettos, who we met last night outside the Old Library. She's dressed differently now, sprawled across a large table by the windows, wearing a bright green T-shirt over white leggings and black gym shoes. She's doing scissor kicks as she flicks through a magazine with a man called Simon LeBon on the front, and the words *Just Seventeen* printed along the top in white. It's 45p. I can't think of anything that I can buy for 45p these days. Those days? My days. Maybe a small chocolate bar.

There's another girl in the corner, painting her nails. She looks like she's spent hours on her make-up, and her foundation must be an inch thick. She's singing to herself. The tune is familiar but old.

Another girl is sitting on the floor surrounded by sketches torn out of scrapbooks and postcard-sized pictures and photographs of paintings by artists I can't quite place from my Art classes. Lichtenstein? No, Warhol. Her eyes are watery though as if she's been crying recently.

Another girl in the room makes a big deal out of stepping over the mess, her arms full of fabric, dropping the F-bomb as she nearly slips on a *Campbell's Soup Cans* print. Younger Mother.

'FML,' I mutter.

'Where are we?' Jasper says quietly beside me.

'We're in Mrs Wharton's school days,' Ani says breathily.

'It's changed,' Jasper says. 'In here, I mean. Isn't this the Computing Centre?'

'It looks like my doctor's waiting room,' Ani said. 'That's so dope!'

'Where are all the computers? Oh, I suppose they didn't have any.' Jasper says. He pauses, taking in the absence of technology. 'We really have travelled back in time. I didn't think it was possible.' Suddenly, as if recovering his thoughts, he turns on Ani. 'This is your fault!' he hisses. 'What are we going to do now? How are we going to get home?'

I turn and face them, drawing them closer to me so no one can hear what I'm about to say. 'Whatever's happened to us, it's not going to help if we burst in and say 'Hi! We're from the 21st Century!'' I hiss. 'You understand me?'

'Of course not. They're more likely to ask us what drugs we're taking if we say that,' Ani says contemptuously.

'There are no guys here,' Jasper says, drawing the hood of my sweater a little lower over his forehead.

'If I'm right, there are no guys at Drake's for years,' I say quietly.

'You okay?' Her voice is unmistakable. Lighter, maybe, and a lot less polished. A lot more like last night.

I turn around, expecting her to realise that she already bumped into us last night, but there is not the slightest glimmer of recognition in her eyes.

'Fine,' I say slowly, drawing the word out.

'Good,' she mimics me, drawing the word out. 'So what's with the hard stares?'

'We're new,' I say.

'We met you last night, don't you remember us?' Ani blurts out before I can bring her up to date with my latest theory.

Younger Mother pulls a face like she thinks we're mad. 'I wasn't even out last night.'

'Bet you bloody were,' Red Stilettos calls from her table throne. She swings her long legs onto the grey tiles and walks across to us, hips swinging. 'I tried to ring you three times, and every time Glenda said you were in your room studying. Like that's even likely.' She waved the magazine under Younger Mother's nose. 'You were off tarting with Patchouli, weren't you?

'I bloody wasn't!' Younger Mother answers, with a smirk.

'Don't expect any of us with brains to believe you, Brookes. We all know that bloke is sex on legs, he's just too damn old and he's trouble.' Red Stilettos smiles at us, bringing us in on the joke she seems to be making. 'Thank the Lord for you lot. Today is well boring, and you just made it less so, new girls. Are you coming tonight?'

'Tonight?'

She pulls a dumb face. 'Fundraiser Disco?'

'There's another Fundraiser tonight?' I blurt out before I can stop myself.

Red Stilettos pulls another face, bounces onto her impossibly long legs and stretches. 'There's one every year. This is the most important event of the year so far! End of this pants term! Start of study leave!' She pauses. 'Well, the most important event until tomorrow night, of course.'

The clouds lift slightly from Younger Mother's face. 'It's going to be the business tomorrow,' she says.

'White jeans tonight, I thought. And I've got this great pink top with cap sleeves,' Foundation says from her nail painting. 'I look great in pink.'

'Thought I'd go in -' Younger Mother looks down and grins. 'Jeans and a T-shirt?'

Red Stilettos sits on the edge of one of the tables. 'That's hardly a pulling outfit, Liz. You got to raise your game if you want a piece of Rob Simmons, girl.'

'Rob Simmons wouldn't care if I was buck-naked. Anyway, I've got other plans.'

'I knew it!' Red Stilettos squeals. 'He's too old!'

'Oh get off my back, Rutherford, who made you my mother?'

'So are you coming to the Fundraiser?' Andy Warhol asks us kindly. 'It'll be a good place to get to know people. You can come with us. It's a rotten time of year to start a new school.'

'You want to borrow something of mine to wear tonight?' Foundation says. 'I got loads of pink stuff. I love pink.'

I am not pink. I have never been pink. I grab Red's magazine from where she's abandoned it on the desk and scan the front cover quickly. '1987,' I say, sure for the first time. 'This is 1987.'

Younger Mother rolls her eyes. 'Space cadets,' she says, and she walks away. It feels like another slap in the face.

'No, don't go,' Ani says. 'The lady downstairs on Reception _'

'Mrs Thompson?' Red asks.

'Yes, Mrs Thompson – she told us to come up here and that Lizzy Whar … Brookes would look after us.'

Younger Mother turns and shrugs and folds bare arms across her plain black T-shirted chest. 'Don't know anyone called Lizzy Warbrookes,' she says.

Red punches her in the arm. 'Don't be a tart,' she scolds, 'they're obviously foreign. Look at what they're wearing for a start. American?'

I look around at my collegiate hoodie on Jasper and at Ani's Fitch T-Shirt. I shrug, and thank whichever gods are listening that there're no dates on either of them.

Younger Mother's mouth curls in a sneer. 'They don't sound like Yanks.'

'We're British, but we were in the States for a few years, yes,' Ani says carefully as if she's working out each idea as it becomes a word. 'Together. We're cousins. The family all came back at the same time.'

Foundation waves her fingers in the air like jazz hands as her nail polish dries. 'Introduce us to the new girls then, Lizzy.'

'I don't know who the hell they are,' Younger Mother snarls. Ani reaches out and gently pushes my chin up so that my mouth closes. I will *not* cry. I *will* not cry.

'I'm Maisie, that's… Jane and this is Ani.'

'Like 'Annie - I'm Not Your Daddy?' Cool,' Andy Warhol says. 'And Daisy like in *The Dukes of Hazzard*?'

'Just Ani. And Maisie,' I say.

They look at me blankly.

'I'm Tracy,' Red says, and I feel bad that I thought so poorly of her last night when she's making a real effort here. If I wasn't already confused for England by all this, the fact that neither she nor my mother recognises me when we met last night is preparing me for the World's Most Confused Person Championships. 'That's Elaine with the make-up,' Tracy goes on. Foundation girl smiles and waggles her fingers. 'The sour puss is Lizzy. The messy one on the floor is Kim.' Andy Warhol looks up, waves and goes back to her prints. 'And that's Claire, up the back, already cramming.'

Some node in the darkest cobwebby corner of my brain is twitching. I remember these names. *Tracy, Elaine, Kim and Claire.*

'No, I'm *trying* to study, or at least I would be if you lot didn't keep on bloody yapping all the time!' the girl with the pile of books shouts without turning.

'Can it, Claire, we've got ages to the exams,' Elaine says dismissively.

'Two weeks!' Claire shrieks. 'Two weeks before mine start!'

Then it hits me. Double History on a wet Wednesday afternoon with Mrs Elizabeth Wharton, my mother and the headteacher of Drake's School, telling us about her life as Lizzy Brookes. How one of them – it must have been Kim – had drawn cartoons of the five of them in the back of her sketchbook: Little Miss Flirty; Little Miss Runaway; Little Miss Serious; Little

Miss Sorted and Little Miss Reckless. She'd never told us who was who. I'm already working it out.

I glance down at the mess on the floor and wonder if the sketchbook poking out from under a purple print of Marilyn Monroe already has the drawings inside.

Tracy draws a circle with her index finger near her right ear. 'Total basket case. Why she can't cram like the rest of us beats me. What're you taking?'

'Physics, Psychology, Media, History, and Class. Civ,' Ani says automatically. She's definitely the brains of our squad.

'Sorry, you're taking how many A-Levels?' At the back of the room, Claire is almost steaming with anger. She slams the book shut and comes over to us.

Elaine nearly spills the contents of the varnish bottle all over her white jeans. 'What the hell is Class. Civ?'

'Classical Civilisations?' Ani says, uneasily.

'Bollocks. How come they get to do cool stuff like Media and Classy whatever when all we get is Latin and German? This place is the pits.'

Tracy strokes Claire's arm like she's calming an excitable puppy. 'Don't mind our Claire. She's always going on about how old the syllabus is at Drake's. Even FCAB started Media Studies this year. Sorry, that's Fletcher Clark's Academy for Boys – the school over the other side of our playing fields. It looks like a museum.'

'Hogwarts,' Ani says.

'No, it really does,' Kim says, frowning.

'Those poor kids in the fourth are all going to suffer. How the hell are the teachers supposed to know what they're talking about with these new subjects?' Claire says. 'They've only had two years to learn the syllabus and get them through it.'

'Brand new exams?' I ask faintly.

'The GCSE next year?' Tracy says.

'Bloody guinea-pigs, that's what they are,' Elaine says.

Claire gives us a look full of pity. 'Fancy having to move house just before your exams. That sucks.'

Jasper and Ani look at me for help. I shrug. How come these people are speaking in English, but none of it makes any sense?

'Is it lunchtime soon?' is the best I can come out with.

'You got classes today?' Kim asks.

Ani shakes her head. Her brain is much bigger than mine. 'They said there wasn't a lot of point.'

Tracy nods. 'At least they got that right.'

'So Thompson said *Lizzy* had to show you guys around?' Elaine says it as if it's the most incredible thing ever to be suggested.

I look at Lizzy Brookes. She's slouched against one of the desks reading the magazine, but she's looking at me, and I nod uncertainly.

She slams the magazine down on the desktop and sighs loudly. 'That cow Thompson's had it in for me ever since she caught me nicking Tippex from the stationery cupboard. I can't be doing with all this crap. Who's coming out for a fag?'

They all look at us.

'Smoking's disgusting,' Jasper says quietly from beneath his hood.

'So shoot me,' Lizzy snarls. 'Another babysitter.' She rolled her eyes theatrically. 'Bollocks. I don't just get lumbered with the new kids; I get lumbered with evangelicals. Don't tell me, you don't drink either?'

A bell rings loudly in the corner of the ceiling.

It's at this moment that I feel like something is breaking inside me. Something is crumbling, and hurting as it crumbles but, in its place, something else is being built. This girl isn't my mother. This is the girl who *becomes* my mother, and there's no room in this living nightmare for sentimentality. Not that there was ever much sentimentality between Elizabeth Wharton and me. Whatever has happened to me, Jasper and Ani, I have to deal with this version of my mother as she is now.

I find my voice. 'I need a piss. Lizzy?' She cocks her head and fixes me with a bored expression. 'Go suck on your cancer sticks. We can find our way around without your help if it's such a problem for you.' I glare at Ani and Jasper, who now look like someone unhinged their jaws.

Tracy snorts and grins. Elaine makes a point of staring very carefully at a painted fingernail. Claire rolls her eyes; Kim pulls a face and looks at Lizzy.

Lizzy Brookes looks at the floor, the tip of her tongue appearing through her gritted teeth the way I've seen it so many times when she's struggling with a dilemma. Then her shoulders sag, and she looks me straight in the eye. 'Smokes can wait. I'm starving. Let's go and get some scoff. We'll show you where the canteen is. The loos are out the door you came in, down the end of the corridor on the left.'

'We'll wait for you to come back,' Tracy says, a smile touching her lips.

'I've not got time for lunch,' Kim says from her sea of artwork. 'Can someone bring me back a filled roll? Cheese and cucumber?'

'We're catching up with the gang after,' Elaine said. 'Don't you want to see Ian?'

Kim blushes so pinkly she almost clashes with her yellow T-shirt. 'No,' she says, tossing a lurid print of a soup can over her shoulder.

'You okay with seeing Brian?' Tracy asks Elaine.

She sighs. 'I'm yesterday's news.'

'This is unbelievable,' Ani says, once we've established that the loos are empty. 'We are in the past! The Portal in the Old Library opened up, and we are in the past with Mrs Wharton and her friends! I told you,' she says gleefully, rubbing her palms together like a little old man. 'I told you.'

'My mother - Lizzy,' I correct myself, 'and Tracy don't recognise us. I know nothing about history and time travel, and I want to refuse to believe any of this, but the only explanation is that if Ani's right, we've come through to their time before they made it through to ours. The date on that magazine was May 20, 1987.' I pause to do a few calculations. 'My mother turned 18 on May 23rd this year. So Lizzy is in Year Thirteen – or Upper Sixth they seem to call it here.'

'Fundraiser this year – I mean, our year - was May 24th,' Jasper says, 'Are we repeating May 24th?

I look at Ani: she's the historian. 'I'm not sure, sorry,' she replies.

'Do you think the Fundraiser Night is significant to the Old Library opening up?' Jasper asks. 'That's what all the stories used to say. The ghosts always appear on the night of the Fundraiser.'

I run out of the loos, down a flight of stairs, peek through a classroom door and at a noticeboard, and then run back to find Ani and Jasper haven't moved. 'Tracy said the Fundraiser is tonight, and there's a poster on the wall on the next landing down. It's May 22nd today,' I say. 'So Lizzy's 18 tomorrow.'

'So they will come through to 2019 from this Fundraiser tonight?' Jasper asks. 'We have to go back with them then.'

'Well, that's just great. As if the first Fundraiser wasn't bad enough; now we have to go to another one?' I sigh.

'Don't knock the Fundraisers. Tradition is important. My mum and dad met at a Fundraiser disco, you know,' Ani says proudly. 'Anyway, this one will be lit. It's in the past! Think of all that '80s music. And the fashion! Like fancy dress, but for real!'

'I can't think of anything worse,' I mutter.

'Fancy dress? I can't even show my bloody face properly here!' Jasper almost looks excited, but he's more terrified than anything. 'Aren't people going to notice us? Won't people notice we've vanished from 2019?' he adds quietly. 'What if our families think we've gone missing? Will they tell the police? Send out search parties?'

'I don't know the answers to any of this,' I say. 'Ani?'

She shakes her head and shrugs. 'Just because they came through to our Fundraiser, it doesn't necessarily follow that they left on the same day in their time.' She sighs. 'We haven't come back to the same day, have we? I wish I could talk to Orla about it.'

Why Orla is important right now, I don't have the time to discover, or to rummage through Ani's very complicated brain. 'Okay. We'd better get back in there. We'd better stay close to them while we decide what to do.'

'We'd better try to act normally,' Ani says.

'Like you'd know anything about normal,' I say. She giggles at me and pokes her tongue out.

'How the hell do you expect me to be normal?' Jasper mutters. 'I'm the only guy in an all-girls' school!'

'Some boys would view that as an opportunity,' Ani says, grinning.

'I'm not some boys.' Jasper rolls his eyes at her, and then his face falls and he stops walking. 'If people find out I'm a lad, they'll take me away and try to call my family. Right now I don't have one. We must stay with Lizzy and the group. It's the only way home for sure.'

The school canteen hasn't changed a whole lot since we visited last, but the menu has, and the prices.

'Soup and a roll?' Jasper says, after reading the chalkboard by the door as we walk in. 'That's lunch? I've not had anything to eat for over 30 years!'

'Soup and a roll for 25p though.' Ani shakes her head. 'That's very cheap.'

'Could be soup and a roll for 5p for all it matters, we don't have any money,' I point out. 'Nothing that would be accepted here anyway.'

Tracy comes over with a tray holding four white bread sandwiches on green plastic plates and a green bowl of nuclear orange soup. A Persil white roll sits on another green plastic plate, and there's pink sponge with an iced top with sprinkles on it. 'Ham sarnies, cheese sarnies, tomato soup (school speciality) and a roll, and tray cake. I had a few dinner tickets saved up,' she says. 'Figured you wouldn't have been issued with any yet. Elaine's used a couple of hers as well.'

Suddenly sandwiches, nuclear soup and pink sponge feel like a feast – I haven't eaten either since my mother did me a microwave Spag Bol about 32 years from now.

Lizzy appears at Tracy's side. 'You don't need to worry about dinner tickets,' she says, 'Mum'll sort them out.'

'You could've said before I used them up!' Tracy mutters.

'You never asked.' Lizzy gives us what could be translated as a kindly smile. 'My mum's the Head Cook and Cleaner here. I told her you're new.'

Lizzy's Mum. The grandmother I have never known; she died before I was born. I feel the tears rise in spite of my determination not to show myself up. I'm not sure I can face all this.

'Mum! This is the new lot!' she shouts, and I turn, and I find myself staring tearily into the eyes of yet another family member.

Chapter Five –You're The Voice (John Farnham, 1987)

'These are the new girls?' Lizzy's Mum asks, wiping her hands on a tea towel draped over her shoulder.

She's maybe a bit younger than my mother is back in My Time; there is no grey in her hair; it's shiny brown like a polished conker shell and cut to curve under her jaw. Under the green cotton-serving apron, she's wearing a pink blouse with a huge embroidered collar, and trousers that seem to be the same width from the tops of her legs to the floor. Her voice is high. It reminds me of the way Lizzy sounded when she saw us outside the Old Library. Last night. 32 years in the future. My brain is sizzling.

'I'm not good with names,' Lizzy says, sweeping her arms to either side of her.

'I'm Ani. This is Ja … Jane, and this is …'

'Maisie,' I say before she can finish.

I'm staring into Lizzy's Mum's eyes. I'm transfixed. I'd heard so much about Glenda Brookes, and I'd always wondered what it would've been like to meet her. Ask her about what Lizzy was like when she was a child, since accordingly to my mother, she was a perfect daughter and a model student.

Strangely, she's staring just as intensely at me. Someone was bound to comment.

'Well, this is lovely.' Lizzy rolls her eyes. 'When you've quite finished eyeballing the new kids, Mum? You're grossing every-one out.'

Nan actually shakes her head as if she's trying to clear a vision or a thought. She looks like someone's murdered her pet dog. 'Sorry, yes. Have you all got enough food?'

I shrug, looking at the lunch for eight on Tracy's tray. 'I think so.'

'And they are taking good care of you?' she says. 'They're making sure you're well?'

'So my Mum's having an eppy, and we're all going to ignore it, aren't we? Good,' Lizzy says, rocking her long auburn hair away from her face. 'You got enough food? Good. Let's go and find a seat before I shrivel up from the embarrassment.'

'Glenda's really kind,' Elaine with the painted nails says as we all traipse after Lizzy towards an empty plastic table for eight. 'Lizzy's Mum, I mean. She looks after people all the time. Especially Kim. And don't think the kind streak missed a gen-eration, either. It really didn't.' She puts a plate of chocolate sponge covered in thin pink sauce on my tray. 'Don't worry about Lizzy. Her bark is worse than her bite.'

Never a more accurate word, I would've thought before, but I say nothing.

We all sit down at the table, and the hard wooden-effect plastic bench scrapes across the floor as we settle. I take a grateful bite of white bread with plain ham; a massive slab of real butter melts on my tongue, and it is total heaven.

Claire, the one who was studying at the back of the Com-mon Room, is staring at Jasper. Jasper is trying really hard to eat his sandwich without dislodging the hood. 'Are you cold?' she asks him suddenly.

Jasper glances at me and shakes his head, but it's no good. She's drawn attention to him, and they're all looking now. Tracy tilts her head to one side. Lizzy is actually peering across into his face.

I see the light bulb moment before Tracy speaks. 'What did you say your name was?' she asks.

'Jane,' he replies, but his voice sounds like it belongs to a five-year-old. He's tried too hard.

I watch Lizzy and Tracy exchange a look. Tracy's eyes are twinkling; Lizzy's are suspicious. 'You want to tell us why you smuggled a fella into our school today?' Lizzy mutters, but there's a hint of a smile on her lips.

'Oh yeah! So he is! Quite a dishy one too,' Elaine adds with a toothy grin.

I've got no response. I only thought to hide Jasper from the teachers, not from the girls. If they all realise there's a boy in the canteen, will there be a riot? Fortunately, Tracy and Lizzy seem to understand this. Elaine is looking excited, and Claire is scowling with disapproval.

'This is our cousin Jasper,' Ani says in a voice I can barely hear.

'Lovely to meet you, Jasper,' Elaine says, all shiny. 'Have some of my pink sponge.'

'Yes, it's super-duper to meet you, Jasper, but this is a girls' school,' Tracy says. 'What're you doing here, mate?'

'He ... didn't have anywhere to go today, so he had to come with us,' Ani says, and she sounds about as convinced of her story as I am.

'Are you starting at FCAB?' Claire asks.

'Yes – but he wasn't allowed to start today, and there was

no one at home to look after him, so he had to come to school with us ...' My voice wilts into the virtual tumbleweed that is rolling around our table.

'You're not allowed to stay home alone?' Lizzy asks, her face slightly crumpled in confusion.

'My parents are bare strict?' Jasper tries to take some responsibility for our failing story, and I don't expect them to buy it, but surprisingly, they seem to and they nod knowingly.

'Why wouldn't they let you start at FCAB today?' Elaine asks.

Salvation comes from an unexpected corner. 'Everything okay with the food?' Nan asks.

Lizzy looks at her like she's covered in dog muck. 'Fine,' she says.

Suddenly, it's all getting a bit much, all of this. Why am I sitting in a canteen that still looks like it was put up during the Second World War as a bomb shelter, eating artery-busting sandwiches with teenage tools while Lizzy sneers into her soup? We should never have gone into the school after Tyler spoke to us. We should have gone straight back to the Old Library and jumped back through that portal-or-whatever-it-is and hoped to whichever God was listening that we could get home again, and that's precisely what we need to be doing now.

'We need to go back to Reception,' I say aloud. 'To sort out some ... paperwork.'

It takes a while to convince Elaine that we don't need to be accompanied back to Reception. Tracy says they'll eat our puddings for us.

On the path leading round to the back of the Main Hall and

the Old Library, Ani is whiter than Tracy's leggings, and Jasper is panicking.

'Do we really have to go back so soon?' Ani says.

'Yes, we bloody do,' I snap. 'I did not buy a ticket for the Crazy Train last night, I bought a ticket for the Fundraiser Disco in 2019, and that's where I want to be.'

Jasper says, 'That girl with the bright pink lipstick was going to skip the sponge cake and eat me for dessert instead.'

'Aren't you just a teensy bit curious though?' Ani stops in front of the two of us. A couple of kids in lower school uniforms nearly walk into her and then scuttle away. 'You've just met your Mum when she was young! And her friends! And your Nan! It must be awesome!'

'It's not awesome.' I can feel the emotion pushing at the back of my throat, but I swallow it down hard. 'I never knew my Nan; she died long before I was born. And that girl ... Lizzy Brookes isn't my mother. She might be my mother in the future, but right now, she's just a snarky biatch.'

'Harsh,' Ani says lightly.

'Not harsh. You saw the way she spoke to us. Like we were worse than shit on her trainer. How in the hell did she ever end up teaching kids?'

'I'd say she's a lot like I'd expected,' Jasper says. 'Your mother has balls of steel. Well, she would have. She's mean to people back here, and she's mean to people in our time too. And everyone still smoked in the '80s.'

'I didn't mean for you to get all salty about this,' Ani says, her eyes wide and concerned.

'I am not salty!' I snap, and then I sigh. 'We shouldn't be here, Ani. You've had a look around 1987; you've proved your point. Can we just go back to the bloody book tomb now and find our way back to normality?'

'She's right, Ani.' Jasper puts a consoling arm around her shoulders. 'We can't stay.'

She huffs and puffs, but she doesn't argue with us.

The thick wooden door to the Old Library has always reminded me of a church door I saw when I was a bridesmaid for my Uncle Paul. I was only tiny, which is probably why I didn't refuse to wear the massive orange dress with puff sleeves and white ballet pumps, and anyway, Uncle Paul told me I looked lovely, so I put up with it. I've always liked him – his eyes twinkle behind his glasses like he used to be naughty – but these days he gets all serious with me about the importance of passing my exams.

Ani pushes against the door. 'I can't move it,' she says.

'You need to turn something,' Jasper tells her, but apart from a big black iron ring in the middle of the door itself, there is nothing to turn.

'No, it's probably locked,' I say. I reach into my pocket and fish out the key that I stole from my mother's office. But when I try to put it in the keyhole, it doesn't fit.

I try it several times: upside-down, switching left and right, but it's no good. This is 1987, and this is a different lock. My key doesn't work.

'It could just be jammed,' Jasper says over-optimistically, and he starts pushing his weight against the door (which to be fair isn't great; my mother used to say that Jasper was built like a whippet), but maybe his heart isn't in it; anyway, it doesn't budge.

What do I mean – My mother used to say? She still says it –

in the future. FML.

'What are you doing out here?' says a vaguely familiar voice from behind us.

Chapter Six – Weak In The Presence Of Beauty (Alison Moyet, 1987)

Kim, her arms laden with the artwork she'd carpeted the Common Room Floor with earlier, is looking confused. 'That's the Old Library,' she says. 'No one goes in there. Apart from the cleaning staff.'

'We were looking for Reception? To collect our dinner tickets?' Ani is doing her usual toe shuffling, and I'm not confident that her mind is going to hold through all this. She's not a good liar, which is usually a positive. Right now I don't hold out much hope for any of us hanging onto our mental stability.

'Well, you won't find any dinner tickets in there,' Kim says. 'I've got to drop off these prints in the Arts Block first, but why don't you come up to the top field with me and meet the others? You can sort out your tickets later.' We have no choice. She must sense our hesitation because she adds with a smile, 'We don't bite.'

Andy Warhol prints abandoned in the block that is now the home of Performing Arts, we walk up past the Old Library towards the sports fields shared by Drakes' and FCA. The girls who weren't so quick off the lunch bell are just making their way out the Top Gate; a low, white-painted farm gate with a blue sign beside it tells people they have found Drake's School for Girls. There are low brick pillars either side of the gate and equally low walls that tail off after about ten metres and would be next to useless at keeping anyone on or off the site. The crowds flow past a clear glass box cemented into the ground, with the word Telephone all fancy and a dancing piper etched onto it, over the road into the Park. Town's too far to walk from here in a lunch hour; it's a good two miles from the Park down to the centre, but if we go through the school down to the Main Gates onto the bottom road, take a left towards town and a quick right, there's a decent chip shop. I live out the back of the Park, on the edge of an estate that stretches right up to the Hospital grounds.

I can't see Lizzy or Elaine. Tracy and Claire are sitting on the grass talking to a boy I recognise. That's weird enough, but the thing is, he's standing next to the fittest thing I've seen in 32 years.

The window licker has bottle-blonde hair like Kiefer Sutherland in *The Lost Boys*. I'd not registered quite how buff his friend was when he was playing the drums in the dark Music classroom in 2019. He's dressed differently to how he looked last night; they're obviously both in uniform now. He's wearing a white shirt with a thin blue and yellow striped tie and smart black trousers, but he's got twinkly green eyes and this crazy dark stickup hair with bleached ends on top like he dipped them in lemon juice; a vertical ombre. I'd known he was hot, but in bright sunlight, he is fit AF. I guess he won't recognise me any more than these girls did.

'See those blokes standing with Tracy? The dark-haired one's Rob, and the other one's Brian,' Kim says as we approach.

'That blonde guy licked the window last night. In the PA Block,' I say without thinking.

'Yeah – that's Brian. He's off the wall. He's Elaine's -' She pauses. 'Well, they're not together any more. It's complicated,' she finishes without explanation. Then she looks at me. 'Sorry, where did you just say you saw Brian licking the windows?'

'New girls,' Brian says and does something weird with his hands like he's playing an imaginary trumpet.

'New girls *and a fella*,' Tracy says, with added emphasis. 'Daisy, Ani and Jasper. Cousins from America.'

'Maisie,' I say, not unkindly.

She smiles broadly. 'You decided to join us then, Kim?'

'I finished earlier than I thought I would,' she says, finally looking away from me.

'A new bloke? At Drakes'?' Rob grins. 'Since when did that happen, and why don't I go there?' He glances at me briefly. 'Hi.'

I smile back, but I can't look at him for long. His eyes. Awkward much.

'Where are those chips?' Tracy asks brightly.

'Jasper's supposed to be starting at FCAB,' Claire says, 'but apparently, they told him he couldn't register today.'

'Not surprised. Hardly a lot of point. Teachers have got a meeting about how to teach the new remedials,' Brian says. 'They're kicking us out after lunch.'

'You can't call people that!' Ani blurts out.

'What, teachers?'

'No,' she says irritatedly, 'that other word.'

Brian looks at her curiously. 'Remedials? Why not? Better than some names I've heard them given.'

'We were going over to Bry's for a jam session this afternoon,' Rob says into the extended pit of silent nasty. 'Will's got the afternoon off work.'

'What do you play?' Jasper asks.

'Skins. You got any skills?' Rob asks him.

'I play a bit of bass.'

'Slap?'

I watch Jasper's eyes glazing over as he struggles to have a conversation in a language we all used to speak fluently in 2019. 'Rock. Metal. Blues. Anything retro.'

'Retro?' Tracy asks.

'Yeah, you know – stuff from the … eig … nine … teen seventies,' he stumbles carefully.

'I bet he plays better than Will does,' Brian says.

Everyone playfully attacks Brian for being mean, but apparently truthful about the absent bassist. My stomach cramps violently. I only had time to have a couple of mouthfuls of the sandwich they clubbed together to get us, and before that, I haven't eaten since 2019. My purse is safely in my locker in Drake's, somewhere in the ether. While Jasper and Ani might have money on them, I don't think it'll be legal tender yet. I'm pretty sure that our current notes would look a lot like Monopoly money. I'm beginning to wish I'd paid more attention in GCSE History beyond the crash course in fashion and music from the '80s.

Fact is, the door to the Old Library is locked, and now our best chance of getting back is to wait until whatever point in Time Lizzy and her friends decide to go through the purple light and go with them. It might be a good thing, waiting. If we'd made it through the purple light, who knows where we would've ended up? Or when? If we go through with Lizzy and her friends, we can be pretty sure when we'll end up.

Five minutes later Lizzy, Elaine and another boy are

back, holding two substantial open bags of chips and we're all sharing. As we sit in the spring sunshine at the edge of the playing fields, I listen to us all. You'd think we've known one another all our lives. Elaine's talking clothes and shopping with Ani, and it seems okay here that Ani's a bit left field with her ideas and tastes. Rob and Ian, the guy who went to the chip shop with Lizzy and Elaine, are on either side of Jasper, and they're all talking about whether someone called Mark King is a better bass player than someone called Geddy Lee. Lizzy and Tracy look like they're hatching a plot. Claire's with me, Brian and Kim, and Claire's talking about her study timetable and the way she's got it all colour-coded, and she doesn't seem to need us to respond, she just needs to say it all out loud to put her mind at rest about the exams. Shame Ani's History exams don't include questions about the Education System in 1987 yet. *'Compare and contrast the GCE A-Level examinations of June 1987 with the exams currently being taken by teenagers of the 21st Century'*? She'd get an A star straight. She probably will, anyway, if we can get back in time for her to take the exam.

'So what're we doing tonight then?' Ian asks.

'Fundraiser?' Tracy says, sarcastically.

'No, I mean, where we meeting beforehand?' he goes on.

'Meet at my place,' Lizzy says.

'We can't all get ready at yours. Your Mum'll have a pink fit with all the sorting out for tomorrow. You want to come over to mine to get ready?' Tracy's asking Ani. 'There's a payphone over by the Gates, you can call your folks and let them know where you're going to be … what in the name of Sod is that?'

I close my eyes. I know what Ani's done; I don't even have to look. It's too much a part of every day to us. Mention giving someone a call and we just pull it out of our pockets like a reflex action. I'm surprised we've managed to keep them in our pockets for as long as we have if I'm honest.

So there it is, in Ani's hands for all to gawp at. Flat with its canary yellow cover and a shiny black screen. Samsung *Galaxy S10*. A communications device that's not due to be even invented for god knows how many years. Ani's smartphone.

'Holy crap,' Jasper has his hoodied head cupped in his hands like a live version of *The Scream.*

Ani starts with the hysterical giggling. It was only a matter of time before the sanity dam burst. 'I didn't think about it! I'm sorry!'

The others are all staring, and she's holding her mobile out like it's a half-eaten rodent present from the cat that she found inside her slipper.

Jasper is by my side suddenly. He looks down at me, and I'm not prepared for the comment. 'Should we tell them what's going on now?' he mutters.

Chapter Seven – I Love My Radio (Taffy, 1987)

Luckily I think he said it too quietly for anyone else to hear.

'No way!' I hiss back.

Ani tries to stuff the phone back in her pocket, but Tracy's having none of that. 'Seriously, what is that? Looks like …'

'It's a calculator,' Brian says evenly.

Tracy looks from the phone to him and then back to Ani. 'Is it a calculator?' she asks.

'Oh yeah. That's one of those girly jobs from Athena they sell up the front desk with the pencil cases and those monsters you stick over the end of your pencil to stop you chewing it,' Ian says.

'Is that what those monsters are for?' Kim asks.

'They don't work,' Brian says, grinning. 'I ate mine.'

'That's a well cool colour for a calculator,' Elaine says.

'There's no number keys or anything. It's just a screen. Like a tiny television,' Claire says. 'How do you input?'

'No scientific functions or anything,' Brian says. 'It'd be less than shit in an exam. Sorry,' he adds sheepishly, as Ani takes the phone back from Tracy.

'So yes, it is a calculator, and actually, I don't care whether it's a girly job of shit or not,' she says breathlessly, pushing it deep into a pocket. 'My dad got it for me from South Korea.'

I can't meet her gaze. I suppose it was better than saying

Carphone Warehouse. Slightly.

'South Korea? How did you get hold of that then?' Tracy asks.

'Oh, her dad's out there quite a bit. With Jasper's obviously,' I interrupt, rapidly spotting the tenuous opening and launching myself into it. 'Her dad's away the moment with my Mum. And her Mum. With Jasper's too. They're all away. Extended family holiday. Just for the olds. Which is why we don't need to call anybody, and why it's so nice that you've invited us over.' I grin broadly. This speech leaves me a bit breathless, and I'm not convinced they're convinced. I probably look a bit manic. I feel it.

'Your parents are all away?' Claire asks, her face full of indignation. 'So close to your exams?'

'They found a cheap break?' Ani tries faintly.

'You've had to register at new schools while they went on holiday?' Claire asks again.

'I get it completely. My parents would do exactly the same,' Kim says supportively.

'So we were saying - you can't all go to Lizzy's for tea, her mum'll throw a pink fit,' Tracy says. 'Especially with Lizzy's big day tomorrow – Glenda's got all that catering to organise.'

'You know she won't mind,' Lizzy says, and for the first time since we've been here, I see a ray of sunshine in her eyes – a spark of happy. 'So I say it's not right that FCAB gets the afternoon off and we don't, so let's all bunk off and go back to mine.'

I can feel my eyes widening like dinner plates. My mother is happy, and it turns out it's because she's suggesting we all walk out of school this afternoon? No, I remind myself. This isn't my mother. This is my pre-mother. My not-yet-mother. There is no point in me being offended, upset, shocked or messed up by anything she does or says. That way only lays more mental health issues.

'You see,' Kim says, and the tone of her voice is odd like she's trying to cover her emotions. 'We're all a bit ... you know.'

I shake my head, no.

'Well Claire's a brainbox and Brian's a complete genius, although his parents are more interested in his sister, and Tracy's parents are practically Stoneford royalty. My parents ... well.' She picks at a bright pink fingernail with her thumb. 'Let's just say none of us really fit in anywhere else, but we fit in with each other. So we always say, if people want to be mates, we're up for it. We don't care whether you're in love with Simon LeBon, George Michael and Michael Jackson, or Bruce Dickinson, David Lee Roth and Jon Bon Jovi. Some people nowadays can be really judgemental.' She looks over my shoulder. 'These people keep me afloat.' She pats me on the shoulder. 'You'll be okay with us. We're not like most kids.'

'Kim's stopping over at mine tonight anyway, aren't you?' Lizzy calls across.

She nods violently, gives me an encouraging smile and a shoulder squeeze, and goes over to Lizzy's side.

'So you lot might as well all join us,' Lizzy says, looking at me again with the small smile.

'If Kim goes home, she'll not get out again until Monday. There's the Fundraiser tonight and Lizzy's 18 tomorrow,' Tracy says quietly into my ear. 'And my folks are having a garden party on Sunday. I'd bet good money there won't be enough petrol in the car to drive Kim anywhere, or no change for the bus, or she'll suddenly get a stack of chores to do again that she only finished that morning. Cinderella has nothing on Kim.' She stands up and stretches. 'Don't tell her I told you.'

'I can't bunk off,' Claire says, and she's almost tearful. 'I just can't! I have too much study, and it's already going to be massively busy this weekend.'

Kim, Elaine and Tracy enfold her in a huge circular hug. 'We love you, Claire,' they chorus.

'I'll go through some stuff with you, Claire,' Brian says. 'Bring your Physics books to Lizzy's. And Chem. You don't need to be stuck in this dump to be revising.'

'There you go, sweetness,' Lizzy says, 'every ugly bug can come to the ball.' She eyes us, and there's no malice. 'Even the new kids.'

Tracy says. 'What time do you get off, Rob?'

'Got to register at 2:15, then we're out,' he says. 'We'll meet you back here at the Top Gates. The whole of FCAB will be leaving, so you can get lost in the crowd. Okay? You coming?' he asks Ian and Brian. He turns to look straight at me and smiles again. 'We're out of here.'

They walk on up the road towards FCAB. I refuse to look at Tracy's face; I can see out of the corner of my eye that she is staring, and I know my cheeks are pink.

'We've got to register too, or they'll know we've skived off,' Lizzy says.

My watch stopped working about 32 years in the future, but Claire's looking edgy; it can't be long until the bell rings for registration.

'Usual way?' Tracy asks.

Lizzy nods. 'Sneak around the back of the History department, through the hole in the fence and onto the top road.'

'You sound like you've done this a few times before,' I say faintly. That's the way we all use now.

Lizzy snorts. 'I spent most of the Fifth getting out of school that way. No one can see us leaving that way from the main offices. Or the Head's. To be honest, they won't care if we bunk off today. Half of 6^2 will vanish after Form Time, I reckon.' They all laugh.

If I'd been expecting anyone today, she'd really not be what I would've been expecting.

'We'd better go in now before the bell goes,' Claire says, a little more urgently.

'Which tutor group are you two in?' Elaine asks me. 'We're 6^2T.'

They all stare at me, and I realise I am no longer in Weirdsville. I am in Madness Central, and we've been travelling by fast coach from Normal Town for a long time. I take a chance, and I glance down at the fitness tracker that hasn't worked since 32 years in the future. 'Bugger! We never picked up our dinner tickets!'

'It wasn't 6^2T,' Jasper says helpfully. 'They were definitely given a different letter.'

'Wonder why Lizzy got asked to show these two around then?' Elaine asks.

We are saved by the bell ringing sharply from some unseen speaker under the eaves of a nearby building. We're all 0-60 in 2.7 seconds. It's impressive; I don't think anyone bothers to respond so quickly to the bell back in the day. Forward in the day, I mean.

Lizzy and the others need to see us come into the building.

'We'll get our dinner tickets and see you up there,' I call.

'Give it 20 minutes,' Tracy calls back as the five of them disappear through a battered set of double doors into the depths of the Main Block.

I head for the New Library on the second floor. I'm banking on there being no teacher here as they'll all be with their classes and tutor groups, or prepping lessons.

The New Library isn't much different from how we know it now, but it's full of books now of course, and there's not a computer or tablet to be seen. As we walk into the room, though, I realise I've made a mistake, and the place isn't empty.

There's a teacher putting books away on a metal rack by one of the vast windows. She turns and raises her eyebrows before I can put us all into reverse.

'Private study. Miss,' Ani says.

More likely than being lost, I guess.

'You should be in Form Time,' the teacher says.

'We're new,' Ani says. 'They haven't sorted out our lanyards yet.'

'Your what?' At least, this teacher doesn't seem quite as much of a monster as David Tyler. 'Never mind. What form have you been assigned to?' She looks over my shoulder, her eyes narrowing as she takes in Jasper, lurking behind one of the taller bookcases, hoodie up, trying to sink into the bookshelves.

'We haven't been given a form either. Yet.' I add. 'We were supposed to go down to Reception to find out where our form room was, but Ani here saw the signs for the Library and just had to take a look.'

'I love books, I do,' she says simply. I'm not sure whether Jasper sneezes, or whether he's unsuccessfully covering up a snigger.

The teacher isn't convinced either. 'Down the stairs. Ground Floor. By the Front Entrance,' she says in capitals, a little less friendly now.

As we are going down the now deserted staircase, Jasper says, 'Now what? We have to get back to them.'

'So we just go up to the Top Gates and wait.'

'So you do want us to go with them then?' Ani says.

'Do you have a better plan?' I snap. 'It wasn't me that got us into this crock of shite situation!'

'And what happens after that?' Jasper says quietly, as we head towards the Third Year Changing Rooms. We say Year Nine nowadays, but the buildings are in front of the History department and still the preferred route for escape. I can't believe my mother used to use it. I suddenly realise that very little at Drake's probably gets past my mother. More to the point, why doesn't she do anything about it if she knows what's going on under her nose? 'I mean,' he continues, 'what happens when everyone goes home after the Fundraiser tonight?'

'Why are you acting like I have the answers?' I say out loud.

'We need that book,' Jasper says.

Sudden laughter from an open classroom window startles me.

'Which book?' I ask.

'The book Orla told Ani about.'

My eyes roll up into my head. 'I told you both already. Orla was taking the piss out of Ani. The whole thing was a joke.'

'And if she was taking the piss out of me, how is it we're here having conversations with old people like your mother who are suddenly as young as us?' Ani asks.

For a few seconds, all I can hear is my heart beating in my ears and the crunch of the gravel path beneath my feet as I consider her comment. As I say, she is left of centre, but she is definitely the brains of our little group, and she has a point. We are here. So does the book exist too?

'That book might have information that would help us,' Jasper says.

'Well, it doesn't matter, does it? Because we don't have the bloody book even if it does exist.'

We're at the changing room block now, and we fall into silence. After checking to make sure no one is watching, we tread lightly past the building, hoping there are no members of staff about. From here, we sidle down to the left, between the wall of the History Block next door and the fence.

Jasper seems to have another crisis. 'What if we can't get home? What happens to our lives? What about our parents? What about - ?'

As if she's read his mind, Ani puts a hand on his shoulder and pulls him into a hug. 'We can get back to the way it was,' she says, her cheek against his.

He pulls away from her and she looks hurt. 'You don't know that for sure. What happens when we get back to where we're supposed to be? What if we've changed the past? You can't change the past, those old films always say the same!'

'This isn't a film, Jasper,' she says.

'We don't have any other facts to help us! If you change things, you affect the future!' Jasper says, his voice beginning to peak out desperate.

'Who's changing things?' I ask. 'Seriously, Jasper, try and get a grip, bro.'

'We are changing things,' he says anxiously. 'Aren't we? Just by being here. We'll be at their Fundraiser tonight, and we aren't supposed to be there. We aren't supposed to be here at all.' He glances across at me. 'And Rob likes you. That was bare obvious to everyone. What kind of crazy would that cause if you two get with the Netflix and chills?' The bell for the beginning of Period Five rings faintly up from within the school like Doomsday. That's if they still call it Period Five. 'This is 1987, and we've not even been born!' he says. 'So if we ever get back, will it be the way it was?'

I've seen the movies he's talking about. I know the drill. Don't mix with the kids from the past. Don't change anything that already happened. Don't get involved, even if you meet a guy born more than 30 years before you who plays the drums and he's as fit AF. Stop the rollercoaster, I want to get off.

Chapter Eight – Another Step (Closer To You) (Kim Wilde & Junior, 1987)

'Will the others be long?' Ani asks.

I shrug. 'Let's wait in the Park under the Big Willow. We can see the Top Gates from there easy.'

The Big Willow is a regular meeting place for Drake's and FCA kids in our day, but to be fair, it's hardly a big willow right now, just an average one. It's one of those days at the end of May when the heat of summer's in the air, with only the slightest fumes of the traffic drifting up from town. Sometimes you get more summer in May than you do in August. We walk down into the Park and settle into the shade of the Willow.

Jasper, still restless, rummages around in a bin until he finds a newspaper that isn't too manky for us to read. We're shocked that Coventry won the FA Cup, and then to top that, we find out there's no Premiership, just a Division One. Jasper knows about Maggie Thatcher and Ronald Reagan because he's taking Gov.Pol, but I'm shocked that was an accident recently where a ferry sank, and people drowned in the English Channel because they didn't shut the doors properly! I've never been on a boat, but I've been through the Channel Tunnel on a train once. Those poor people on that boat.

Jasper can't believe the TV listings. 'BBC1.Terry Wogan; I remember him. Didn't he use to be on *Children in Need*? Then there's a bloke called Paul Daniels doing a magic show, and an American soap called the *Colbys*?' he says, 'On a Friday night? It's worse than UK Gold. And there are only four channels listed here! Don't they even have cable yet?'

'It would be exciting to stay, wouldn't it? Just to watch everything we know is going to happen, happen?' Ani tucks a stray lock of hair behind her ear.

I sigh and shake my head no. 'We have to get back, Ani.'

'I know. I'm sorry,' Ani says. I look across at her, and she's staring at her knees. 'I didn't realise it would end up like this.' She looks up, and her eyes are all bright and sparkling in the sunshine. 'I didn't mean to make everyone salty. I thought it would be fun, seeing the past. Living in the past. Like living in a history book!'

'Book,' Jasper repeats after a moment's pause. 'That reminds me of something I meant to say earlier. The book Orla told you about. You said she told us it was in Maisie's Mum's office.'

'I did,' she agrees.

'Well, what if maybe it's still there? In the same office?'

'Well, it's to do with the history of the school, so I guess there's every reason it could be there already,' Ani agrees again.

I can hear birds singing in the Willow above us. 'So, what are you thinking about now?' I ask.

'We go searching for Orla's book?' he asks. 'In the Head's Office?'

'And then we can slip off somewhere quiet and find out how the Portal works!' Ani says, clapping her hands like a seal hopeful for snacks.

'Makes sense,' Jasper says.

I'm glad he thinks so. Who even is in charge here now, and how exactly are we supposed to get into their office? 'I still think we're better off sticking with Lizzy until they all go through the Old Library. We know they're going to. It's just a case of when,' I say.

Jasper shrugs, and nods. 'I still think it's worth getting our hands on that book if we get the chance.'

'Or if something goes wrong,' Ani adds, her voice uncharacteristically dull.

At 2:30, we meet the others back at the school gates.

'You don't all need to go and get ready yet, do you?' Rob says.

'I'm going to need at least a couple of hours,' Kim says, her face deadly serious.

'You don't need that long,' Ian says. She blushes. So does he. So that's cute then.

'We've got a couple of hours we can kill,' Elaine says. 'Let's go down town to the burger bar.'

'We can see if they've got the new Def Leppard LP at Our Price?'

'I don't think it's released for another couple of weeks,' Rob says.

'I'm broke until I get my pocket money at the beginning of the month anyway,' Claire says.

'We were going to have a jam at my place,' Brian says.

'Someone's bound to kick off about the noise at this time of day. Come back to mine,' Lizzy says. 'Mum's at work until four,' and against all my natural dislike of history, I can't help myself but feel excited at seeing my home 32 years ago.

I've always known my mother had lived there with my Nan Glenda and my Granddad Henry and her brother Paul before I was born, and that the house has passed down through the family for as long as anyone can remember.

I live at the far edge of the Park, and during the winter, you can just about see through the leafless branches of the trees in the Park up to the roof of the Performing Arts Block at Drake's and the tallest turrets on the Old Library. It's no mansion, our house, but with three floors it is big enough for all the family to stay over at Christmas and still leave a couple of rooms spare. Detached and built in pale grey stone like a lot of the grander houses on the other side of Stoneford, it has several quirky tall chimneys that never served much of a purpose. Behind the house, there's a long back garden that leads down to a garage, and a carport with a motor home parked on it that we haven't used since my brother Blake went to Uni.

When I was small, the kids at my primary school said I lived in a castle and they called me stuck-up. Those kids I knew at primary school don't get in my face these days. My mother is a head teacher, my dad lives in Torcombe with his new girlfriend, and my brothers Lucas and Blake are working two jobs each to get through Uni: we aren't rich, we just inherited a big house, and my mother's mean. My mother hates it if I take people home. She's always busy. Teachers are always busy. They don't have time to make snacks. They don't have time for anything other than their job.

'Sarnies at Lizzy's gaffe,' Brian says. 'I'm in. Cheaper than burgers.' He plays the little imaginary tune on his fingers.

'Jamming can wait,' Rob agrees.

'Okay,' Tracy says. 'Lizzy's it is.'

Normally, I don't think my house is anything special, but today, as we walk over the brow of the slope in the Park down towards it, it looks like something out of those picture post-cards you get at the seaside, with the sun shining down in just the right places. Nowadays, there is an estate built behind it, the one Jasper lives in; you can see it as you come out through the bottom gates of the Park, snaking its way up east towards the motorway and then down towards the General Hospital. We call it the Poets' Estate because of the names of the streets. Now, as I look down, that land is still covered by the orchards and the overgrown meadow where I used to play when I was a tiny kid. Jasper's talking to Rob about guitars, but, as I watch, as he glances over at where his house should be. When he looks away, his face is paler.

We walk down the front path past the apple tree in the centre of the garden and pile in through the back door, through a retro stripy red and blue plastic windbreaker into the kit-chen. I don't know who's more shocked when my Nan, Glenda, comes through from the dining room and does a double-take. Lizzy should've realised something was up when she didn't need her key.

I can't work out whether Glenda is shocked that Lizzy's home, or that she managed to find so many people to bring home for tea. 'Lizzy?' she says, and it's like an exhalation. 'Why are you here?'

'I could ask you the same thing.' Lizzy crosses her arms and pulls a face. 'Don't sweat it, Mum – 6^2 had PS this afternoon, and FCAB is shutting for teacher training.'

'You didn't think to mention this to me at lunchtime?' Glenda asks. Lizzy shrugs. Glenda shakes her head and stares at Jasper.

'This is Jasper,' I say, into the abyss. 'He's at FCA. B! I'm Maisie, and this is Ani.'

'Hello, Mrs ... Brookes?' he says carefully, in his best I'm-going-to-impress-the fam-with-my-manners voice.

'Call me Glenda. Mrs Brookes makes me feel like I'm at work.' Glenda's eyes are unnervingly bright. 'A boy? At Drake's?'

'Long story, Mum, don't start. Got anything to eat?' Lizzy asks.

'Dinner?' Glenda asks unsurely. 'I don't want to let you lot down, but I hope you're not expecting me to provide a hot meal for a dinner party at a moment's notice! I've got a lot to do! Big day tomorrow!' She winks at Lizzy.

'Dinner party,' Lizzy snorts. 'Jeez Mum, you're so old-fashioned. Just a snack. Few sandwiches and crisps?' she asks and looks back at us all. 'Well, maybe just some crisps,' she adds. 'Is Dad home yet?'

Glenda shakes her head. 'He'll be back sometime this evening while you're out. Paul should be back any time though. I'll see what I can rustle up. Last day good?'

'Great,' Lizzy says. 'We'll be in my room.'

As we all troop past her, I try not to look, but I can feel Glenda's eyes boring into my back as we disappear into the hallway. It's unsettling, but right now, I am excited because I'm going to see something special. I'm going to see my mother's room when she was a kid. Why's it special? Because it's my room in my nowadays. I know I said I wasn't into History. But this is nothing like a visit to a regular museum. Ani's right.

Against one wall, there are white fitted double wardrobes

with a little mirror and dressing table between them. There's a piebald china pony on the white painted dressing table, and a clay hedgehog with a blue and green glaze, fired by her arty headteacher. She liked Art. I know about the hedgehog because she told me; it was one of her favourites ever lessons at primary school. Make up is strewn across the white surface. Names I've never heard of beside names that are still familiar: Terra Africa face powder, No. 17 black mascara and Poncho Pink lipstick, a bottle of Ysatis perfume, Jovan musk oil and a tiny glass bottle labelled Patchouli.

Against another wall, there's a record player turntable under a lid filled with coloured lights, and original vinyl records and tape cassettes stacked beneath it on two shelves. On the other side, there's a bookcase stacked with stories from when she was a little kid, plus some additions like *Lace*, *The Thorn Birds* and *Endless Love* – even I know there's a load of sex in those. On the walls, the posters are a weird mix of one guy with long, massive, blonde hair in a pair of eye-wateringly-tight striped trousers that show his Everything, Michael J Fox with the DeLorean car in the first *Back to the Future* film, Tom Cruise in *Top Gun,* a sailor in a white uniform kissing a girl in a white dress on a busy street full of shops, and what look like a massive pair of soulful animal's eyes in a mystic sort of grey swirl - all over the top of flowery blue wallpaper, and a crocheted multi-coloured spread over the blankets on the bed.

It's nothing like my room any more, but somehow, that's okay. Rob sits on the floor next to Ian, and Kim copies them; Ani asks Lizzy where the loo is, and they walk out onto the landing together; Elaine sits on the bed next to Tracy, and they start talking in hushed tones; Brian and Claire sit on the other side of the bed and open one of the colossal books she's been carrying since we left Drake's.

Jasper dives into a collection of multi-coloured cardboard sleeves beneath the turntable. 'Nightflight to Venus?' he asks in mock disgust after pulling one particular cardboard sleeve out. It's blue, and some people that look like they're dressed in cooking foil are bursting out of a fake moon on the cover. 'Boney M?'

Lizzy comes back into the room. 'Don't you take the piss out of the mighty M,' she says, flicking long red hair off one of her shoulders. 'You can't have a decent party these days without a bit of Boney,' He laughs. She laughs too, but I don't think she's laughing for the same reasons Jasper is.

The first strains of pure '70s pop pour into the room from the little boxy speakers on the white bookcase. Jasper seems to have put the Boney M record on the turntable.

'Mum, where are the snacks?' Lizzy yells through the door behind me.

As if by magic, Glenda appears at the top of the stairs, smiling unexpectedly broadly, and even more unexpectedly passes me the tray laden with snack foods I never heard of, like Golden Wonder Sausage and Tomato crisps and Jungle Fresh peanuts along with a few I recognised: Blue Riband bars, Caramel wafer bars, plastic beakers and a couple of metal jugs of what looks like weak orange squash. 'All here, love. Sausage and Tomato okay?'

'My fave,' Lizzy beams and takes the tray from her. 'Jasper, this is wank. Put Def Leppard on. 'Pyromania'. Do you like Def Leppard?' she says to us.

Ani snorts. 'Def Leppard? Like a blind elephant?'

'Not heard of Blind Elephant,' Lizzy says, giving her a

strange look. 'Are they heavy?' As Ani dissolves into a pool of gibbering sniggers, I've pretty much given up all hope of her ever seeing ordinary again. 'I suppose you're into Prefab Sprout,' Lizzy says moodily. 'Steve McQueen'?' She takes one look at my blank face, makes a pfft sort of sound, carries off a bag of Sausage and Tomato crisps and goes and sits down next to Elaine and Tracy.

Glenda coughs and gives Jasper a meaningful look. He doesn't get it for a moment – then he turns the music down.

'Come off it, Mum, it's not that loud,' Lizzy starts and then she realises that Glenda is holding out a red velvet box. 'What's that?'

'I was going to give it to you tomorrow at the party, but you'll get so many other presents tomorrow, and I figured you might like to have it for the Fundraiser. Happy 18th, chicken.'

Lizzy is off the bed like a shot and, although she's got her back to all of us, I can hear her sigh of pleasure.

'Oh Mum, that is the nuts.' She reaches into the box and pulls out something shiny on a chain and slips it over her neck. When she turns around, everyone makes noises of approval.

I'm a bit shocked.

Lizzy is showing us all a silver key on a silver chain around her neck. It's probably six or seven centimetres long, and it's identical to the necklace she still wears to this very day, or at least, my very day, not this one.

I've just witnessed the day she was given it.

'It's just like your one,' Lizzy says to Glenda. There's a tremor in her voice. She moves forward quickly, throws her arms around her mum, and then as if she's remembered where she is, she steps as quickly back. I've never seen my mother show this kind of emotion. It's strangely unsettling to see her like this.

Glenda nods, and there is definitely moisture in her eyes. 'I'll tell you all about it in a couple of days. You just enjoy your special weekend.' She peers around Lizzy at me then and says, 'You don't have to stand there holding the tray for them, love, even if you are new here.'

Chapter Nine - Ever Fallen In Love (Fine Young Cannibals, 1987)

Pyromania. I remember my mother streaming this album for me on the smart speaker in our kitchen a couple of years ago. She told me it reminded her of being young and happy. I hadn't thought about it at the time, but I'm wondering now if that meant she wasn't feeling happy when she played it for me. I laughed at her at the time because I was so surprised that my conservative Head Teacher of a mother liked rock music, even if it was well old. She laughed back at me and said I had no idea about what her life was like, and now I see that she was totally on point with that.

I don't have a type or a thing where music's concerned – I just like what I like – Pyromania, this old, cheesy album from the 1980s, is full of songs that make you want to link arms or punch the air with your BFFs and sing along, with cider if possible. It's a popular choice here too. Tracy, Lizzy and Elaine are dancing in what carpet space is available in the bedroom: Lizzy threading her new silver key in and out of her fingers as she chatters happily to her two friends, Elaine casting the occasional smile down at Jasper as she shakes her booty in the hope that he might notice. Brian's nodding to the beat as he scribbles a few ideas on a notebook he's grabbed from a nearby shelf to explain something to Claire and Ani, who's back from the loo. Jasper is staring up at the three girls dancing. He's fix-ated on them, and as I'm watching, he turns towards me, and there's the strangest look in his eyes like he's just realised the enormity of what seeing this moment in time must mean to me.

Before I can take a deep swallow of air to control my breathing, things are changing around me again. A different drumbeat kicks in and Rob's on his feet, reaching down for my hands. Without considering what might happen, I let him take my hands in his, and he's pulled me to my feet, and we're dancing.

Kim smiles by the bookcase with Ian, stuffing her face with pink wafer bars like there's a shortage. I register Lizzie's look as she glances across at me. Bugger. Does she think I'm hitting on her hottie? She can't be that stupid. Or am I the stupid one?

This song though, it's not some grime act on the club scene, this is 1987 Rock Music in Capital Letters, loud with big messy hair, double denim and big exposed muscles protruding out of skin-tight vest tops and impossibly tight jeans.

'We do a cover of this,' Rob says to me, 'in our band.'

'I'd like to hear you guys play,' I tell him.

'We're not that great.'

'Bollocks,' Brian and Ian say at the same time, without ap-parently looking up or moving. Rob laughs; I guess he doesn't care that they've overheard him, or what they thought about what was said.

Ian has grabbed Kim around the waist, and they are now dancing in a way best suited to a different song. Has *Dirty Dan-cing* even been released yet? That Patrick Swayze guy's not up on the wall, so I guess not: I know he was a big favourite of my mother's.

Ani's got distracted by whatever Brian's drawing, Claire is thumbing through one of her enormous school books, and Jasper is smiling and talking to Elaine, who has finally sat down next to him.

If anyone notices when Rob leans across to me and asks if I fancy a bit of fresh air they don't say a word, so I'm surprised to see Tracy's hand on my arm before I can reply because I hadn't even noticed her watching us.

She pulls me nearer to the door. 'Can I have a quick word before you disappear off with our tall, dark dishy?' she whispers in my ear.

I imagine Tracy's like a cross between your BFF, your big sister and the voice in your head that says "are you sure you're doing the right thing?" when you know bare well you aren't, but you don't care. I'm not sure what I'm getting myself into, but I smile an okay? at Rob, and he nods and turns back to Lizzy's record collection.

□

Along the first landing, past the stairs to the second floor, in the bedroom at the end, there are football team and band posters on the wall – Megadeth, Metallica - and it smells like someone exploded an aftershave bomb. I realise I'm looking at my Uncle Paul's room. If my mother – Lizzy – is nearly 18, Uncle Paul's at Uni, he's a couple of years older than her.

Outside Lizzy's bedroom on the landing, Tracy leans over the wooden bannister and peers back at me.

'What's it to be then?' I ask. ' Back off shorty, you've only been here for five, and you think you can poach?'

'I'm not altogether sure what you just said,' she says, 'but it sounded a bit fresh. Don't be a bitch. Doesn't suit you. Rob's gorgeous, a really nice bloke.'

I sigh. 'Explain it like I'm five?'

'We thought …' She pauses and twirls some stray hair around her finger. 'We thought he and Lizzy were going to seal the deal tonight. It's been on the cards for weeks.'

'So you are telling me to cancel.' I look back at her, but she's looking down over the bannister to the bottom of the staircase.

'Maybe I shouldn't interfere. I mean, nothing's ever settled really, is it? Wasn't that long ago that we thought Rob and Yvonne were the real deal, and Elaine was all cosy with Brian. Now Eve's up at Cambridge, and Elaine says she's besotted with Neil Thorpe. I guess it doesn't matter. None of us is even going to be around for much longer.'

'What? Why?' I ask, thinking of her in her red stilettos at my Fundraiser in 2019 last night.

'Uni? We're all going to be on opposite sides of the country if it goes to plan.' She looks up at me then, and she's smiling. 'Maybe I'm just saying, be careful. Don't piss Lizzy off. She's my bestie. I want a happy Summer before we all go our separate ways.'

I smile weakly. I see your bestie; I'll raise you a mother. 'You don't need to worry about that. I'm not looking for a boyfriend.'

Tracy punches me gently. 'You aren't interested in Rob?'

'I didn't say I wasn't interested. I'm just not in a position to commit,' I say, carefully.

She nods. 'So what gives with your sexy bassist?'

'Jasper? Oh, he's my bruv.'

'I thought you said you were cousins?'

'I didn't mean my real brother. He's just – you know. Part of the squad.'

'Squad?' She shakes her head. 'You Americans have a bizarre way of talking. Is he hooked up with anyone?'

'Hooked up?' I ask faintly.

'Is He Involved With Anyone?' she says as if I am three.

'Jasper? No. Why?'

She smirks. 'If it's an open playing field, I may just take an innings,' she says.

'It's not exactly an open field,' I say, as she goes back to Lizzy's bedroom door.

'I think Elaine might get in there first anyway. Warn him off,' she laughs.

'I'm not sure he'll need warning off Elaine,' I say, but it's not for me to tell her why.

Rob's standing in the doorway already, and I wonder how much he's heard. 'Okay for that walk now?' he says.

I smile and follow him down the stairs in spite of the swarm of butterflies that just arrived in my stomach.

At the bottom, he stops and turns back to face me. 'There's a pretty view at the bottom of the garden.' I'm already wondering why I agreed to this and whether or not we might be better having a chat back upstairs on the landing. 'Would you like to see it?'

We go down the passageway and back out into the kitchen. Glenda's not around, I figure she's in the front room, using the TV to shut the music out from upstairs. All the doors to the front room are closed. We slip into the kitchen and out the back door, and I realise instantly why I wanted to come outside with him.

The garden is the same as mine but so different. We walk down the steps away from the back of the house, past a battered old shed on the left that looks just like the one we have in my time, the one I'm not allowed inside because of the power tools and the weed killer.

Past the brightly-coloured stone patio on the right that my mother told me Granddad Henry laid in the '80s, past a stripy deckchair in a prime position that receives the first rays of summer and a perfectly green lawn with tiny white and yellow plants beginning to bloom around the borders. Then on further: past strips of green leafy shoots in the ground and poles with more climbing wispy plants; a greenhouse stacked with shelves of black plastic plant trays with tiny stalks waiting for someone to put them in the earth, another shed and finally we're walking down the side of the garage on the left to where an old caravan stands parked. There's a small wooden cross in the grass by an apple tree. It's my garden, but so much of it isn't.

'Is it open?' he asks. I try the caravan door. It's locked. No surprise, really.

My stomach is churning suddenly. I go to the corner of the van. Somehow, being able to still see the house gives me a sense of security. Bugger if I only know why. I'm so out of my depth now, I could be standing on the top of Canary Wharf up in the City, and I'd still be bloody drowning in the Thames.

He leans against the van, looking out over the fields and orchards that come right up to the unmade road that links my garage to the street. Where they build Jasper's house. Maybe Rob lives over there now with his wife and five kids. Grandkids.

FML.

'They'll probably build houses over there in the future,' I say out loud.

He laughs; it's a wicked, throaty laugh. 'Everything changes,' he says, looking away from the fields, directly back at me. 'So how long have you been in Stoneford?'

'Feels like we arrived yesterday,' I say.

'You like it here so far?'

'It's all a bit of a mess up here if I'm honest,' I touch my left temple with a slightly shaky finger.

He nods, serious face. 'It's a big trauma, moving house. Your cousins seem sound though.'

'Cousins? Oh, yeah, they are. When Ani goes off on one though, that's Netflix worth buying popcorn for. She's no noob though – she's got brains. Jasper's dope.'

Again, the laugh, a bit more wicked this time. 'You're funny.'

I think I've probably said too much. 'You think so? Thanks.'

'You've got the weirdest way of speaking. I like it though.'

He's edging closer as he speaks, so slowly you can hardly tell he's moving at all, except now I swear I can smell the sweet scent of the conditioner that his clothes were washed in, and if I turn my head, I would see the dark specks of stubble lying just below the surface of the skin on his upper lip and chin. He's totally hot with his black trousers and white shirtsleeves rolled up to his elbows, unbuttoned at the collar now with the school tie loosely hanging against his chest.

I'm standing very still, wondering how close he's prepared to get, and why he might want to. My heart is thundering against my rib cage, and his arm brushes mine. All the tiny hairs on my arm stand up and send tickly shock waves down to my fingers, and I can feel his fingers gently lifting mine and weaving our two hands together.

But we're on a different playing field altogether, me and Rob, and I don't know that it's doing me any good standing here, holding hands with him, acting like I know what I'm doing when I'm all tied up in knots already, and I know I should be cancelling as fast as I can and getting away, leaving the opposing team - because this beautiful guy, standing to the side of me?

He's old enough to be my father.

Chapter Ten – Incommunicado (Marillion, 1987)

My heart feels like it starts beating again when the motorbike pulls up beside us. We both step away from the other and next thing I know, I'm looking through a visor into the cheeky, teasing eyes of my Uncle Paul.

In my nowadays, Paul's got a shaved head to cover the fact that he's lost most of his hair. He's a bit of a chubba because, as he's always telling us, he likes to live well since he can afford it. My mother says he likes to drink well and that's half the problem, and then they start on at each other, but it's always in fun. Uncle Paul can always be relied on to snap my mother out of a downer. She always seems younger when he's around. She laughs more. Lately, he's been uptight with me, though, keeping on at me about my exams, telling me it's my only chance to get away. Like I don't get that?

Paul punches Rob on the arm. Rob grins and hits him back. 'Won't ask what you're doing out here,' he says. 'Where are the others?'

'Lizzy's room,' Rob says.

'My old man back yet?' he asks, pulling off his helmet.

'Just Glenda, drowning the music out with the telly,' Rob says.

'Who's this then?'

I realise I'm staring at Paul as if one of the photographs on the albums upstairs in Lizzy's room has come to life and ridden a motorbike up to Nan's garage. Right now he looks nothing like he did last time I saw him; now he's what you imagine if anyone says "80s rocker': faded denim jeans that look like someone spilt bleach all over them, worn black leather biker jacket and shoulder-length fluffy reddish-brown hair that's gone a bit flat but is a long way from the balding uncle I know. Under the jacket, I can just make out a black Megadeth T-shirt over a flat toned stomach, and as he bends over to put his gloves in the box at the back of the bike, I can see a guy on a hospital bed on a woven patch that covers the whole of the back of the jacket, and the words Anthrax. If Lizzy's 18 tomorrow, Paul's 20 and reading Law at Exeter Uni.

'Maisie, this is Lizzy's brother, Paul. He's at Uni,' Rob adds.

'You back for her birthday?' I ask, and it comes out as a bit of a squeak.

'Wouldn't miss it. You coming in or you staying out here?' He can't quite disguise the smirk.

'We're coming in,' I say, looking at Rob. I've had enough tension. Rob nods; the sweetest of smiles on his lips.

Reunions between brother and sister over, Paul is back in his room, and noises like a sack of kittens being murdered are coming out from the cracks around the door. Back in Lizzy's bedroom, the scene's shifted slightly. Elaine and Jasper are talking about what they want to do when they leave school. Tracy, Lizzy and Claire have found a stash of magazines, and they're on her bed talking about Tracy using Sun-In on her hair and getting a shaggy perm to make her look more like Charlene from a new Australian soap called *Neighbours*. Kim and Ian are sitting together on the floor at the bottom of the bed talking in hushed tones, close enough to touch. They're not holding hands or anything, but something's altered since I left the room.

Then I see it. Ani is sitting next to Brian on the bed. He's talking to her with his hands, his eyes are all twinkly, and she is glowing with pleasure. Claire's moved away with her books. I feel a bit weird about this. I mean, Brian's like Rob. They are both the same age as my mother. Jasper's right; we should be thinking about these things, not changing the past and not changing the future. Thing is, when I look at Rob, I can only see how gorgeous he is. I bet Ani isn't seeing an old man in front of her either. What if when we get back to where we should be, my mother has a surprise visit from her old school friend and he recognises me? My stomach suddenly lurches three inches lower. What if when we go back, *my mother* remembers me? Do people recognise someone if they haven't seen them for 32 years? You'd remember them if you travelled through time with them, wouldn't you?

Ani looks up at me then as if she's read my mind, and I feel like I can read hers because I know what she's thinking, I'm sure of it. They've never known anything different. We have. If they get together tonight, she has to do so knowing Brian's old enough to be her father. Rob's old enough to be my father.

I turn around, and Lizzy is now sitting at the front edge of her bed, staring at me as if she's been willing me to notice. My instincts are tingling on point.

'I think it's about time you told us what's going on,' Lizzy says quietly from the bed.

I manage to hold her gaze. 'What d'you mean?'

'Did you think we wouldn't notice?'

She can't possibly mean what it sounds like she says. I look at Rob, but he's giving nothing away. I stall for time, standing up to distance myself from Rob. 'Notice what?'

'You're no more American than we are.'

I look down, and Ani has the look of a rabbit in the headlights of an oncoming lorry. Brian puts a hand on her arm. Jasper looks from me to Lizzy. No one seems shocked by this comment apart from us three, and I realise that somehow, they're all in on it.

I don't know whether to feel worse or better. I stand before her, like the kids who piss her off now she's the Head Teacher. I am so over all this already. I just want my life back. I even want my mother back again. 'You're right,' I cave. 'We're not American. And we're not cousins.'

Ani draws breath sharply. Jasper puts his forehead on his hands. Kim claps her hands like she's just won a prize and gets up of the floor from next to Ian. 'I knew it!' She sits down next to Lizzy.

 Lizzy just nods. 'Okay,' she says in that quiet, almost menacing voice. 'I'm going to tell you what we girls think is going on here.'

Well, this should be interesting.

'I think you got caught on site this morning by one of the staff and had to make up all that stuff about starting at Drake's.'

More interesting than I predicted, then.

'I don't think the Receptionist told you to look for me at all. I believe you made that up too. Not sure how you got my name though.'

I can feel my mouth starting to curl up at the corners.

'That's why you were on site with a boy. You're from out of town. You didn't know it was a girls' school.'

I'm beginning to feel like I traded faces with The Joker. 'It's not what you think.'

'But we're not wrong, are we?' Lizzy asks.

No one says anything for a few seconds.

'Are they right?' Rob asks. I can feel him trying to get me to look at him out of the corner of my eye.

'Your clothes are all baggy, and your jeans are torn,' Kim remarks.

'To be honest, I think that's a really good look. It could catch on,' Elaine says.

'Your hair's all flat like it's been ironed, and you've hardly got any makeup on,' Kim continues. No one replies. Clearly, that's not a good look here, as they are all concerned about it. 'You look like I expect I looked, the first time Lizzy found me sleeping rough under the Willow.'

Now, that really wasn't how I expected her to finish that sentence. In fact, I need to sit down, so I plonk down on the carpet.

'Sleeping rough?' Ani echoes.

'My stepmother and my dad are very traditional,' Kim goes on, lacing her fingers together in her lap and kneading them like dough. 'They don't believe teenagers should have the free-dom we have. They don't let me do things other girls my age are allowed to do. They don't -' She falters, and suddenly, my heart lurches for her. Ian's suddenly up on the bed as well, and he's taken her hand.

Lizzy is a step ahead of him. She threads an arm determinedly through Kim's. 'Kim's folk are strict, and they don't let her out. She used to run away when anything was happening, sleep rough in the Park and tell her parents she missed the last bus. Then they'd bollock her for the next month. When she finally told us;' she punches Kim's arm gently, and Kim smiles a watery smile; 'when she finally told us what was going on, we worked stuff out. Mum helps. We can work it out for you too.'

Kim slides off the bed and on to the carpet beside me. 'You're runaways, aren't you?' she says, her elfin face solemn with intensity.

It's not a bad cover story, as cover stories go. Will it last us until we can sort out this mess? The jury's out, but it's better than American Cousins. I look at Ani, and she's looking down at where Brian hasn't moved his hand. Elaine is smiling at Jasper. Exhale.

'You're not wrong,' I reply carefully.

'How did you know to ask for Lizzy though?' Claire asks.

'Saw her name on a folder as we came into the Common Room,' Jasper says quickly. Claire pulls a face, but even if his quick thinking hasn't impressed her, it's impressed me, and Elaine, so it seems.

'Okay. So we were right. And we can sort everything out, but now it's the start of a mega party weekender, so party first, problems another day. It's about time we left, I reckon,' Tracy says. 'You want to come back to mine, Ani? I got this great red silk bomber jacket that would be fab with your hair.'

'Ani can come with me,' Claire says firmly. 'I want to pick your brains on some of the Physics we were looking at this afternoon. I can lend you some gear to wear.'

'Bugger off, Claire, it's supposed to be a party, not a study date,' Tracy growls, but Ani is on her feet.

'No, I'd like to come with you,' she says gratefully to Claire. 'Don't be salty about it, please Tracy?'

'Don't be what?' Tracy blinks once. 'You may not be American, but that dialect is funky.' She waves her arm. 'Fine. Go dork together. Elaine, you want to come and play?'

'I'll get my stuff from home,' Elaine says.

'Maisie can stay here with Kim and me,' Lizzy says firmly. 'That's cool with you, yes?'

'Absolutely,' I say.

'We better be motoring too,' Rob says. 'You come with me, Jasper. I've got some stuff you can change into if you want to.'

'What? Oh yeah, thanks a lot,' Jasper replies, his voice unnaturally high.

Two by two or three, they all leave the room. Rob gives me another of his sweetest smiles as he goes, and I get a panicky feeling.

'Are you still going to get off with Rob tonight?' Kim asks.

I turn sharply, but before I can put my foot in it, I realise she's aimed the question at Lizzy.

'I don't think so.'

'Why not?'

Lizzy sighs. 'Just because things looked good with Rob, he hadn't made me any promises. Besides, he seems really into Maisie now.' I open my mouth to protest, but she laughs and shakes her head. 'It's cool. Rob can't take his eyes off you,' she retorts. 'You may not've been watching him, but I have. It's fine. I've met someone else, anyway.'

'Someone else?' Kim squeaks.

'I told you,' Lizzy says patiently; 'Patchouli.'

Kim breathes out hard. 'He's too old.'

Lizzy giggles. 'You sound like Mum.' She looks at me. 'He'll be okay though, Rob, I mean. So long as his new crush feels the same as him.'

Kim looks across at me, and her mouth forms a perfect 'o'.

I realise their point a little too late. 'Oh no,' I say, 'no. I'm not looking for anything like that.'

Lizzy laughs. 'Why not? Don't you fancy him?'

It's not as easy as I thought to lie. 'Well, he is fit as.'

'Fit as what?' Kim asks. 'Well, he drums, so that keeps him fit.'

Lizzy laughs again. 'He's wicked hot, and he's clearly into you. Bingo.'

'*Bullseye*,' Kim says.

'Got to love a bit of Bully,' Lizzy says.

I get the feeling I'm trying to speak a different language again when Glenda's voice trills up the staircase.

'Do we need to be ringing Kim's Mum soon?'

'Be right there,' Lizzy says.

Kim looks at me. 'I have to make my younger brother's packed lunch for school, mop the kitchen floor, clean the toilets and the washbasins, feed her brother's guinea pigs, load the washing machine and make my packed lunch before I get any time to shower or have breakfast.'

I don't know what to say, so I just pull a face. Things at home with my mother weren't great, but she never treated me like that.

'Dad'll tell me I can go somewhere, and then the car will be needed for something else, and they won't let me use the phone to tell Lizzy.'

Okay, that did sound a bit much.

'Once, they'd agreed to let me go to a party, and when I got home from school and opened her wardrobe to start planning my outfit, it was stripped bare. Nothing left but knickers and tights in my drawers. Even my bras had gone as well.' She nods at my shocked expression. 'Stepmother said they were dusty and smelled of mould, and she had to wash the lot. That evening. An entire wardrobe of clothes. I lost it with them that time, and ...' Her voice breaks then, and I put my hand out quickly.

'Kim, listen, you really don't have to tell me this stuff, you hardly know me ...'

She shakes her head no and takes a deep breath. 'They told me if the party was that important I could go in my knickers, and once the washing was done, they locked me in my bedroom for the rest of the weekend without any food for being cheeky. So you see, Lizzy's family looks after me now. Lizzy's family always look out for people who are down on their luck. And the point is - she'll look after you. If you need her too.'

She almost runs out of the room and down the stairs.

'Shouldn't you follow her?' I ask, my stomach churning with concern.

Lizzy shakes her head. 'She'll be okay.'

'She really didn't need to tell me all that personal stuff,' I say.

'Yeah, she did.' Lizzy sits on her hands. 'She needs to get it off her chest every now and then, especially with new people. It's kind of cathartic, but it's also a test.'

'A test?'

'She thinks if people still want to be her friend after hearing her story, you're worth having around.'

'Who wouldn't want to be her friend after hearing that?' I exclaim. 'You'd have to be bloody heartless.'

'Seems like you're going to be worth having around then.' She smiles and gets to her feet.

'I didn't think you liked me,' I blurt out as she goes to leave the room.

She looks back at me then, and there is a genuine shock in her eyes. 'Why wouldn't I like you? I don't even know you,' she says. Her head droops a little, and she sighs. 'So, here's my story. I'm crap around new people. I get defensive. I never know what to say, so people think I'm a bit up myself. That's about it.' Her voice trails off without explaining, and my throat constricts to the point that I can say nothing in reply. 'Mum's been taking in what she calls her waifs and strays for as long as I can remember, and if you need our help, it's yours. Anyway, come downstairs for the Ritual.'

It's funny how a couple of sentences can completely change your understanding of what makes someone tick. I'm starting to wonder if I ever really knew my mother at all.

So it turns out that the Ritual was that if something significant happened socially, Kim wouldn't catch the bus home after school. She'd pack some clothes in her PE bag that morning, go back to Lizzy's place when school finished, and then ring her Mum to say she wouldn't be home until later. Her Mum would start to rant, and then Glenda would step in and reason with her until the woman had no choice but to step down. Of course, Kim would pay the price later, but Glenda would hide loads of snacks into her bag which kept her going if she was locked up, and since Kim did all the washing at her house, so far, we'd got away with it. If it happened at Drake's now, you'd hope someone official would step in, but it seems you can get away with it in Glenda's time. I guess they never hurt her where you can see it, her parents.

At the bottom of the stairs, she looks at us, and Lizzy gives her a big bear hug. She takes a deep breath, maybe two. Then she lifts the phone, a large handle, attached by a plastic spiral away from a dark red plastic wedge. There seems to be a circular dial on the front of the wedge with holes in it. She puts her finger in different holes and makes the dial rotate. It clicks back to its original position, and she starts again. I'm guessing this is a phone, but it takes so long even to make the call. One of the numbers is 9, and it takes forever to go back to its original setting. Wouldn't it take forever to call an ambulance if you needed one? And where's the privacy when you're having your conversation in a hallway?

I open the door into the lounge, and I'm temporarily overwhelmed by more history. Cork tiles over a fake brick fireplace, cream and brown patterned carpet that gives me a headache if I stare at it for too long, brown velour furniture, and the tiniest screen seems to be showing the opening credits to something called *Montreux Rock Festival Preview* on the telly. My Granddad Henry's chair is in front of what my mother still rather pompously calls the bureau, where she keeps all her bills.

Glenda looks over from her favourite armchair by the fire as we walk in. The fire's not on, but she always sits there anyway. 'Need me yet?' she says.

Lizzy nods and goes back out to the hallway, where Kim is

speaking into the large mouthpiece.

Glenda gets up and turns the telly down, and we both wait as Kim goes through the motions. 'Who was that dishy boy with you earlier?' she asks quietly.

'Rob?'

'No, the boy that came in with you new kids.'

Kids? I'm 18 in 32 years. Charming. 'His name is Jasper.'

'Nice boy. Very polite. Is he going to the Fundraiser?' I nod. 'I don't think he should spend too much time with Lizzy,' she says out of the blue.

My mouth falls open a little bit. 'Why do you say that?'

'Just a hunch.' She looks at me again, that same odd look she gave me in the canteen.

Something in the way she says that makes me edgy rather than resentful – it doesn't feel like racism, it's something else, and I'm instantly cold in my fingertips and my toes. 'Lizzy will explain everything,' I say, hoping that she never needs to.

In the hallway, Kim holds the phone away from her ear, and I can hear her mother's voice from where we're standing, shrieking about responsibilities on the other end. Lizzy's making urgent shapes with her hands.

Glenda's on the case immediately, all weirdness forgotten. 'Mrs Fox? Hello? Yes, hello, it's Glenda Brookes here. Mind if I call you Mary? Lovely.'

Kim steps away from the phone like it's an armed grenade. We go into the front room and sit down on the carpet. The *News At Six* comes on. We've got just over an hour to get ourselves looking gorgeous for the Fundraiser Mark Two.

Chapter Eleven – Shattered Dreams (Johnny Hates Jazz, 1987)

Just over an hour later, me, Lizzy and Kim walk away from our house to where the back entrance to the Park joins my road. Lizzy's looking every inch the eighties' rock fan girl again, but it's not exactly like the first time I saw her. This time she's wearing blue jeans that look like someone's thrown a cup of acid over them before spraying them onto her legs. The bottoms are tucked into saggy socks and black trainer boots with Reebok sewn onto the side. A simple grey T-shirt clings onto every curve she's got, and her hair is crimped with an iron and preened into classic big hair backcombed wildness. She's wearing a denim jacket and a pair of fake Ray-ban Wayfarers sunglasses.

Beside me, Kim is Madonna to Lizzy's Rock Chick, her light brown hair held back with a brightly patterned green and orange silk scarf, a little floaty tiered purple skirt over black Lycra crop leggings and a pair of cute black suede boots that she calls 'pixie', and weirdly, one short white lace glove. A black vest top sets her off. She looks amazing, but I don't have the confidence to bare that much skin, so I opted for black jeans, red vest, black Converse and a short black blazer that's fitted to my waist. Not exactly my usual look, but not like so much fancy dress either. There's not going to be a pair of straighteners in town for another two decades; I couldn't face the crimping irons, but at least no one's going to judge my fluffy hair tonight.

Lizzy's got something she calls a gas mask bag over her shoulder, yellow canvas fabric with the names of her favourite bands drawn in felt tip all over it. Inside are our contributions to the party: a couple of brown bottles of 1080 cider from the fridge, a big bottle of Thunderbird Blue alcohol that Paul gave her as we headed out the door and a packet of cigarettes in a bright blue box marked Dorchester. When we walk into the Park, I can see Ani, Claire, Elaine and Tracy waiting by the Willow where we sat and chatted on earlier on in the day. Ani's looking fine. Perhaps the clothes are a bit pinker than she'd usually choose, but the pink jeans and a white T-Shirt are fire against her dark skin. If Brian thought she slayed this afternoon, he's going to be lit at the sight of her now.

Tracy and Elaine are in full-on '80s Day-Glo: their hair all backcombed with bright silk scarves tied under and in a bow on top; vivid short leggings under colourful tight short skirts, bare lower legs and high heels with impossible spikes; little double-breasted cropped jackets cut short at the waist over even shorter tops showing their stomachs.

The boys turn up next. Brian can't seem to help to gawp at Ani, and I can't deny Rob looks dope. He's got this whole '80s movie star vibe going on for him in bleached-out jeans and black trainer boots, with a white T-shirt and a light grey jacket with the sleeves rolled up to his elbows so you can see white and black pinstripe lining, and the thing is – he looks good. Jasper's usual style is only slightly tamer: hair a little flatter; jeans a little tighter; T-shirt a little baggier. Ian and Brian are cool in black with biker jackets similar to one Paul was wearing earlier.

Take your places, ladies and gentleman: it's showtime.

We pour the contents of our bags and jackets out onto the grass. Tracy's managed to find two litres of Diamond White, Ian and Rob produce a few cans of lager and Claire's pinched a few shots of vodka from her mum's drinks cabinet. I reach over and grab the bottle of Diamond White, as it's the only name I recognise, but after one swig I nearly barf - it tastes like meth in a green plastic bottle. I take another swig to steady my nerves. We can do this. We can cope until they go back through the Old Library. Lizzy thinks we're runaways and she'll sort something out.

I take another swig from the Diamond White as it passes around the circle. This stuff really does taste like meth, or what you'd expect meth to taste like, but somehow it's okay when your sole purpose in drinking it is to get wasted entirely as quickly as possible.

By 8:15, the drink's gone, the whole bloody lot, and I feel pissed; not the way I've got used to feeling pissed but this is sugar rush pissed. I'm up for a marathon run, or an all-night disco. This is dangerous, and I don't give a shit. This is the Fundraiser 1987, I am back here, and I can do what I want. I can get off with Rob. Watch me!

Kim's got my arm as we all get up. 'You okay, Maisie?' she asks, all concern as seems to be usual for her.

'High on life,' I reply, with a grin. She shakes her head and gives a wry laugh.

'I'll take it from here.'

I look up at Jasper as he offers me his arm. I take it, Kim smiles and moves away. I'm not looking at Tracy or Lizzy, but I can feel their eyes on us. I am not even thinking about Rob, whether he's watching us or not. Honestly. I really am not. I am just linking arms with a boy friend like I'd link arms with a girl friend.

'Here we go again,' Jasper says quietly. 'Same shit, different decade. What exactly are we doing here?'

'Not doing exactly the same shit,' I say, conscious that my own words are a bit furrier around the edges than usual.

'Not exactly with the same people,' he adds.

'Not exactly wearing the same clothes, either. You look good, though.' I squeeze his arm. 'We're in 1987!'

'How bevved up are you?' he asks, smirking at me.

'I'm fine.' I pat his hand patronisingly, and perhaps a little harder than necessary.

'Brian seems really into Ani.'

'And Elaine seemed keen on you back at home – Lizzy's I mean.'

'And Rob would rip my arm off to be walking here next to you now.' He steadies us both and starts walking again. 'Maisie, it's like *Back to The Future.*'

'No, it's not, unless Rob lent you a pair of Calvin Klein underpants. No! – don't tell me. What about it?' My voice sounds slurry. Surely I can't be that drunk.

'In the film you don't change the past, or you mess up the future!' Jasper says uber-dramatically.

'Thing is though Jasper, this isn't a film set. This is something else.'

'This is just crazy, and if I knew how, I'd already be doing something to get everyone back where they should be!' he hisses at me.

I find myself prodding him somewhat hard in the chest. 'Why would you want to do that?' I grin.

Those words drop into the middle of us and detonate like an atomic bomb.

He stops walking, so I stop walking. 'Why you say that?' he mutters quietly, and the spot I'm standing on doesn't feel all that still.

'Well right now, I'm not all that bothered about going back,' I reply, and a giggle slips out.

Then we're facing each other, and suddenly I'm concentrating hard on the silver zip at the bottom of his jacket, but it keeps going in and out of focus. 'Maisie. You don't mean that. You were all worried about being here earlier. You're wasted.'

'I like Rob,' I say.

'He likes you too. He dropped a few hints. He's a decent guy. Got a great setup in his dad's garage.' I can see the others walking on ahead without us. Rob's walking between Tracy and Lizzy, Brian with Ani and Claire, Ian between Elaine and Kim. They haven't noticed we've stopped moving. 'He is good blud,' Jasper continues. 'But he's – Maisie, he's crusty. Ancient.'

'Well, not right now he's not,' I reply cheerfully.

'Will you two move your arses?' Tracy screams back at us from the main school gates.

I hadn't realised we're so close to the school, but now I can hear the bass pounding from the open Hall windows. We've walked past the caretaker's house on the bottom road and then towards the main entrance at the front of the school.

This time yesterday when I heard the bass pounding from

the windows, I was going to meet Lizzy and her friends. If I'd known I would meet Rob, what would I have done? Would I have gone home?

I don't think so, somehow.

Me and Jasper walk up to join the others. I still can't bring myself to look Rob in the eye. I'm fed up with thinking about the implications; I'm fed up with the feeling I ought to be responsible. I need a holiday away from Responsibility City. I can hear poppy, lively, happy music blasting out of the Main Hall as we walk through the School Gates, up to the main entrance to pay, get our hands stamped and move into the building.

Suddenly Tracy's grabbed my hand, and she's pulling me away from Jasper. He holds on for a fair while until he realises that the boys are staying in the entrance hall, and us girls are heading for the Hall itself.

The curtains are different; they're heavier and darker than the blackout blinds I remember. There's hardly a boy dancing, but I can just about pick them all out, loitering on the edges of the action in groups around the room. I can almost hear them working out which of us they're going to target later.

At the front of the Hall by the doors to the entrance hall, there's a table with water and soft drinks to buy, and a nervous couple of olds staffing it. Next thing I know they're playing a song I recognise but couldn't name. I'm eternally thankful that Kim, Elaine, Ani and Claire dance; me, Lizzy and Tracy slink into the sidelines.

'I have never danced to bloody Five Star, and I don't intend to begin now,' Lizzy says.

'So have you made your choice?' Tracy asks.

'About dancing to Five Star?'

'Don't act smart. Are you going to stick with Rob or break your heart over that bloke who works in the Hippy shop?'

'Stop pushing me into stuff,' Lizzy replies unsteadily. She's pretty much as drunk as I am. 'You think I'm such a player? Make your moves on Rob and see if you get what you want. We already know he doesn't want you.' She waves an unsteady hand at me.

'That's a really bitchy thing to say, Brookes!' Tracy exclaims. My head is beginning to spin rapidly, and suddenly I don't feel so good, and the last thing I need is Lizzy and her best friend having a row.

'Well, I don't want to get off with Rob, and you keep on at me about it,' Lizzy roars, although her words are almost drowned by the music. 'I told Maisie to go for it if she wants to. Rob fancies the pants off her, it's written all over him. I want something a bit more mature.'

'Bloody Patchouli!' Tracy shouts back. 'I don't trust him! He's going to break your bleedin' heart.'

The boys are walking into the back of the Hall. They've bought the drinks, and as they get closer, I'm overwhelmed with a desire to run away. It's not the music; it's not even the bitching between Lizzy and Tracy. My head feels like someone has forced cotton wool balls in through my ears, and my mouth feels full of grit. Everything I knew is in my face now, chafing against my skin, yelling at me to wake up and get a grip, make a choice, move on. I'm only just about dealing with Lizzy as a person rather than my future mum; I can't deal with her drunk and fighting yet. Who is this Patchouli they keep on about? I don't ever remember her mentioning him in any of the stories she's told us, and you know what? I'm freaked. Finally, I'm freaked, and I run back to the main entrance to find some space. Or maybe somewhere to vom violently is a better description.

Waving my stamped hand at the teachers on the door, back outside the entrance I'm close enough to hear the music; I drop down onto the grass and stare down at the bottom road that passes the school, watching cars driving up towards the chippy, and in the opposite direction going down towards town. People are still queuing to get in. I know they're there, but I don't look at them. I close my eyes against the lights, trying to make my lurching stomach hold on to its contents.

Am I bothered about going back to where we should be, or am I just a mess? Mixing drinks is never a good thing. I suppose I shouldn't be surprised that someone would come and find me, and I'm not surprised by who shows up.

Chapter Twelve – Is This Love? (Alison Moyet, 1987)

How can I feel so excited and terrified at the same time? How can I stay here in 1987? How can I even have considered the possibility? No matter how much I might want to stay, I've got to get back to where I belong. We've all got to get back. My cheeks are wet. I'm an embarrassment, sitting on my own at the Fundraiser and crying like this. Whatever I want, I have to get us back to where we should be. Don't I? I wipe my cheek roughly.

'Don't cry,' he says. So here he is, fast becoming the main reason for my confusion.

'I'm fine.' More of the hugest tears of my life leak onto my face. 'Well, maybe not so fine.'

Rob sits down on the grass beside me, draws his legs up and gently pulls me against him, leaning around and rubbing the tears from my face with his thumbs, rough but gentle, dismissive but caring. 'Don't cry,' he says again.

'Everything's a mess,' I say.

'Not your fault,' he says.

'You don't know that.' The tears are dropping out of my eyes now like a dripping tap. 'Maybe it's not my fault but I ... I don't know what to do to make it better!'

'What do you want to do?' he asks. 'Do you want to go home?'

Of course - I'm a homeless runaway. 'Do I want to go home right now?' I turn to face him. It feels like there are millimetres between our noses and our lips, and my breath catches in my throat. I hold my position like a standoff, but he's not moving either. 'Home?' I say. 'You don't want to know the truth.'

'Are we playing truth or dare now?' he smiles.

'That might be dangerous,' I say, smiling back in spite of everything.

'I can take the truth.'

'Maybe I want the dare instead,' I hear myself saying.

'Let's stay with the truth for now,' he says, his voice kind, not accusing. I guess he can't work it out; if there's such an attraction between us, why won't I act on it?

I clutch at the first thing that comes into my woolly head, to try to have a reason for all these hysterics. 'They told me you were with Lizzy. She told me to back off. In the nicest way possible.'

He stares forward. 'I heard what Tracy was saying to you earlier. Before we went to the caravan.'

'Oh,' I reply, still hiccupping tears.

'Lizzy and me, we've known each other for donkeys,' he says.

'Donkeys?'

'Ages,' he frowns. "Our families go way back. Lizzy's cute, but there's always been someone else around for both of us. We're just really good mates. You know how it is when all your mates think you'd make the perfect couple, and you end up getting together just because they think it's a major league done deal, and it ends up being a massive mistake?'

No, not really. 'So the two of you were never planning on

getting together tonight?'

I can feel his arm enfolding me, as he shakes his head, no. 'She's after some bloke who works in town, and me - well, I had my head turned this lunchtime.' His words in my ear are like velvet has a voice, and his breath is warm against my neck. 'So I've told you my truth,' he says, and I swear every part of him is closer to me than he's been before. 'Are you going to dare me something now?'

I'm leaning up against him, head turned, and we're practically nose to nose, and he's got one hand on the side of my face, and the other has found one of my hands. This is make or break. This is the choice. To be honest, it's no choice. I'm so glad I haven't been sick. 'Dare you to kiss me then,' I say quietly. Don't make me explain myself. I'd like to see you refuse a kiss in this situation.

I can feel his lips touching mine, soft as candy floss scented with mint and he's sliding his hand hesitantly over my hips, wrapping it around my waist, and I am sinking in the quicksand that's developed under my feet. The softest, gentlest lips he has, and as they start to part over mine, I hear shouting like voices inside my head. No, they aren't inside my head. It's Jasper.

'Need to talk to you now, Maisie!' he snaps.

'Bit busy here, bro,' I say, still looking at Rob. Rob moves away from me but only just; his lips are so close to mine it's like there's an electrical current buzzing between us.

'Maisie, for God's sake! Listen to me! I can't find Ani!' Jasper shouts.

'You can't find Ani?' I ask, and even before her name's left my mouth, I think I know what he's going to tell me.

'She's gone off somewhere with Brian,' Jasper says. He looks uncomfortable. 'I think they like each other,' he says as if he's trying out every word before it leaves his mouth. 'That's what I wanted to talk to you about. I mean, I know what you said earlier. I know what you said, but it isn't right, because I mean, on the face of it we're all the same age, but I don't think it can be good, you know?' He pauses, and I'm conscious of his eyes on Rob. 'I'm not sure what's right and wrong about this, but it's like you said - Brian's like – her age now, isn't he? I mean back where we came from? And him?'

It's difficult to ignore the meaningful looks he's giving Rob, or the puzzled looks Rob is giving him in return. I can feel my tired legs starting to kick in the water, and I'm suddenly soaring to the surface of sober through the weeds of uncomfortable conversations. Okay, maybe not so sober just yet, way too flowery with the poetic observations. 'But unlike us, they've got no idea what's ahead of them,' I say, staggering to my feet, feeling like someone's just slapped my face.

Jasper looks down at his Vans. If I'd been sober, I've have realised I wasn't thinking straight earlier. All that talk about wanting to stay here. Jasper's a worrier. Now we're all sobering up, all he can see is that one of his BFFs is sitting way close to a boy who's old enough to be her dad, and the other one has vanished with someone the same, and reality is hammering on his front door with a baseball bat. 'We have to find Ani! What if they go back through the Old Library tonight and we're not with them?'

'Jasper – am I on your turf here?' Rob asks seriously. I turn around. He's still sitting on the grass, both legs up, elbows resting on his knees. It suddenly occurs to me that I met Rob in the

Music Room in the PA Block last night. Maybe if we just stay close to Rob -

'Sorry, Rob. Can you give us a couple of minutes please?' Jasper says.

Rob says nothing for a few moments. This boy, he's kind and thoughtful; he's not like most of the guys at Drake's or FCA, and I feel bad that he's getting dragged into our drama when he doesn't even know it's happening under his nose. He's on his feet now.

'No, don't send him away. Please,' I say into the sudden silence. 'It's not his fault, Jasper, come on -'

'I can't talk to you if he's here,' he says.

'You want us to go and find Ani? We can all of us go and find Ani together. We don't have to split up.' I need a glass of water; it feels like my throat is full of dust. 'Where is everyone else?'

'Some of them are in the Main Hall dancing. They wouldn't come after you because they said - well, they were right,' he says lamely, looking at the floor. 'But I can't find Ani. We all need to stick together, Maisie!' he suddenly blurts out regardless of Rob being there. 'We can't mess around in the past! You said so yourself! Why have you changed your mind?'

I haven't the balls to trash him for talking so openly. 'I haven't changed my mind! At least -' Then I realise somehow I have, and that I'm making a colossal mistake. I look back at Rob. 'I'm sorry.'

He pushes his hands deep into his pockets. 'So you two are together?' he says, without looking at me.

I look at Jasper. 'No, but -'

'I don't understand then,' he says, and he looks so forlorn, and I am lost, and this is the thing: I don't want to lie to this lovely boy any more. Maybe it's still the cider talking, but I can't see how to make this right, without calling in the truth. The real truth, not a flirty game.

The words are out of my mouth before I can change my mind again.

'We're from the future.'

Jasper's face snaps around to stare at mine in complete surprise. 'For fuck's sake, Maisie!'

'Come again?' Rob says.

Five, maybe ten seconds pass. I slither back down onto the grass next to Rob, and Jasper sinks down beside me. I look at Jasper. We've known each other forever, Jasper and me. We started nursery school on the same day, and we've been BFFs ever since the time he stole my red crayon and I smacked him over the head with the yellow plastic spade from the sand play area. We can finish each other's sentences on a good day. Today, he can read my mind. He nods, almost imperceptibly.

I pull the *iPhone* out of my jeans pocket, where I hid it when I was changing at Lizzy's. It's the latest model for 2019 and my early birthday present. Mum gave it to me the morning of the Fundraiser. We all stare as I toss it onto the grass between us.

'Why are you showing me your calculator?' Rob asks lightly.

'It's not a calculator,' I say. 'This is an *Apple iPhone. Ten-R.* Two hundred and fifty-six gig.'

'A phone?' he repeats faintly. 'That's not a phone. Where are the wires? How does it connect?'

'It's a phone. It's also a camera, a music player, a video player and a games console,' Jasper says.

'A … what the hell are you on about?' Rob asks, and for the first time, I can hear the tension in his voice.

I mentally cross my fingers and hope the battery hasn't died along with the signal. I've got 4% left. It's enough if I choose my next moves carefully.

First, I hit play. Bastille comes out of the side speakers; the music is tinny but audible. Rob's eyes widen, and he moves back from it, almost imperceptibly, but he says nothing, and his eyes don't leave the screen, which is now telling him that doom days are coming, scrolling the lyrics for him, telling him how long the song will last.

I end the song. 3% left. Time and my battery are running out fast.

'What is that? Some kind of Walkman? Where do you put the tape?' he asks.

I open my Gallery and pray that the picture we took on the day of our Fundraiser is still there. I'm hoping to find the picture of us at the bottom of my garden, brandishing the cider, the estate where Jasper's house is built stretching away into the distance on the other side of the road behind us.

Photo found, I thrust the phone into Rob's hand, and I watch as his brain finally fries. 'This is a picture of me, Ani and Jasper,' I say. 'It was taken last night, at the bottom of my garden between the garage and our motor home. You can see we're wearing the same clothes we were wearing when we met you. We were about to go to the Fundraiser. In our time.'

'This is …' He trails off.

'Lizzy's back garden. In just over thirty years,' I say.

'Those houses,' he says hoarsely. 'There are houses. Over the back road.'

'They haven't been built yet,' I confirm, my voice low.

'It's the Poets' Estate,' Jasper says flatly. 'I live there.'

Rob stares at the image. 'So you're telling me you live in Lizzy's house. In the future?' he says. His voice is too low. This isn't going to end well.

'Lizzy is -' Jasper begins.

'Unaware of any of this.' I glare at Jasper, and he takes the hint. Don't ask me why I think it's safer to tell him about our predicament and not my future mother, but I do.

The three of us look at each other for a few moments, and then Rob laughs. 'This is a stunt, right? Are you two from *Beadle's About* or something?'

'I don't know what you're talking about,' Jasper says.

Rob looks at Jasper, down at my smartphone in his hands, and then at me. So I tell Rob about the Fundraiser in 2019, how Jasper is at Drake's with us, how Ani convinced us to go scratching around in the Old Library because a friend in her History class found a book that said it was a portal – but then I stop. I don't think I should tell him about his future. Something is stopping me from telling him how we click in the PA Block in thirty-two years. And I'm definitely not telling him that Lizzy is my mother.

'In 2019, I'm 18, but Maisie hasn't had her birthday yet,' Jasper says. 'We don't exist yet here.'

'So I'm... what ... 50, in 2019?' Rob asks. When neither of us replies, he laughs again. 'I am! 50? Well bugger me, that's a turn up for the books.'

'We're supposed to go back to 2019 tonight. And when I do get back to tomorrow, what happens then?' I hear myself asking. 'Think about it, Rob! I've drunk too much; I shouldn't have made you think I have a choice here. We have to get back!'

'If you were a runaway like you told us you were,' he goes on quietly, 'you'd be in the Upper Sixth, and I'd be the same at FCAB. We would be friends, all three of us.' His beautiful green eyes drip honey into mine. 'Maybe more than friends, Maisie. Wouldn't we?'

I've broken out in a cold sweat. We're staring at each other, and as the seconds stretch out into a full minute, I realise my world is changing in the backdrop of the scenes we're playing out here.

'Maybe, yes.' I look into his green eyes, reflecting the lights from the school back at me.

'Okay, maybe you're right, but we need to go after Ani,' Jasper says unsympathetically, and I stand beside him, looking down miserably at Rob, having to choose. And it shouldn't be a difficult choice between my BFF and the boy I just met, but it is. It's as simple as that. It just is.

I tell him, 'Come and help us find Ani.'

He stands up. 'If you didn't want this, you only had to say so.'

I wasn't expecting that. 'No!' I hear myself telling him. 'Didn't you listen to what we just told you?' And the world's suddenly rushing in my ears, roaring like a tide coming in - I can't stop the change.

'Oh, I listened,' he says miserably. 'You think we haven't all seen *Back to the Future*?' I'm not sure how to reply, but it seems he's not waiting for an answer. 'You didn't have to come up with some whacko story about time portals and the future to put me off, and I don't know how in hell you got your calcula-tor to play that song, or what special effects you used to make those houses appear in your photo, or even how that photo is on your calculator and not printed out like normal photos in an album ...' He trails off. His face is a mask of emotion: disbelief, humiliation and confusion. He looks me straight in the eyes. 'I'm not a perv. You could've just said no. I thought it was what you wanted. I would never have kissed you if I thought you didn't want me to. I'm not that sort of bloke.'

As he walks away, I feel like someone's slapped me, and that I deserve it. Another big fat tear seeps down my cheek.

I feel soft fingers winding their way around mine. 'Maisie, I know you're hurting, but we have to bounce and find Ani,' he says gently. 'He doesn't believe us. He thinks you made it up to explain why you didn't want to fix up. He won't say anything to the others.'

'You think I care about that right now?' I snap, pulling my fingers away from him.

Now it's Jasper looking miserable because of me. FML. I look up towards the glass front of the entrance hall. Suddenly noises come rushing back in: laughter, music and chatter. The bubble has burst.

'We need to find Ani,' I mutter. I can't even.

Chapter Thirteen – C'est La Vie (Robbie Nevil, 1987)

Half of me, no probably three-quarters of me wants to run in and find out where Rob has gone, but when we're back inside the Entrance Hall he's already vanished, and I have to focus. If Ani is with Brian, that's potentially not good. I've always looked out for my mates, now, even more, I need to make sure everyone's okay tonight and protect what kind of a future we might have if we ever get back to it. And Jasper's right. If Lizzy and her friends are going to go through the portal in the Old Library tonight, then we all need to be with her: me, Jasper and Ani.

I walk back through the entrance hall, Jasper close behind. Teachers are standing around out here – they're more on it than the ones in our day – so there's not much other going on. I go past them, and I can feel them eyeing us, probably wondering whether to confront us over where we've been, but I wave my stamped hand at them, and they say nothing, and I push the double doors open into the Main Hall.

The lights are out apart from the ones flashing from the DJ's rig. The place is rammed, and it's hard to make out faces, let alone one I recognise. I stand for a while and watch people, taking a little time. This is not my Fundraiser. People don't know me, and I know very few of them, but it must have been a big event, this Fundraiser, because there are no boys in class at Drake's yet, and right now the Main Hall is full of them. There're so many crowds of cliques that I don't know where to begin to look to find the one I've ended up with. A load of girls in ruffled skirts and bright cropped tops are dancing in a big circle; another group are almost solely in black and denim, and yet another are all pastels and gym shoes with cardigans slung around their shoulders. I watch as a group of boys pace around the ruffle girls, and although I can't hear, their body language is making decisions, pulling rank on each other, who's going to score, who's going to walk away empty-handed. It's like the cattle markets I'm used to at home, but with tons of neon and big hair. Finally, I spot some of who I'm looking for.

'Tracy, Lizzy and Claire are dancing over there,' I shout into Jasper's ear, pointing forward. 'Can't see the others. Who are we missing? Kim, Elaine, Ian, Ani, Brian - and Rob of course.'

He nods. 'We need to find Ani.'

We walk further into the middle of the hall, striding purposefully towards where Tracy, Lizzy and Claire are dancing. As we get closer, I spot a rack of boys in black and denim standing off to one side, watching them. Jasper turns and nods at them, and they nod back, grinning and nudging each other as if he sits with them in double History every week and he's the first of them to get lucky. Amazing what you can get away with if you show enough confidence.

'There you are!' Lizzy says, flinging a drunken hand around my neck. 'Take it you did the dirty deed then?'

'What?'

'I told you, don't worry. That one over there in the Maiden T-shirt looks all right. Might make his night later!'

'Good idea. Where's Ani?' Jasper yells at her. Lizzy shrugs and goes into a set of moves clearly designed to attract maximum attention from the onlookers.

Claire leans over. 'She was here, then Brian came over, and the two of them went off somewhere,' she shouts, cupping my ear. 'They went out the fire doors towards the Old Library.'

What is it with that bloody building?

'Claire thinks she's with Brian!' I cup my hands and bellow into Jasper's ear. 'Out the back. Head for the Old Library.'

'Let's get out of here,' he mouths, his eyes rounder than the lights on the DJ's desk.

It's a relief to be able to talk again outside. I wonder whether my mother has to follow some regulation or other about the noise levels in discos between now and there. I swear it's louder in that hall tonight than it was yesterday.

We walk up the familiar path towards the Old Library and I have a push against the door just in case, but it's still locked. I look past the building, across where the tennis courts will eventually be built, over the fields towards FCAB, trying to make out two figures sitting on the grass, or standing, talking or ...

On the edge of the area near to the top road that leads down to the school gates, standing under an unlit lamppost with the fading daylight filtering down and framing their faces, I can see two people holding each other, kissing. One of them I recognise.

'Is that Ani and Brian?' Jasper whispers.

'No,' I reply, peering more closely to check. 'It's Kim and Ian.'

He breathes out dramatically. 'So we found them at least.

Would Brian have gone on across the field towards FCAB, or gone back into one of our departments?'

I remember Brian in Lizzy's bedroom earlier in the day talking to Claire and Ani about Physics, and then when he showed Ani his drawings, how awestruck she seemed and how excited they looked to share all their ideas with each other.

'He doesn't go to Drake's. He might've taken Ani to see one of his projects.' I pause, staring out across the darkening fields. 'He was showing her some drawings of robots earlier at Lizzy's. But surely he wouldn't be such a tool to attempt to get into FCAB now?'

'Wasn't he the one you said climbed up and licked the window when you were in the PA Block yesterday?'

It's a fair point. Brian's clearly on the safe side of certifiable, still crazy enough to attempt anything to impress a girl that likes Physics, and Ani's just bare weirdo anyway, so she'd definitely go along with any suggestion made by a clever boy who likes her.

'Probably worth a look.'

Five minutes later, chest heaving from a quick jog across the fields, we're drawing closer to the imposing brown brick building that is Fletcher Clark Academy, now solely for Boys. Looks a lot like a cross between Hogwarts and prison, FCAB, and it hasn't changed much since I walked past it yesterday, except for the lack of a new concrete computing block out the front. We've just run straight across the land where that's going to be built.

With its rows of dark windows reflecting the sun setting behind us, tonight it looks like it's in Hell. There's one car parked in the staff car park; it probably belongs to the care-taker. You don't usually enter FCA from the front; you walk around the sides of the building and go through the narrow brick passages to your form room. I've been here a couple of times for enrichment classes, and I've been to a couple of Fund-raisers here too, although FCA rather pompously calls them Community Events. But then FCA is a bit up itself, not like Drake's, with its 1950's shabby chic, flat-roofed glass-fronted four-storey buildings that behave like fridges in the winter months and greenhouses in the summer.

I don't believe for one second that we're going to get into FCA, I mean it's getting on for nine in the evening. Jasper's not saying much. He leads me right up to the right of the main doors they apparently only open to parents and visitors on Speech Day, and round the side of the building, through a covered walkway and then we're standing in a pretty cool quadrangle, like something out of a University campus, but smaller.

'Bloody hell,' he says.

Last time I saw this place, it was little more than a tree in the middle of a few walkways leading off to different parts of the building, but in 1987, it looks like the Head of FCA wants his school to look like it's a fee-paying private job. A flashy brass plaque on a plinth tells anyone passing that this is 'The Grotto', tended by an after-school club every week. Nowadays the guys call it the Grotty. It's been called that for as long as I remember, but it's not that grotty now. There are traces of blossom left on the little apple tree in the middle of the square, purple tulips so dark they're almost black planted around the base, wooden benches with brass plaques remembering old students, and a couple of other flower beds coming into bloom.

I sit down on one of the benches. 'Not exactly grotty, is it?' I say. Jasper laughs and sits beside me.

'FCAB is run with a bit of an iron fist.'

I almost lurch out of my seat as the unexpected voice carries over from a dark corner, and Jasper isn't far behind. 'The Head's got this big tradition thing going on. Thinks he's running Eton. You get caught on the grass, and it's automatic detention – or so the boys tell us.' A shadow moves forward and puts a foot heavily on the grass. 'No one to stop us doing it now, though.'

'Lizzy?' I ask as my adrenalin rush slows. 'What're you doing here?'

The figure moves a little further forward, and she's not alone – she's with the boy in the Iron Maiden T-Shirt that she was eyeing back in Drake's Main Hall. 'I thought you were going after Rob,' she says, looking at Jasper.

'Oh, no. It's not like that with Maisie and me,' Jasper says quickly, sitting back down.

Maiden slings a lazy arm across Lizzy from behind. 'Sure it's not.'

'No,' I reply, feeling a little irritated, sitting down again. 'It's really not.'

'So you keep saying,' Lizzy says casually. 'What you doing over here then if it's not for that?'

'We were looking for Ani.'

'Why would she be here?' Lizzy reaches into her pocket, pulls out a packet of cigarettes and goes about lighting two up, and placing one tip out between her for Maiden, who takes it between his lips like they've been practising the move for months.

'She's with Brian,' Jasper says.

Lizzy grins. 'Match made in heaven, that one. Marriage of the nerds. Leave it out, I'm talking,' she snaps back at Maiden, swatting a hand away that clearly indicates his desire to do what they came over to the Grotty to do.

'Perhaps you should stop talking then and listen to me instead.'

This time I'm on my feet a second before Jasper, and at first, we're looking frantically around; we can't see where the sharp retort has come from. As my eyes adjust, I can just make a tall figure standing at the end of the covered walkway.

'Bugger it,' Lizzy mutters under her breath. 'It's Tyler.' As he strides towards us, she grinds the barely-smoked cigarette into the ground beneath her Reeboks. It's hard to tell from her body language how they're feeling, she may be big with the tude these days, but she's not about to give a teacher grief. This is 1987, and this is her form tutor.

'A little off the beaten track, aren't we?' Tyler moves forward and peers at us all in the rapidly fading light. 'Having a party, Miss Brookes?'

'Something like that, Sir,' she says.

'But not with the usual posse.' He frowns into my face. 'Although didn't you two cross my path earlier?'

'Apparently so, Sir,' I say, trying to copy the exact non-committal tone that Lizzy uses.

'So this is twice in the same day I've found you out of bounds. Perhaps you would explain to me why you're here, and not deadening your hearing receptors in our school hall right now?'

'It's exactly for that reason, sir,' Jasper says.

Tyler peers at him over non-existent half-moon spectacles. He has that look off really well. 'And you are?'

'Jasper Lau, sir. I'm in Year … er, the Upper Sixth here at FCA, sir. FCAB, Sir. I wanted somewhere quiet to talk to Maisie, and this seemed like a good place to come.'

'Jasper Lau?' He takes another look. 'So now we have the name of the boy trespassing on our school premises earlier on. You come here now, do you?' Without waiting for a reply, he continues. 'So I've got one of my sixth formers planning a party in another school, and now I've got a couple who tell me they find the Disco too noisy and want somewhere quiet to chat. Is it a full moon?'

'We're not a couple,' I say. Why doesn't anyone ever listen?

'Sir, I know it sounds weird but …'

'It does not sound weird, Lau, it is weird. Turn out your pockets, all of you,' he barks. 'And empty that bag while you're at it!'

In my day, he'd never be allowed to do this, but on this day? I've pulled the smartphone out of my pocket before I've even thought about it, and before I can put in back into my pocket, Tyler's grabbed it.

'What's this?'

'It's my calculator,' I blurt out, hoping beyond hope that it's got too dark here for him to see it clearly.

Tyler lifts it up to what's left of the light, lowers it, and stares at me. 'I fail to see how this will help you pass any examinations … Name?' he barks.

'Wharton. Maisie Wharton. Sir.'

His eyes narrow. 'I fail to see how this contraption will help you pass any examinations, Miss Wharton.'

'Just as well I'm not taking Maths, Sir.'

I can hear him inhaling, and I grit my teeth and hold my breath. That was too much. This is 1987 – you don't answer back. But, instead of ripping me apart, he takes hold of the cigarette packet Lizzy's pulled out of her gas mask bag, and suddenly I notice that she's tensed up.

Lizzy's cigarettes do not impress him. I mean, why would they? Foul habit. He sniffs at them, once, twice and then he gives her a look. Where do teachers learn that look? Is there a course on that look when they are training? She looks down at the ground and starts digging the toe of her Reeboks into the soil.

Tyler unbelievably hands me back my smartphone. 'Get yourself a Casio FX-7000, much better quality,' he snaps. 'I'm taking you all back to Drake's. We will not tolerate students leaving the site during Fundraisers.'

'Mr Tyler, seriously, sir, we were only having a bit of fun,' Lizzy exclaims. 'Come on – it's the end of the term. You love the end of the term, you know you do.'

Please tell me she isn't flirting with her teacher?

'You should've thought of that before you dragged me all the way over to this place to smoke marijuana. Move,' he snaps and points out of the Grotto.

We go, and he follows. Like I say, it's 1987, and apparently, that's what you do. But I know my mouth is fixed in a perfect 'o' shape.

I can feel Jasper at my side silently fizzing like a wet firework, but he's got enough common sense to realise this version of the education system's not weighted in students' favour, and he keeps his mouth shut. The journey back to Drake's seems to take twice as long as when we came over. I glance across at the top road, but the kissing figures of Kim and Ian entwined under the lamppost have vanished. We haven't found Ani or Brian; I need to sort things out with Rob, and my mum's being accused of smoking weed. Things were complicated enough before we got to the Fundraiser.

The Head's offices are up on the fourth floor of Drakes' main block, above the Sixth Form Common Room, next to the classroom my mother uses to teach her History classes and a couple of store cupboards. Tyler's switching the lights on as we climb the staircases. We haven't spoken a word to one another since we left the FCAB site.

We approach the familiar unpainted wooden door, but now with a plain white label stating 'M.J Copperfield, Headmistress.'

'M.J. Copperfield's the headteacher?' Jasper says.

'Headmistress,' I hiss. 'Who were you expecting? My mother?'

'What's that?' Tyler snaps.

'Nothing, sir,' I say, and I elbow Jasper in the ribs for good measure.

Copperfield is on the phone when Tyler opens the door, and I can see her waving him away. He ushers us into the waiting area. My mother's waiting area is real executive now – all soft low seating and glossy educational magazines and fliers on a little beech effect coffee table, a water dispenser in the corner and framed examples of Year Eight Textiles up on the walls. This waiting area has a few wooden kids' chairs jammed back against the partition wall, and one dog-eared poster about head lice vigilance. I sit down on one of the chairs; the boys stand. Lizzy slides down the wall and sits on the floor. Eventually, Miss Copperfield opens the door.

'You wanted to see me, Mr Tyler?'

'Yes, Miss Copperfield. I'm sorry to inform you that I found these children trespassing on the grounds of Fletcher Clark Academy for Boys when they should have been downstairs at the Fundraiser Disco. I then discovered some additional serious issues.'

'I see.' She does have half-moon spectacles, and she peers over them. Real old school, she is. I wonder if Lizzy learned that look from her. 'You had better all come into my office.'

Ten minutes later, Tyler's relayed his story to her; she's given each of us a chance to speak and interrupted each of us before we can finish the first sentence, and now she's holding Lizzy's cigarette packet out like a hanky someone spat in.

She sniffs it, wrinkles up her nose and opens it at a random page. 'You say these are yours, Miss Brookes?'

'I'm over 16, Miss,' she says. 'I'm trying to give it up, but it's hard with all the pressure of exams.'

'That is as it may be, but one appears to contain marijuana.'

I stare at her as if she's transformed into a badger. It's not just an accusation then. My future mother is a pothead. Jasper is looking around the room, staring at shelves and bookcases, everywhere except at Lizzy or Copperfield.

Lizzy doesn't seem at all fazed. 'I wouldn't know what that smells like, Miss, so someone must've planted it on me.'

'In your cigarette packet.' She turns her shark eyes onto Maiden. 'Why were you trying to get into your school at this time of night?' she snaps suddenly.

'It's not my school,' he replies, unfazed. 'I came with a mate who goes to FCAB. And it's not my bloody reefer either.'

Copperfield's eyelids close slowly and then reopen. She leans back in her chair and puts the tips of her fingers together in a perfect steeple. 'And you've been caught here at lunchtime, and now on Fletcher-Clark after school hours, all on the same day,' she snaps at Jasper. 'You!' she snaps a moment's later.

He blinks twice and appears to come back from wherever his brain was hiding.
'I'm having a bit of a day being in the wrong place at the wrong time,' Jasper replies, straight-faced. 'Sorry, Miss.'

'Do any of you understand the meaning of the phrase "*loco parentis*"?' she asks.

'I sat my Latin GCSE, Miss,' Jasper says.

'You mean your 'O' Level.'

The recovery takes him less than a second. 'Of course, Miss. *Loco parentis* means in place of your parent,' he says.

'When you come to a Fundraiser Disco, your parents put your welfare into our hands, and they expect us to confine you to parameters we can police. They do not expect us to allow their children to break into deserted school buildings or sneak off for drug-fuelled moonlight trysts.'

Drug-fuelled moonlight trysts?

'I am 18 in a couple of hours,' Lizzy says with quiet determination.

'But you are not 18 now! And until you leave this school, you are under our care when you are on site, and you follow our rules!' She's gone red in the face. Shit, Lizzy. Shut the hell up! Even I can see you don't mess with these '80s teachers. Is she going to try to hit our knuckles with rulers, or throw chalkboard rubbers at us like you told us they did? Is she going to call the police?

'This packet never existed,' Copperfield says quietly and drops it silently into a wire mesh wastepaper basket at her feet. 'However, we clearly cannot trust you on the premises any longer tonight. I am left with little choice but to ask your parents to collect you early.' She reaches across her desk for a large, cream vellum notepad and a long-handled, thin black fountain pen. 'There are barely 30 minutes left before the end, in any case. Miss Brookes, your telephone number, if you please.'

'79380.'

'And the Latin scholar?'

'I'm Jasper Lau, Miss.'

'Telephone number, Lau.'

'I don't have one,' he says, eyes still unblinking at the discarded drugs.

Copperfield gives him a very effective half-moon killer look. 'You don't have a telephone at home?' she asks.

'No,' he says. 'Not exactly, Miss,' he adds.

Not at all, Miss. He doesn't have a phone at home. He doesn't have a home. They haven't built his bloody house yet, and his mum's just a bit on the young side to be expecting her 18-year-old son home from a school disco any time soon, Miss. She's probably revising for her own exams. Miss.

'Not exactly?'

'We do have a phone, Miss, but my Mum couldn't afford to pay the bill, Miss.'

Copperfield leans forward onto the desk, takes her glasses off, folds them and places them lightly on the desk. She is turning pink again. 'Miss ... er ... Wharton? You only started at Drake's today as well, so Mr Tyler tells me?' I stare at her as if she's asked me to take shorthand in Mandarin. 'Your phone number, please.'

'I don't remember it,' I say simply.

'What don't you remember?' Copperfield snaps.

Tyler starts thumbing through the large slate grey filing cabinets at the back of the room. She looks up at him, and he shakes his head.

'Her number. She doesn't remember her number; it's a new one. Her parents are on holiday anyway,' Lizzy chips in quickly. 'Jasper's too. They are all in ... Majorca.'

Jasper nods like a plastic dog on the back parcel shelf of a 4v4 on an off-road circuit. 'On a package tour!'

Lizzy glances at me, but I shake my head as slightly as I can.

Copperfield picks up her glasses, puts them on and does her half-moon eye trick again. I guess she's wondering how Jasper's Mum can afford Magaluf when she can't pay a phone bill. There goes another nail in the Lau household's dysfunctional coffin. 'So you are staying where?'

'They're staying with me,' Lizzy says.

Tyler closes one cabinet drawer and opens another. Again, she looks; still, he shakes his head.

'And the Spare?'

Maiden looks at her.

'Close the door on your way out,' she says, picking up her pen.

He blows a kiss in Lizzy's direction. 'It was a blast, babe,' he says, as he disappears out of the office and shuts the door behind him.

'What a wanker he turned out to be,' Lizzy says.

'Language.' Copperfield leans back again, twiddling the fountain pen in her fingers like a little baton. 'Study leave or no study leave, I will be expecting to see either your mother or your father at the earliest convenience, Miss Brookes. I am working here on site all week,' she says, and there's definitely a light of triumph in those grey ferret's eyes. 'Go and wait in the other room while I make some calls.'

'Close the door on your way out,' Tyler tells us in staccato, and we all file out like Year One in Assembly.

Sitting in the waiting area, I don't know whether to laugh or cry. Lizzy and Jasper are sitting cross-legged on the floor, murmuring to each other. Somewhere down all those flights of stairs is Rob; maybe Tracy will have decided to hook up with him. Maybe Kim and Ian will have stopped snogging long enough to notice we've disappeared. I could believe things are as bad as they're going to get, but I know they can get a whole lot worse. I can hear Copperfield on the phone, but the words are too quiet and calm to be distinct through the closed door. Forget what Glenda's going to say and do to Lizzy. We need to get back to the Old Library and go home. The longer we are here, the worse it gets.

By the time Copperfield opens her office door again, the clock on the wall says there are only fifteen minutes of this Fundraiser left.

'You are all to remain in here until the disco has ended,' she says. 'I have gotten hold of your mother anyway, Elizabeth.'

'Mum doesn't drive, Miss. We make our own way home,' Lizzy points out. 'We live close enough.'

'Strangely enough, that has occurred to me since your mother is a member of my staff,' she replies.

Ouch.

'The fact remains that you will spend the remainder of the Fundraiser in my waiting room. I won't have delinquent boys messing around with my girls and plying them with drugs. Miss Brookes, your brother will be accompanying you, Lau and Miss Wharton off the premises.' She shuts the door, and Tyler stands there, staring at us.

'I am seriously displeased with you, Elizabeth,' he says gravely.

No one laughs. I'm not even tempted. Discipline was so much easier for teachers in the '80s. He shakes his head and goes back down the stairs towards the last of the Fundraiser.

'Delinquent boys?' Jasper repeats faintly.

'Bloody hell,' Lizzy says. 'This is a major balls-up. It's going to go down like a sack of sick with Mum and Dad.'

'They'll go ape about the drugs, I guess,' Jasper asks.

Lizzy snorts. 'Drugs? Jesus, it's not Charlie, it's a just tiny bit of grass.' She sighs. 'They'll be more pissed off with Paul for giving it to me.'

I put my head in my hands. I must be sobering up: my head is killing me.

'At least you were lucky she didn't call the cops,' Jasper says.

'Don't be daft. Drake's precious reputation as a virtuous girls' school is far too important to Copperfield to go squealing to the pigs every time she finds one of her sixth formers with grass,' Lizzy laughs. 'At the weekend, she probably smokes all the joints she confiscates.'

We sit in silence for a few moments.

'So why are you three on the run?' she asks.

That was a curveball. Jasper and I look at each other and stare back at her, temporarily lost for words.

A slight blush lifts on Lizzy's cheeks. 'Sorry,' she mutters. 'Not tactful. I didn't think. I was just wondering about what to say to Mum about the three of you.'

'It's okay. My mum's not exactly around much right now,' Jasper replies carefully.

'And what about your mum – is she around?' Lizzy asks me, and what must seem like an innocent question to her pushes me over the edge, and I burst out laughing. 'Right,' she says, frowning slowly, 'that wasn't really an answer I was expecting.'

'It's complicated,' Jasper says, elbowing me as I try to rein in my battered consciousness. It's not typically Jasper who has to keep it together; I'm usually the one propping him up.

'Don't sweat it. You don't have to tell me anything. I told you, I'd look out for you. Mum'll be cool with it,' she says.

'Even after the phone call from Copperfield?' I ask, getting myself straight.

Lizzy finally looks a bit sheepish. 'Well that won't help,' she says, 'but God knows how many times Mum's helped Kim, how many times Kim's had to stay over at ours to be able to go to parties and discos. Mum's always helping people who're down on their luck. I admit this will be the first time I've asked her to put up boys overnight, so I'm just hoping she's feeling generous and understanding - after being told I was off in the grounds of another school with a guy from another school with joints and fags when I should've been dancing safe and soundly in my own school hall like a good little girl.' She blows air out through her lips in a tuneless whistle. 'Didn't think that one through really, did I? No, it should be fine. It's my birthday tomorrow. Major party.' She reaches into the top pocket of her jacket, pats it and sighs. 'Bugger, I wish the old bag hadn't confiscated my smokes.'

Frankly, to me, it looks about as likely as chocolate rain that we're going to have a bed for the night.

Then Lizzy gets to her feet, and we look up at her. 'Going somewhere?' Jasper asks.

'You know something? I bloody am,' she says. 'Bugger this waiting around for the hammer to fall. There's nothing to stop us walking out that door. I've pretty much left school, and she can't stop me from taking my exams. They won't expel me for walking out of here, and even if they wanted to, Upper Sixth's over bar the shouting.'

I turn to find Jasper standing beside me, his eyes full of horror and all the bravery he's been feigning has drained away. 'We'll get into shit loads of trouble, and your Mum will never let us stay,' he says, and his voice has dropped to a whisper.

Chapter Fourteen – Stand By Me (Ben E King, 1987 (1960))

Lizzy pats him on the shoulder like he's five.

'You're cute, but you worry too much,' she tells him, with a grin, and he blushes.

Seconds later we're creeping down the staircase away from Copperfield's room. Once we're a few flights down, and far enough away that our feet won't be heard, we freefall the last staircase or two and run headlong into the Main Hall, which has turned into a riot of couples. They're playing the final slows. I'm staring at each pair trying not to look like a sicko, or a tosser, or a sick tosser, as I try to pick out someone I recognise.

Lizzy strikes lucky. First, she spots Ian and Kim dancing about a third of the way down the Main Hall. I see Tracy talking with one of Maiden's friends, and then I see them, and I realise how relieved I am. Ani and Brian are dancing by the curtains, and when she sees us, she almost breaks into a run and leaves Brian standing. She flings her arms around my neck and nearly pulls me to the ground. I can see the curtains moving a little to the left and go over to investigate. Someone has opened a fire door. We step outside.

'Where have you all been?' Ani squeaks. 'I was starting to panic about getting home! To your place, I mean,' she adds. 'To

Lizzy's place. Which place do I mean? Everything's all muddled!'

'I told you we'd find them,' Brian says, stepping out of the wall of music. 'Where have you been?'

'Long story.'

'We were looking for you,' Jasper says, appearing through the fire door.

'Okay, not such a long story then.' I look around as Ian and Kim join us. 'Has anyone seen Rob at all?'

'He's with Claire, getting some drinks,' Brian says. 'Elaine's doing her usual. It's all a big act. She knows we're over. She wants Neil Thorpe anyway. She's thrown a complete wobbly.'

'Thrown a wobbly what?' Jasper asks.

Brian laughs and punches him lightly on the shoulder, which, let's face facts, is no answer. 'Take my advice? You'd be better off with Tracy, mate.'

Tracy steps out through the open fire door with Claire, and to my total embarrassment, Rob. 'We tried to find you lot and we couldn't,' Tracy says, 'so we were hoping Elaine had found you instead, but obviously not. So we need to go and find her.'

Lizzy says, 'We need to get out of here more.'

'Why?' Kim asks.

'Long story,' I say.

'The other story wasn't all that long,' Ani says.

'We got caught over at FCAB. They found my joint. They called my mum,' Lizzy says.

'Okay, another not such a long story after all,' I say, shrugging.

Claire's jaw drops to her chest. 'You got caught in FCAB with grass? What in sod's name were you doing? – No, don't tell me,' she says, doing a fabulous talk-to-the-hand although she'd have no idea what I mean by that. 'So we need to get out of here because?'

'We were told to wait for Paul up in Copperfield's office,' Jasper says. 'But Lizzy got bored, and we left.'

Claire's eyes roll. Ani puts two hands dramatically over her mouth. Rob and Brian let out a shout of laughter. Lizzy grins, and Tracy pats her on the back. Ian kisses Kim's neck and she giggles, and I lose the will to live. Just for a moment.

Another few seconds later, we're jogging up the path that runs up past the Old Library and out to the Top Gates. A minute or two after that and people are milling around us, getting ready to walk home or collect the lifts waiting for them a respectful three hundred yards down the Top Road.

'So where is Elaine?' I ask.

Tracy sticks her hands on her hips, pointedly eyeing first me and Jasper, then Ian and Kim, who are standing arm in arm, then Ani and Brian. 'She's gone all schizo again because she saw the two of you together, which hasn't exactly helped matters!'

'Get off my back,' Brian says, pleasant on a razor edge. 'I'm a free agent, or I was.' He smiles cutely down into Ani's upturned happy face. 'Elaine went on a date with that Neil bloke, and you bloody knew about it and never told me!'

'Mate, everyone knew about that,' Ian says. 'That's not news, that's chip paper, son. Get with the skinny.' Brian scowls at Ian, who shrugs, and they both put their arms more firmly around their new girls' shoulders.

'Anyway, we managed to get Elaine out of the Hall as the teachers were all looking at her and if they'd come close, they would've smelt the booze,' Tracy pushes her hair back from her eyes. 'Then we'd all have ended up in Copperfield's office. We sat her out the front, and I came to find you, Lizzy, because you can always calm her down, but I couldn't find you, and by the time I got back out there, she'd scarpered.' She glares at Claire and Kim.

'Don't you give me the evils,' Claire snaps, 'we're hardly going to hold her down and pin her to the floor, are we?'

'Perhaps we should go back and look in the loos,' Kim says.

'How's she getting home tonight?' Rob asks.

'It's Friday. Her folks'll be up the Club,' Lizzy says.

He frowns. 'No point expecting any response out of them until tomorrow then.'

'I'll take her,' Tracy says. 'Mum won't mind. You can't all stay at Lizzy's – Glenda will have a pink fit.'

'You should go back in and look for Elaine,' I say. 'But I don't think me, Jasper or Lizzy should go back in there, Tyler and Copperfield'll be looking for us by now.'

'I'll go look,' Tracy said.

'I'll come to help you,' Claire says.

'Meet back in the Park when you find her. By the Willow, okay?' Lizzy calls.

'We need to leave now anyway,' Ian says. 'Mum and Dad'll be here to collect me, Rob and Bry in a minute and your brother will be here for you lot. Listen.'

He's right. There's no music pounding out of the school hall.

'All the more reason to get away from here then,' Lizzy says.

'The Fundraiser finished,' Ani says. I look at her, and her meaning is clear. The Fundraiser is over. Lizzy didn't take her friends through the Portal in the Old Library tonight. They're still here, and so are we.

Before I can process the situation, Kim is grabbing onto my arm, linking it through hers. She squeezes the top of my arm gently. 'I thought you'd gone off without me,' she says sadly.

'As if we would.' I reach down and squeeze her hand. Something about her brings out a nurturing instinct I never knew I had.

'Glenda's cool,' she says. 'Lizzy's Mum? She won't turn the three of you out.'

'Lizzy said that,' I reply, 'but that was before she got busted for drugs.'

Kim unexpectedly lets out a hoot of laughter. 'You do talk so funny! Busted for drugs … ha-ha. It was only a joint.'

I shake my head, and I only hope Glenda's going to be as relaxed about this as everyone expects because I don't think I ever heard the story of how my mother got caught with drugs at her final Fundraiser the first time around, and how hysterically funny it was, and I'm not sure how she's going to react.

It's colder now and The Park doesn't feel as friendly and comfortable as it did in the May sunshine earlier. From the Willow, we can still see the top road, busy with cars collecting people and the sounds of laughter. I'm listening out for the roar of a motorbike. Rob is standing with Ian up on the road; Tracy and Claire are still in the school building; Ani and Brian are behind the Willow, talking in the darkness. Jasper is speaking in low tones to Lizzy, and her reassuring pats on the shoulder don't seem to be calming him down at all.

I'm sitting at the foot of the Willow with Kim. 'You want some time alone?' she asks me.

'With who?' I ask before I can check myself.

'You know,' she says confidentially.

'Really. It's okay,' I assure her, the heat flooding my face.

'Well, I'd like to go and wait by the road with Ian anyway ...'

'Kim! You're okay here!' I say, a little more forcefully than I might've dared before, but she smirks in the light from the bright orange streetlamp and skips away and, to be honest, of course, she wants to be with Ian and not me.

So, Lizzy didn't come through to our time at the Fundraiser tonight. When did she come through, and how and why? And how long can I stay here and resist the gorgeous boy wandering down from the road towards me? The grass is slightly moist from the heat of the day. I'm dragging my fingers through it when I hear him approach.

'So you got caught over at FCAB,' he says, after a few moments shuffling his DMs.

I look at his feet. 'We were looking for Ani and Brian.'

'Why did you go looking over there? They've been in the Main Hall most of the evening.'

Figures. 'It seemed like a good idea at the time,' I say.

The silence feels endless.

'Are you okay?' he asks eventually, crouching down to my level.

'Are you okay?' I ask back.

'I asked first.'

'I'm fine,' I lie.

'Are *we* okay?' he asks.

So I can't deal with another black cavern of nothing. 'I wasn't trying to cancel you earlier,' I say.

'Cancel me?'

'Cut you off. Fake you out. You know.'

He pulls the cutest face. 'No, I really don't.'

'I wasn't trying to get rid of you,' I say slowly like he's five.

He bends down and sits next to me, knees pulled up against his chest. 'Okay.' He picks at a blade of grass. 'Okay then. So what was all that about earlier then?'

I look at him, and I feel like crying again all of a sudden. Gorgeous boy, Mr 18-Going-On-50, what will I do to my world if I have one more kiss with you? What have I already done? 'The truth?' I tell him out loud, and my voice wobbles a lot, but maybe he can see the hopelessness in my face, because the darkness that was in his eyes last time I told him has vanished, and it's been replaced by something else. Fear? Concern? But not anger, at least.

'I don't think Mum's going to let you guys stay in the house tonight,' Lizzy says. I am so lost in Rob's eyes that I didn't hear her approach. 'And if I ask and she goes nuts, she'll insist on getting you back to wherever you came from so me and Jasper have come up with a plan for tonight, and I'll sort something out for after the party tomorrow.' She looks down at the two of us and smirks. 'Sorry, was I interrupting something?'

'We've been trying to sort out a plan,' Jasper says tightly, 'and a bit of help from you might have been good.'

'We were just talking,' I say sourly.

'So what's the plan for tonight then?' Rob says, his voice a little sharper than usual.

'You can bunk down in the caravan for tonight. There are two double beds when you pull out the benches. It's not cold tonight. I'm going to get the keys off Paul.'

'Are you now?' There's an unexpected movement behind the two of them as they tower over Rob and me and I realise who it is a few seconds too late. 'You've got exactly ten seconds to explain to me why Mum got a phone call from your bloody Head telling her you'd been caught smoking weed with some bloke over on FCAB, and why I had to come away from fixing Dave's bike and get you!'

I look over Lizzy's shoulder. Paul's standing there, crash helmet in hand, and as I look past him, I can see the bike propped up on the road next to where Kim and Ian are still kissing.

Chapter Fifteen – Can'tcha Say (You Believe In Me)/Still In Love   (Boston, 1987)

Then he grins. 'Impressive work, sis. I'm proud of you. For a shortarse, you've caused one hell of a riot back indoors,' he adds. 'Bloody fine timing too - Dad's come home just in time to stop World War Three.'

My heart's been stuck under my tongue, but thinking about it, Paul would never pull rank on Lizzy for wading in shit: he was in it too often himself. When our family get together at Christmas, if Mum and Uncle Paul have too much Prosecco, the stories start about how he was always up to some depravity when they were young. Have I ever heard the story of how she got caught at FCAB with a strange guy and the cannabis he gave her? To be honest, I can't remember.

There's a gravel path through the Park from the Bottom Gate that gives out onto our road. Should have realised he'd use the shortcut.

'Sorry to drag you into this,' Lizzy says, turning to face us.

'No, she's not sorry at all, she's an inconsiderate bitch,' he answers her, but there's a smirk on his lips as he speaks. 'I had to leave bits of Dave's bike all over the garage floor. He's well chuffed.'

'What kind of mood is Mum in?'

'Oh, you know.' He picks absentmindedly at a mark on the

visor of his helmet. 'Copperfield rang her and told her you've been caught;' he puffs his chest out and speaks like the Queen; *"in flagrante delicto* on the grounds of Fletcher Clark Academy for Boys with suspicious substances"*; his voice returns to his usual deep drawl, 'and then she rang back to say you ran off, so Mum's throwing a street party. Dad's just having a beer.'

'*In flagrante delicto*?'

'Look it up in a dictionary, Einstein. You could've picked somewhere a bit classier than the Grotty.'

'Bloody cheeky git of a big brother. I know what it means, I just wasn't.'

'So you say. Who's this?' he adds, looking up at Jasper.

'Jasper,' he says, putting out a hand.

Paul shakes it and looks at Rob and me. 'I saw you two down by the van earlier, didn't I?'

Lizzy gives me a look mixed with surprise and then turns back to him. 'They need to stay with us tonight, Paul.'

Paul breaks out a soft laugh. 'Oh, you have got to be taking the piss now Liz …'

'I'm serious! It's important,' Lizzy says, grabbing onto his arm and pouring big begging puppy eyes into his. 'They've got nowhere else to go. I can't exactly ask Mum and Dad, can I?'

'Well, you can try,' he says. I look down and suddenly realise Rob's taken hold of my hand. 'But if you want to see 18, I suggest you don't bother.'

'Paul, I need to put these guys up in the van tonight.'

'The van is not classier than the Grotty,' he says, laughing.

'Be serious.' She smacks him on the arm. 'I know you had a key cut.'

I can tell she's got him by the reaction before he checks

himself. 'You know nothing.'

'I've seen lights on down there in the middle of the night.'

'That was probably Mum and Dad having a back-to-basics bonk.'

'Eww.'

I thought mentioning the rents' bonking thing was sick enough without them bringing animals into it.

'It wouldn't be them, Paul. Come on, I know you have a key.'

He pulls a black packet of cigarettes with JPS printed in gold letters out of his pocket and lights a cigarette with a silver box.' Why'd you lot need to stay in the van for the night?' he asks, looking at Jasper.

'Don't ask,' Jasper says.

Paul shakes his shaggy blond hair. 'Liz, what is it with this family and people who live with certifiable parents?' He draws deeply on the cigarette and exhales. The smoke is like a blue veil over my face for a second or two, and then it's gone. 'Okay. Say I can get hold of a key. What's in it for me if I lend it to you?'

Lizzy bites her lip. 'I'll do your washing-up duties for a week when you're home for the summer.'

'Two.'

'No bloody way!'

'Two, or no key.'

She pauses. 'I'll only do it for two if you tell Mum they're your mates if she asks any awkward questions.'

'Didn't Mum meet them earlier?'

He's right, of course.

Lizzy sighs. 'Can you just think of something to cover my back if it comes to it, and give me a break, Paul? After the party, I'll come clean once they're all tanked up, but it's my birthday. I don't want them on my back.'

Paul took another deep drag of the cigarette. 'You could've thought of that before you went off shagging in the Grotty with an eighth in your pocket.'

'There was no shagging involved! Jesus,' Lizzy exclaimed.

'Yeah, I can just see Mum now, jumping up and down saying, 'it's okay Mrs Copperfield, there was no intercourse, just a bit of grass," he says in a falsetto.

'They need to sleep in the van, Paul,' she says.

Paul picks up the helmet from the ground. 'We'd better get home. Where's Kim?'

It's not long before we're walking back along the pathways that cross the Park back to our house. Paul's wheeling his bike and Jasper's talking to him about Ozzy Osborne. Kim's on one side of me, her other arm tucked through Lizzy's, Ani's on my other side as the boys were finally picked up from the Park. Tracy and Claire never came back from trying to find out what happened to Elaine.

The only thing I'm sure of is that if I can rely on any of the girls in 1987, it's still Lizzy, I know she will make sure we're safe. Because somewhere in the wild, off-the-chain rebel brain that is Lizzy Brookes, there is my mother, and whatever else she's been like in my life, in this life, she looks after people. She said so. Kim said so.

'Elaine is such a wild card,' Kim is saying. 'The last Fundraiser I was here, me, Lizzy and Paul waited with her for her parents to come and get her because she lives a bit further away. They blamed the traffic, but we could all smell the booze on her mum's breath – Elaine didn't say a word to any of us until two days later when Brian asked her out.'

'So where do you think she is?' I ask.

'She'll turn up,' Lizzy says encouragingly. 'She always gets home.'

As we walk, my mind wanders. Is Jasper's Mum going frantic because he hasn't come home? Has she called the police yet? And Ani's parents, are they texting all her friends? When we landed here did the holes we left behind seal up seamlessly, or are we still there? Do Ani's parents even have an 18-year-old daughter called Ani? And is my mother going to notice I'm not around?

'Maisie?' Kim says, more insistently.

'Sorry?'

'I was talking about us all going over to Tracy's on Sunday. Tracy's dad wants to try out one of those new outdoor camping grills called a Barbie Queue that they have on *Neighbours* and *Home and Away*. They sit on the beach on Christmas Day in Australia and cook shrimps on a grill. We're going to sit in the garden until the sun goes down, paddling in the pool, drinking cider and lager and eating beef burgers and sausages. Will you come?'

'It sounds amazing,' I say kindly.

'Assuming I can get there,' Kim says sadly.

'Assuming I can get there and I'm not grounded for a month after my birthday,' Lizzy says.

'Glenda's cool. It's not like you were caught having sex at FCAB,' Kim says.

'No, just a doobie,' I say, trying to keep my disapproval out of my voice.

Lizzy giggles. 'It's my birthday in 90 minutes!'

Paul unlocks the front door and, as I step over the threshold, I can hear someone turning the television down in the lounge.

'Is that you, Paul?'

'Yes, Mum.'

'Tell Lizzy to come in, please.'

Lizzy opens the door into the lounge. Paul touches me briefly on the shoulder and slips away down the corridor into the kitchen, obviously heading out through the back door to go back down to the garage. Kim gives me a brief hug before disappearing up the stairs. I don't know what to do, so I just stand there framed in the doorway, with Ani and Jasper on either side of me.

I can see Glenda standing by the television, her cheeks flushed pink, and I can just see the thick red hair of my granddad Henry over the top of the other armchair. He was completely bald by the time he died.

Lizzy dives straight in. She's got balls. 'Mum, I know you're angry with me, but whatever else I did wrong, I did not have sex tonight!'

I'm sure if I had one of those ultrasound receptors or the kind of technology that can detect space noise or some other thing that Brian and Ani would spend hours explaining, I'd be able to hear the word 'sex' bouncing off each surface in the room over and over again like a squash ball in a court. Instead, it's just bouncing around my brain. I'm so not comfortable with the word 'sex' and my mother being in the same room.

Glenda's cheeks glow even pinker. 'You went off with some strange boy when you should've been at the disco. And you were smoking joints at FCAB!' She looks over at the door then – at me, Ani and Jasper, caught in her glare like Ninja Cat. 'Why are you all here?'

'It's okay, Mum, I'm walking them home,' Paul says, suddenly reappearing from wherever he disappeared to.

'Why?' she asks, her red eyes narrowing.

Paul slings an arm around my shoulder, and I flinch just before I realise what he's trying to get her to believe and then grin stupidly.

She sighs and nods. 'Don't be late. I need you to help with setting up tomorrow.' She turns back to Lizzy. 'Do you have any idea how embarrassing it was to get those phone calls from Marguerite?'

'Can't you two keep the noise down? I was having forty winks,' answers a deep voice that I miss with a sharp ache in my guts, and two arms are flung up in the air, one wearing the silver chain bracelet that I never saw my Granddad without. 'Here's my special birthday girl, causing a rumpus again and breaking your lovely mother's heart. Come over and give your old dad a kiss, chicken.'

I want to stay and watch, but Paul is moving us on, and I'd probably cry anyway, and not be able to explain why. Grabbing jackets from the coat hooks on the wall at the foot of the stairs, we tread lightly over the hallway carpet through into the kitchen.

'Had to go and find the key. You're going to have to keep the lights off,' Paul says, taking his arm off my shoulder, 'and be somewhere else before six, in case Dad goes down to get anything from the garage. You are coming to my sister's party, aren't you? It's going to be a blast. Mum's booked Divine Morrissey and a couple of other local bands to play a gig at Trinity.'

He opens the back door, and a strange man is standing there with a wrench.

Chapter Sixteen – Caravan Of Love (The Housemartins, 1987)

It's as much as I can do not to cry out.

'Dave, you prat,' Paul mutters.

'You made me jump!' I hiss, heart hammering its way out of my throat.

'Going somewhere?' Dave whispers, grinning.

'More of Lizzy's fugitives,' Paul says. 'Staying over for the party. Mum's giving the pothead a grilling.' They both laugh. 'Good thing the old man's home to soften the blows.'

'Shouldn't have given her the grass, mate.'

'Early birthday present. Dad'll be more pissed off that she didn't share,' He turns to me and winks.

'There's already two more down there,' Dave says as we walk past the old shed. 'One said he hadn't finished saying goodnight, and the other said he hadn't even started.'

Worry and excitement dance in my stomach, and Ani just giggles.

Jasper sighs. 'Great. Can I stay up here with you?' he asks Paul hopefully.

'You'll be snug as mugs in a couple of car rugs. And if you'd rather stay up here, you've got a serious death wish going on. Or you've got it bad for my sister,' Paul adds, his voice softening unexpectedly as we walk silently past the greenhouse down to the caravan. 'Once you're in the caravan, you're on your own.'

'We owe you one,' I mutter.

'This is not one. This is at least two. Weeks' worth of washing-up on Lizzy's part,' he whispers. 'Maybe she's the one who's got it bad. Rob? Brian? You've got company.'

He puts the key into my hands before I can ask him what he means, disappears into the garage behind us before I can negotiate, and two figures appear around the back of the van, silhouetted against the pale light from the garage window. They must've convinced Ian's mum to drop them off here.

After a heart-stopping moment or three as the key stutters in the lock, I push the door handle down to unlock it, and we all slip into the van.

I remember Granddad's caravan from when I was small. He refused to get rid of it when he was alive because he said it reminded him of fun times with Nan. We part-exchanged it for our motor home. I guess my mother wanted to keep up traditions.

The van is quite vintage, but I'm guessing it's quite high-spec for its day, with its little cupboard of a chemical loo, kitchen hob, fridge and seating that converts into what can just about pass for double beds at either end. There's an old wood-effect radio on a cream and orange plastic-covered shelf, next to a white pod of what must be a tiny television screen with a circular indoor aerial on top, as well as some puzzle books and pens. There are lit tea lights in the window that faces away from the house casting just enough light to see by, and drawn curtains in the windows that don't. Somebody has thrown some old car rugs in and pulled the seating out and made makeshift beds with the cushions.

'This is wicked,' Brian says and plays the little tune on his make-believe trumpet. 'Let's put Radio 1 on; we can catch the end of the *Friday Rock Show*.'

Rob takes my hand and starts to move towards the candle-lit end of the van. 'I need to talk to you,' he says.

I open my mouth in preparation to agree, but Jasper is at my side. 'Forget it, blud,' he says firmly. 'You think I'm sitting in the middle while you two couples swap fluids? Cancel that.'

Rob, to his credit, looks a bit put out. 'I need to talk to all three of you,' he says, 'but I think Ani's busy, and you'll forgive me if I don't hold your hand.'

'No, we're sweet,' Ani says, to my surprise, so we all move into the lighter end of the van.

'Did Lizzy get a load of crap from her Mum?' Rob asks, as we settle against the cushions.

I shake my head no. 'Not compared to what I'd get if I were found with drugs at FCA. B.' Or would I? 'Paul thinks she'll get away with it, all things considered with it her birthday and her Dad being home.'

'So, when you were up in that headteacher's office,' Ani asks, 'why didn't you look for the book?'

I rub my face with grubby hands. I need a shower, and I so don't want to be talking about this in front of Rob again, and especially not Brian. 'Can we not do this now?'

'The book that explains the portal is in your Head Mistress's office?' Brian says unexpectedly.

Jasper looks at Brian, then at me. I look at Brian, then Jasper, then back at Rob. Rob looks at Brian.

'Not our Head Mistress; Lizzy's – I told you,' Ani says patiently.

'Tell me again what makes you think it's in there?' Brian

asks.

'Well, it was there last time when Orla saw it, so it's as good a place as any to start looking. It'll be an artefact of some sort, like an old school ledger.' She looks back at me. 'Surely you could've had a little peep while that headteacher was ranting at you? We agreed that we would search the office?'

The small shadowy fingers cast by the flickering tea light dance over her cheeks.

So much has happened, I forgot about looking for the book.

'I did have a quick look around, Ani, but it wasn't easy while the woman was giving us a grilling,' Jasper says. 'Plus you never told us what it looks like, and why the hell are we having this conversation now?'

Before Ani can reply, someone else speaks, and it's Rob. 'So you've been told all this stuff about time travel as well, Bry?'

Brian nods. 'Maisie told you then? Amazing, isn't it?'

Rob takes a deep breath. 'You believe this story?'

'Sure thing, mate. Why wouldn't I believe it?' Brian leans back against the orange cushions and puts his arms behind his head. 'Time travel phenomena have been around for decades.'

'Films aren't real, Bry, come on …'

'Not film, Rob. Don't be a dick. This is science.' Brian leans forward, and his voice takes on an almost teacher-like tone. 'Even Einstein admitted time travel was possible, and that we just needed to master it. Who's to say they aren't from the future?'

'Maisie doesn't look anything like Michael. J. Fox,' Rob says, but he doesn't sound serious, thankfully.

'Science, Simmons! Physics! Why can't the Old Library at Drake's be a wormhole through Time, a rupture in the continuum? Why can't they be from the future? Look at the way they speak. Have you had a close look at one of their Smart Phones?' He says it like it's two words.

'I …' Rob attempts and fails to get any further.

'Yes, he did.' Jasper steps in. 'We showed him. The music player and camera?' he adds, looking intently at Rob.

I produce my smartphone again from my back pocket. Ani whips hers out from somewhere. She's got the *S10*, and it's still holding onto a couple of percents. 'Mine's dead. Run out of battery,' I explain. 'You have to charge them up using electricity.'

'Ani's is a different make,' Jasper says.

'Like Amstrad and Sanyo?' Rob says, staring at the two little blocks in our hands.

I have no idea. 'I guess so.'

'How did you get here?' Rob asks.

'I told you,' I say. 'We came through the back of the Old Library at Drake's. Ani's friend read about it in a book.'

'And this book?' he asks. 'It's in Copperfield's office? What does a book have to do with all this?'

'My friend Orla said she saw it up there a couple of days before we came through. She was left in the office while Mrs … our Head Teacher dealt with an emergency,' Ani says, glancing nervously at me. 'She saw the book and skimmed the first few pages. She said it read like it was the history of a portal in the Old Library. I think if we can find it, we can find out more about how the portal works. So that we can get home again.'

'That photograph you showed me,' Rob says.

Uh-oh. 'What about it?' I ask.

He runs fingers through his fringe; his hair looks almost golden at the ends in the faint glow of the tealights. 'It was taken down here. In your time. Why were you taking a picture at the bottom of Lizzy's garden?'

I hold my breath and hope to anyone who's listening that Ani hasn't told Brian about Lizzy being Future-Mum-of-Maisie – but he just looks at me intently.

Then I hear it. Faint but unmistakable. The sound of a door closing in the near distance. I'm saved by the click.

Jasper licks the fingers on one hand, reaches up and snuffs out the tea lights with a low crackle and hiss. Rob's off the bed, under the level of the window and he's pushing the door handle upwards with a satisfying clunk to lock us in. He slides back next to me as I hear them getting closer. Footsteps. Coming down the garden path. And as he grabs the car rugs up over our heads and we curl our legs and feet up under us like foetal spoons, the footsteps grow louder and louder, stamping down over the concrete slabs as if they don't care who hears. Wouldn't Glenda be trying to catch us out?

The footsteps stop next to the van

I'm concentrating so hard on being silent, creating a void that I can slip into that I'm only dimly aware of how close I am to Rob, how deeply my fingers are digging into the hands he's wrapped tightly around my middle, the warmth of his breath on the back of my neck. There's shuffling outside. They're listening. We're listening too, and I am going to burst. Any minute now the key will be in the lock. Any minute now the torch will be in our faces. Any minute now we are busted and we'll have nowhere to spend the night. I can hear a strange rustling. The person is pushing something under the door.

'Just in case,' Dave whispers. 'Safety first, boys and girls. Oh, shit! Not you as well. What is it with you kids tonight?

Shagathon?'

The door swings open, and Lizzy's red hair is unmistakable, red-framed in the moonlight. Dave sniggers; a minute later we hear the roar of the bike, the one that he and Paul clearly managed to fix, and then there is silence again, apart from the rushing of the blood in my ears.

'Shit. I thought we'd had it then,' Brian calls across quietly.

'I think that was the joke,' I say, aware of how closely Rob's holding me against him as I pull the car rugs away from our faces. They are scratchy.

'What'd you mean? What did he put under the door?' Ani asks.

'Condoms, at a guess,' Jasper replies.

I can almost hear Ani blush. 'What, he thought we'd have sex in here? With each other? I mean -'

'We know what you mean,' Lizzy says. 'Thought you'd all be worried about what happened to me, but I see you got visitors.' She holds her arms up in the air and touches the frame above the door. 'So, I'm 18 now, and the folks have cut me some slack. Party starts here! Dad even let me nick some of his fags. You hoping for a threesome or you want to join me outside?' she says pointedly at Jasper.

Jasper is on his feet; they are out the door, and it closes before I can register what she said. Ani and Brian move next, down to the other side of the van nearest to the house. The van is in darkness, and my heart is thudding suddenly. I can't move. I can feel Rob's breath against my neck.

'So, you really are time travellers,' he says eventually.

'You believe me now then.'

'It's difficult not to in the face of so much hard evidence.

The little wireless phones and the photograph. And what Brian doesn't know about science isn't worth knowing. Bloke's a genius.' I can feel his lips, gently moving against my ear. 'To be honest, I should've believed you. The more I thought about it, the more I thought you couldn't make something like this up. I was going to tell you I thought I might've acted like an idiot, then Ani started blurting out about books.'

'Yeah, she's a great blurter,' I say fondly.

'I'm really sorry, Maisie. You must think I'm a right prat.'

'It's okay,' I tell him. 'I wouldn't believe me either.'

'I couldn't work out why you were fobbing me off before, you see.'

'That sounds a bit intimate.'

'I mean, telling me you weren't interested.'

'That would be a lie,' I confess, and feel his lips curl into a smile against my neck, 'but it's not okay, Rob, we can't all just stay here.' I turn to face him, although I can barely make out his features. The seating cover beneath us feels rough against the skin on my arm. 'This isn't the way things are supposed to be.'

'Maybe you're wrong. Maybe the portal brought you here because this is where you should be?'

'You mean like Fate?'

He snuggles down against the nylon cushions that double up like pillows and pulls me across him gently so that I end up with my head propped on his chest. 'Fate. Destiny maybe. I don't see Ani wringing her hands and weeping at the thought of being here.'

'It takes a lot to faze Ani. Jasper's worried.'

'He didn't look too worried when he leapt out the door

after Lizzy.' He pauses, and in the silence, I can hear Ani and Brian murmuring to each other at the other end of the caravan, and unmistakable sounds of lips meeting over and over in the darkness. Rob's chest is rising and falling a little faster now, and his fingers are stroking through my hair. I have goosebumps all over my back and my arms.

No one's made me as confused or excited, as happy or scared, or filled me with as much anticipation as Rob Simmons has. From the moment he smiled at me on the Top Road at lunchtime to this moment in the darkness, I've felt like I belong with him. I feel like I've always known him. Are we all supposed to be here together?

'I think Brian's quite sweet on Ani,' he says, and suddenly he's entirely still beneath me like he's holding his breath. Ani giggles and there's movement at the end of the van, moonlight casting shadows against the closed curtains. 'And I think I might be quite sweet on you.'

'You think we should get going, Rob?' Brian calls down.

'Probably not a good idea just now,' I say, as Rob traces soft fingers gently against my spine, up and down. My T-shirt is so thin; I might just as well not have it on. The thought makes me blush.

'You still think Glenda might hear us?' Brian asks.

'Wouldn't want to risk it,' I say, putting my hands around Rob's neck, and the almost but not quite, near but yet so far, close miss kisses that've been sending me mental with should-I-shouldn't-I anguish are blown away by the real thing; stomach-swooping, make-me-want-to-shout-out-loud kisses that make me feel like I've never kissed anyone before in my entire life, like I never want to leave this caravan in 1987. I've never

ever felt like this, like my insides are leaving my body through my belly button, like I want to cry, sing, jump in the air, laugh hysterically. I mean, there have been boys, boys I met at Burger King for a coffee, saw a couple of films with, but there haven't been many *boys*. It's always been me, Jasper and Ani. We just fit right together. This feeling that I have right now under this car rug in this caravan kissing Rob Simmons, it makes me feel like I can do anything I want, and this new world has been waiting for me to start living in it.

'Rob? It's after twelve, mate – I told the olds I'd be home by now,' Brian says a little later from the far end of the caravan. 'I don't want them to stop me from going to Lizzy's party. You know they won't cut me any slack. When do you want to go back?'

'Not just yet,' Rob says, tickling the skin on my cheek as he kisses it again.

'Say five minutes then?' Brian asks, a little more anxiously

'If we leave it much longer than that, it could be dangerous,' Rob says.

'Dangerous?' Ani calls down. 'You mean you won't be able to get back into your house before morning?'

'Sort of,' Rob says, and I can feel his lips and tongue teasing the skin on my neck.

'Sort of?' Ani repeats.

'Ani?' he says, looking up at me.

'Yes?' she says.

'Any chance of putting this chat on hold?'

Chapter Seventeen – Crush On You (The Jets, 1987)

They are gone ten minutes later.

We all know they would've stayed longer, but Brian was getting so twitchy about the risk of being grounded that there was nothing else doing. Jasper came back into the van a few minutes' later, and Lizzy repeated what Paul had said to us earlier; we're expected at her party.

We try to get some sleep, but if Ani and Jasper manage to get some, I don't – I'm too troubled by waves of doubt that seep back into my thoughts almost as soon as Rob leaves. As the sun begins to climb above the trees that mark where Jasper's house will eventually be built, we creep out, along the dirt track that connects the garage to the main road, up to the road that will eventually become the proper road leading down into the estate, and make our way past the front of the house to the Park.

Once we are under the Willow, the tension between us bubbles to the surface.

'So what exactly were the two of you doing in that caravan?' Jasper snaps.

Ani giggles. 'You need to ask?'

Jasper covers his face with his hands and pushes his fingers so hard into his eye sockets that I think he's going to injure himself. 'Maisie, I thought we'd been through all this!' he exclaims.

He is making me feel even guiltier than I do already, but my first reaction is defence. 'So what were you doing out there with my mother?' I ask. 'Smoking?'

'Don't be disgusting, you know how much I hate it,' Jasper says.

'What then? You were out there for ages.'

'We were talking.'

'What about?'

'My family and hers.'

'Jasper, you didn't tell her -' Ani says, breathlessly.

'What kind of a tool do you think I am?' he snaps, pulling his hands roughly away from his face and waving them about. 'I'm a runaway, remember? We were talking about our plans for the future. As runaways.'

'That can't have been easy,' I say carefully, but too late, he's snapping at the unintended bait.

'No, it wasn't. But it's okay for you two, isn't it? Playing *Love Island* with two fifty-year-old men who know we're from the future but don't seem to care about it any more than you do? But I can't tell my new friend, can I? Oh, no.'

'Jasper, she's my mother,' I say, again carefully, because this swamp I'm wading into is way too sticky for comfort.

'If she's your mother, Rob's 50 and so is Brian,' he replies, scuffing the toe of his Vans in the dried-out grass.

'Brian is 17, not 50, you tool,' Ani says.

'All right then – she's not my mother now, but she's going to be and can you imagine if we all rock up at her party tonight and say 'Happy Birthday! We didn't get you a gift, but I'm your daughter! Surprise!'

'They will assume we'd been smoking Paul's weed if we do

that,' Ani says solemnly. 'We need to find the book, so we can work out what to do with the Portal. Brian thinks there's a possibility we can still see each other once we know how to control it -'

'Control it?' Jasper asks. 'What you mean, have him come to visit you every Friday after Uni for Netflix n' Chills, hoping you don't bump into his 50-year-old self on the way home from buying snacks? What about our exams then? Our careers?'

'Now you sound like Mrs Wharton,' Ani laughs and then stops abruptly when she sees how serious he is.

'I am trying to do what I think is best,' I say. 'But it's hard.'

'Is that what you were saying to yourself last night when you were locking tonsils with Robbie-boy?' he taunts, and as I open my mouth to protest my lie, he says, 'Oh, don't even bother to deny it. You want to make your bloody mind up, Maisie. One minute it's, 'oh we must get back to 2019,' and the next it's, 'oh, it won't hurt if I boff the fit drummer."

Impatiently, Ani says, 'I like it here, and I like Brian.'

I punch him this time. 'Back off, I didn't boff him.'

'I didn't boff your mother either.'

I shove him again, maybe a bit harder than usual. 'Jasper! That's ratchet!'

'We need to find the book because it might tell us what to do to get home,' Jasper persists. 'Not because it might come up with a way to help us have relationships with people who are already old! We need to be in our own time, and right now, all we know is there's a Portal in the Old Library. Does it always link 2019 and 1987? We don't know where it goes, or what it does! We could get back into the Old Library and end up anywhere in Time! We thought they would come through the Portal tonight, and they didn't, and we have no idea when that's going to happen! Am I the only one here who's thinking about these things?'

'Please Jasper, don't get upset,' Ani says, and there's a wobble in her voice. 'Of course we have to go home eventually, but I don't see how kissing someone is going to do any harm.'

'You don't know that,' he says moodily.

'All right!' I shout. 'All right. We'll go and search for the bloody book as soon as we get a chance, but right now I need some more sleep before I go to my bloody mother's bloody 18th birthday party.'

Fortunately for me, they must've thought I was about to lose my shit, and they leave me alone for a bit. They're not wrong, but I also just want to wallow in memories of Rob's kisses for a few more minutes – in case it's the last time it can happen.

My head feels like a tonne weight on the grass, but someone's shaking me. When I see who it is, I'm wide-awake like a sprung lever, tonne weight or not.

'What the hell are you doing there?'

Paul's crouched beside me. Ani and Jasper are stirring, rubbing their eyes beside me. A few people are wandering about. We must look like the vagrants we're pretending to be. 'Going to have to be nicer if you want me to keep your little secrets, Maisie.'

'Don't be salty. Is something wrong?' I say, a little more calmly.

'Message from my sister, who is currently drowning in an

avalanche of wet birthday kisses from elderly aunties and can't get away.'

'And you could?'

'I've been sent on a mission to find gaffer tape from the ironmonger in town. So Lizzy's taken about 300 phone calls so far this morning, and it's only bloody eight-thirty now, but one of them was from Tracy. Amongst other things, she said they couldn't find Elaine last night, and she can't get hold of her this morning.'

How did these guys cope without smartphones?

'What about the others? Has Claire tried to call her?' Ani is at my side now.

'They both tried, but both mums are getting stressed about them using the phone so much. Everyone's meeting at the Top Gates in about,' he checks a wristwatch with hands, 'about ten minutes. Lizzy can't make it for obvious reasons, but she says can you go and help out?'

Ten minutes later and we're jogging in a groggy sleep-deprived stupor across the Park towards the Top Gates, and Tracy and Claire are already there, with Rob, Ian and Brian. I realise it must be serious – Lizzy really has rallied the troops.

Rob wastes no time to coming to my side and sliding his hand into mine.

'Good night's sleep?' I smile at him.

'You forgot the subtext that said last night rocked.'

'Put each other down, will you?' Jasper says, irritably.

I glare at him. I can hold hands, can't I? Surely that's not going to change the world? Only mine.

'Green's not a good colour on you, Jasper,' Tracy claps him

on the back.

'Don't be a wanker, honey.' She ruffles his hair.

'So Elaine's still missing?' he asks, scowling at Tracy, and rolling his eyes as Ani plants a massive kiss on Brian's cheek.

'It's just another of her stunts,' Brian says, throwing a proprietorial arm around Ani's shoulders. 'It's got 'Attention Seeking' stamped all over it. I only came because I approve of the current company.'

'He means me,' Ani giggles and he nods and kisses her on the temple. Tracy and Claire look at her, and then each other. I guess they realise that Ani's not just a passenger on the crazy train; she's driving it.

'Whatever her reasons, we should still check that she's okay,' I say.

'Where would she go if she didn't make it home last night?' Jasper asks.

Tracy looks at him as if he's just told her how to pass her exams. 'Genius! Major genius!' She turns to me. 'You never said he was sexy with a brain as well?'

'Objectification much?' Jasper remarks, but I know that face; the stormclouds lift a little.

'So, if she's not home -' I begin.

'She's with the guy in the band,' Jasper finishes.

'Her parents were on the lash last night, so there's every chance they haven't surfaced and won't realise she's not been home,' Claire says. 'We need to try and get her back before they throw a wobbly.'

'Is a wobbly like a hissy fit?' Ani asks. No one replies.

'Anyone know his address?'

Tracy shakes her head. 'Lizzy does; her mum's been talking

with Neil about organising tonight's party, but we can't gate-crash this afternoon to ask her, it was one of the terms.'

'The terms?' Jasper asks.

'Glenda wanted a full-on garden party for Lizzy with all her relatives and a buffet in a marquee. Lizzy wanted a band and loads of booze, and she kicked off,' Rob says.

'She did?' I'm not half as surprised as I would've been two days ago.

'Yeah, she's got a good heart has Lizzy, but she's a bit manic at times.' The others laugh in agreement with him.

'Anyway, they came to an arrangement. If Lizzy would agree to play nice at her mum's party, she could have a proper piss-up with her mates at Trinity in the evening,' Ian says.

I know the Trinity. It's still a deconsecrated church on the north side of Stoneford, a vast cold cavern of a stone temple that's been a kind of magnet for up and coming bands in the area, amateur dramatic groups and alternative arts scenes for as long as I can remember. There's a drop-in day centre there nowadays, with food and clothes banks and a play area for toddlers, plus a few counsellors.

'Divine Morrissey are playing,' Claire explains. 'With Black Diamond and Girl's Talk. Everyone's coming. They've been planning it for months.'

'Morrissey? He's a tool,' Jasper says.

'Morrissey is way cool,' Claire retorts with a frown.

'Neil plays the skins for Divine Morrissey,' Rob adds quietly, for my benefit, 'here, Morrissey is cool.'

'No accounting for taste,' I reply.

'Neil's a mate of my brother Will,' Brian says. 'I think he's local.'

'So, we'll touch base with Elaine's parents to cover her tracks, then we'll just go through the phone book 'till we find something that sounds likely,' Ian is already walking away.

A quarter of an hour later we're all standing on the pavement outside Elaine's house. Her dad answered the door, and he looked worse than all of us put together. He seemed confused by the crowd of teens at his door and had no idea whether Elaine was in, and when he checked her room, he said the bed was made so she'd obviously gone out early. Then he turned green and shut the door on us, and now we're standing around wondering where to go next.

'So much for giving her a cover story,' Claire leans against the wall.

'There's a phone booth at the end of the road,' Tracy says. 'Should have a phone book in it. I say our next stop is Neil's.'

The booth is like the one outside Drake's. It's glass and it has a heavy black and chrome receiver inside and a slot to put coins. There are four addresses we think might be Neil's in the phone book. I'm amazed no one has pinched the book; you couldn't leave books lying around in public places in our day.

We decide to split up for the search: Tracy and Claire are trying a house on my estate, or Lizzy's I should say; Ani and Brian are going to a maisonette on the far side of FCAB; Ian and Jasper are trying a place down by the chippy and me and Rob are going to a flat in the centre of town near the railway line. We all agree to go back to the Park once we've checked out the addresses.

Me and Rob walk out of the Park onto the top road and turn left. It's a good walk down Town Hill, but I'm not complaining.

The sun's warm and the air's cleaner and I still can't help feeling the euphoria I felt last night as we chat. It's a good mile or two down the top road: past Drake's Top Gates, the school quiet now, onto where the top road joins the bottom road, past a few pubs with doors just opening to the public and finally down the long steep hill towards the main railway line.

The address we're looking for is in the basement of a big, brown brick, purpose-built block opposite the railway station, four storeys high with an intercom on the left of the door. I hit the button next to the number.

'Yeah?' someone says eventually, the voice cracked and artificial through the intercom.

'Is that Neil Thorpe?' I ask.

'Who's asking?'

'D'you play drums for Divine Morrissey?'

'Who is this? Piss off -'

Rob moves me gently aside. 'No, hang on. I'm Rob Simmons, you know me, mate. I drum with Fallen Angel, Will Walkers' band. I'm looking for Elaine Longhurst.'

In the static, I can hear muttering.

'Fallen Angel,' I say, grinning.

'Who's there with you?' Neil says, eventually.

'I'm with Maisie Wharton,' he says. 'Elaine knows her, she's one of the new girls.' A moment or two later, there's a low buzzer and a click. Rob pulls on the handle, and the main door opens.

The flat is set beneath the level of the road. The railway line runs up one side of the building, with the road and the station running perpendicular to it. The steps down are uncovered concrete, and the light in the passageway is broken. It smells faintly of chip fat and damp leaves. I knock on the door.

A man opens it – he looks about Paul's age. He's got significant dark stubble right now, his hair's all tousled and sticking up in all directions in a very un-eighties way, and he's wearing nothing but a blue towel around his waist. He's a good-looking guy, no question about it.

'All right, Neil. Is she here?' Rob asks. 'Elaine?'

Neil waves us in. To the right, I can see an unmade bed through an open door, so I turn left and walk through into an open plan living area, with a coffee-coloured leather corner sofa, and a massive stereo system with a turntable on top like in Lizzy's bedroom, and a tiny TV in the opposite corner. Off to one side of the room, there's a door through to a narrow kitchen. I can see grass and trees through a small window at the back.

Elaine's in the kitchen, standing beside a steaming kettle. She's wearing what must be one of Neil's shirts. As we walk in, she grins, runs out of the kitchen and flings her arms around Rob theatrically, like he's some long lost friend who's paying her a surprise visit.

He peels her hands off like she's got suckers. 'Where the bleeding hell have you been?' he says, not unkindly.

She takes a step or two back and pulls a face. 'Here?'

'You didn't think about letting any of us know? The girls are throwing eppies.'

'Thought you said he was your mate, not your dad,' Neil says from behind me. I turn and watch as he lands heavily on the sofa, reaching out for a gold and white packet with Marlboro Lights printed on it and lighting one with a cheap yellow plastic garage lighter. He offers me the pack.

I shake my head no. 'We were worried,' I say.

'So worried that you all buggered off at the end of the Fundraiser and left me there.' She flounces over to the sofa and helps herself to a cigarette.

'It wasn't like that,' Rob says.

She eyes me above the flame as she lights up. 'Looks like you got lucky then.'

'Not exactly. We went looking for you at FCAB. We got caught by Tyler,' My voice comes out all clipped. 'Me, Jasper and Lizzy were stuck up in Copperfield's office for ages. They found marijuana in her pocket.' Okay, so it's not strictly true, but hey.

For the first time, she has the sense to look a bit sheepish. 'Oops. On her birthday and everything. Is she in loads of trouble?'

'Seems not.'

She makes a sound like a cat throwing up. 'I'd have got shot if I tried to pull off a stunt like that. There's no justice.'

'You could've rung one of us this morning, Elaine,' Rob says gently, sitting beside her.

'Been busy.'

'Brian was worried too, you know.'

Elaine unexpectedly throws her arms up in the air. 'Well, good then! Because he's the one who dumped me! Why am I getting all the grief here? Why don't you ask him why he decided to humiliate me at the Fundraiser?'

'He didn't humiliate you, he dumped you after you went after Neil here,' Rob says. Neil looks at the wall and blows a ring of grey smoke at it. 'He asked Ani out because he likes her, and you two were finished. Sweet Jesus, Elaine, do you expect every bloke in Stoneford to just line up and wait so you can take your pick of them whenever you feel like it?'

'You don't know anything about what I want!' she shouts at him, but I can hear tears at the back of her anger.

'This is what I know about it,' he says evenly. 'Brian's my bud. You want to screw Neil, you go for it.' He takes hold of my hand and stands up. 'All you had to do was tell Brian it was over. Next time you go AWOL, just ring one of the girls. They've been going mad with worry about you. I love you Laney, but you can be a heartless cow sometimes.'

'Legendary,' Neil says, as I follow Rob back to the front door.

He slams the door shut behind us and walks determinedly towards the steps. 'There's no reason for her to be so selfish,' he says, striding hard towards the concrete steps. 'It's Lizzy's birthday, and all she can think about is herself.'

'Maybe she really does like Brian, and she's trying to make him jealous,' I say, trying hard to keep up with him.

He shakes his head and slows down. 'No. She just wants him to want her; she doesn't want him back. We were together a couple of years ago, and she can be lovely, but she's always on the lookout for the next bloke. Brian's well rid.' He stops and leans against the wall, pulling me to him gently. 'I'm sorry.'

'Why sorry?'

'You don't need to be getting involved in all of Elaine's crappy problems.'

He strokes the side of my face gently, and leans towards me, taking my silence as consent for another kiss. What he doesn't realise is that every millimetre his lips move closer to mine, it anchors me more securely in 1987 with him.

I know Jasper's right. We do need to find the book. I just

hope that Ani's right; I hope it can help us turn all this into a happy ending because I can't help myself but want to be with Rob Simmons.

I only faintly hear the click of the door behind us as it opens.

Chapter Eighteen - Big Time
(Peter Gabriel, 1987)

'Any chance of you two coming back inside?' Neil asks from the doorway, the half-smoked cigarette between his fingers sending fumes into the corridor. 'Only she's started sobbing all over the bloody sofa. My old man'll be back in a bit, and he hates crying women.'

'What's the point?' I ask. 'She wants to be with you.'

'I put her up for the night, I didn't bloody well propose.' He can clearly see the surprise on my face, and he laughs. It's not a pleasant sound. 'Like it's any of your business, but I don't screw schoolgirls, babe,' he replies. 'I met her for coffee once; she asked if the band could help out a friend who needed to take some shots of the band for a school photography project.'

'Kim,' Rob says, nodding.

'Next thing I know, she's hammering on my door gone midnight saying she had nowhere to go. I didn't even know she knew where I lived!'

Rob's already turned, and he's walking back down the steps, so I follow him, feeling like I'm watching one of those awful sitcoms that make you squirm in your seat, but you can't help yourself but keep following the car crash.

Back in the front room, we find Elaine with her knees pulled up to her chin, and she's grizzling over them like a toddler who's been told Santa is dead. I sit down beside her and pat her on the shoulder.

She throws her arms around my neck instantly and bursts into sobs. 'I'm such a cow! I'm so sorry! I didn't know what to do about anything, and Brian looks so happy with your friend, and I went and sat over by the Music Block, and I watched you all run past me, and you never came back, so I went and sat in the Park, and you still never came, so I came here!' she sniffs and splutters at me. 'You never came to look for me!' There's a whining edge to her voice now, and I can just about see Neil and Rob exchanging looks out of the corner of my eye.

'We did, Elaine,' I say. 'Honestly. Loads of people were looking for you. Tracy and Claire. We went to FCA … B, and that's where we got caught by Tyler, and like I told you, Copperfield grounded us for the rest of the disco.'

'Why would I go to FCAB?' she wails.

I sigh. The lie is getting a bit thin.

'Look, get your clothes on, and we'll go find the others, yeah?' Rob says. 'Your dad thinks you slept at home and left early. By the way, he looks like shite; it must've been a big night.'

'Friday nights are always heavy nights,' she says melodramatically, but she pads off obediently in the direction of the bedrooms.

'Nicely handled,' Neil says, stubbing the cigarette out in an overflowing green glass pub ashtray and looking hard at me. 'Don't you sing with Fallen Angel?'

'Me? No,' I say. 'I'm one of the new girls.'

'You're thinking of Lizzy Brookes,' Rob says. 'You do look a bit like her,' he adds thoughtfully, looking at me, and my heart is in my mouth. Of course I bloody look like her, she's my mother!

'Skins?' Neil asks Rob.

'Skins,' Rob replies in agreement.

'Sweet. She said her bloke dumped her,' he says.

'He dumped her because he thought she was seeing you,' I reply.

'Seeing that?' He snorts. 'No way. That's too much like hard work.' He walks off to the bathroom.

'I wonder what she sees in him,' I think out loud.

'He does have a point about the high maintenance though. Elaine's a good laugh and she's no bunny boiler, but she's got the emotional stability of a tree frog. No excuse for it.' He sits down on the leather sofa, avoiding the full ashtrays and empty crisp packets. 'Unlike Kim. Kim's parents are actually her dad and stepmother, who she's been calling her stepmonster ever since we saw St Elmo's Fire. That woman is truly evil.'

'I know. She told me.'

He sighs. 'Elaine moans just because her parents sometimes like a drink at the weekends, and they aren't always around to pick her up.'

I pull a face and look back to the bedroom door that has been pushed closed. 'How do we let everyone know we've found Elaine?' I ask. I'm finding the blocks on communication in 1987 a little frustrating. No point telling Elaine to hurry up. I might as well ask Neil when he's planning on taking her out again.

'We'll go back to the Willow and wait for them,' he says.

It's gone 10:30 by the time we leave the flat. Elaine tried to act all cool and sexy like she hadn't just snotted unattractively all over the sofa, but Neil was very distant. He pecked her on the cheek and said he hoped to see her soon. I thought even that might add fuel to the fire, but she's pretty quiet as the three of us trudge back up the hill towards the Park.

'Where are the others?' she's asking.

'Looking for you,' Rob says.

'Where?'

'All over the place. Let's go back to the Willow, and hopefully, the others'll be back there by now.'

But there's no one at the Willow when we get there, and although we wait for another 15 minutes, no one turns up, so we decide to make our way back to Rob's house, and it turns out it's full of the people who should be in the Park, who gave up waiting for us a lot longer before.

Rob's house is a little deeper into the estate on the other side of the Park, and he lives next door to Claire. Rob's mum Valerie is in the kitchen with Claire, buttering bread for what looks like sandwiches. She looks at me a bit longer than necessary; maybe it's just interest though, so I try not to squirm. In the front room, Ian, Jasper and Tracy are on the floor watching a sports show called *Grandstand* on the small screen in the corner. Ani's laid out on the sofa and Brian's sitting on the floor in front of her, stroking the heads of two beautiful greyhounds, one fawn, one black and white. Rob disappears up the stairs. Elaine sinks quietly to the carpet beside Ian.

'You okay?' I ask Ani.

'Feeling a bit funky,' she says. 'Probably just need to eat something.'

'Good night?' Ian says, fixing Elaine with daggers of a look.

I can't bear the thought of another scene. 'Give her a break.

She's had a rough night,' I say quietly.

'Well, I've had a rough morning trying to find her.'

I don't know whether Elaine's too tired to react, or whether she genuinely feels she's overplayed her sympathy vote, but she says nothing for once.

I sit on the edge of the sofa. 'You do look crappy,' I tell Ani. 'Sorry. You sure you're just hungry?'

'Who made you my dad?' she jokes, but I can hear her heart's not in it. She coughs and splutters a bit.

Valerie and Claire bring in two plates of sandwiches, cut in triangles from Persil-white bread with the crusts cut off. Valerie puts one dish on the floor in front of Ani, peers down at her face and frowns. 'I don't like the look of you,' she says. 'I think I ought to try to give your mother a call.'

'It's fine,' Rob says, coming back into the room from the hallway. 'She's just got a stinker of a headache.' His voice is entirely break-free. 'You don't have to ring anyone. We're not little kids, Mum.'

'No, of course you're not, Robbie,' Valerie says evenly, putting the other plate of sandwiches next to Tracy and Ian, who dive in. 'Old enough to vote now, aren't you?' The phone rings and saves us from more of her awkward questions. 'That's probably Lizzy,' she says, walking through the other door from the kitchen out to the hallway where another massive plastic hunk of a white phone waits on a glass table at the bottom of the stairs. 'She's called for you at least five times in the last hour.'

I've barely perched next to Jasper on the sofa when Valerie re-opens the door from the hallway. 'Not who I thought,' she says. 'Someone called Neil Thorpe wants to talk to you about a gig?'

Rob's in the hallway so quick that he doesn't close the door properly behind him. Jasper's beside me like a shadow; I guess Ani's feeling too rank to move but Tracy's on her feet, sensing a mystery. Elaine remains glued to the screen, apparently.

Claire's settled down next to Brian and the sandwiches. 'I brought your clothes back, Ani. Mum washed everything for you – thought you might want them for tonight.'

'Thanks, that's really kind,' Ani says.

'Hello?' we hear Rob say into the mouthpiece.

'I can lend you some stuff as well Maisie, I'm only next door,' Claire says.

'Yeah, all right thanks. How did you get my number?' Rob says.

'Cheers,' I say. Ani looked good last night, so I'm hoping I'll get the same treatment.

'Oh yeah, I forgot you know Will,' Rob says.

'I'm not sure I'm up for a party,' Ani says.

'Course you are,' Claire thumps her on the arm gently. 'You can't miss Lizzy's party! And it's at Trinity!'

'What kind of a proposition?' Rob says.

Tracy and I both look back at Elaine, who's not moved from her place on the red and cream patterned carpet next to Ian, and we both know she's not interested in the rugby game, but the way she's sitting makes you believe she thinks it's the most exciting thing she's ever seen.

Rob almost drops the receiver piece. Tracy pokes me in the ribs, trying to get information. Jasper's just curious, tapping his fingers in a pattern on the carpet.

'You serious?'

'Why you offering it to us? We're not indie.'

'Well, of course we're going to be there, you case, she's our mate.'

'I'll have to check it out with the others.'

'I'll get back to you before that.'

'Sure. And thanks.'

'Don't be a jerk, it's not a problem.'

He places the milky white cups of the phone receiver back on the hook on top of the central unit and turns to look in at us all. 'One of the support bands has dropped out of Lizzy's party. The singer's got bronchitis, and they can't replace him at short notice. If we want the gig, it's ours. We'll get no more than four songs, and we're first on. But it's a slot.' His voice has gone all croaky.

'No shit! Really?' Tracy says, and she's already skipping from foot to foot. 'At Trinity? Playing for Lizzy's party? That's bloody brill!'

'The biggest gig Fallen Angel has played so far is at the Community Centre for Claire's 17th,' Brian says from behind us once she's finished. 'You know we'd kidnap small children in return for a chance to play at Trinity, Rob.' His eyes are sparkling.

'Black Diamond are playing after us,' Rob says, ' so he says it doesn't matter what we play. Look, I know Will is going to be okay with it, but what about Lizzy? I thought she didn't want to play at her own party, and that's why Glenda and Henry never asked us?'

'Lizzy always wanted to play at her party, you morons,' Claire calls over, 'it'll be her best birthday present ever.'

'It was Glenda that wasn't keen originally,' Ian says from

the TV.

'This is an emergency,' Tracy says. 'She'll come round.'

'You better let Kim take your press photos,' Elaine says.

As they all start to chatter excitedly to each other at the tops of their voices, Rob swings me round in a *La-La Land* twirl and hugs me close. 'He said he owed us a favour after the situation with you-know-who today, and the other band have genuinely let him down, so he said we were quits.' He nearly squeezes my chest flat as he mutters the secret into my ear. 'We've got to get hold of Lizzy! Oh God, I hope Glenda's up for it.'

Ah yes, Lizzy, who on top of everything else, I now discover is the lead singer of Fallen Angel. Two days ago, I watched Elizabeth Wharton, headteacher, mouth the words to the school song from the podium at the front of the Main Hall for our leaver's assembly. My mother told me she always mimed the words, as she couldn't sing and she didn't want to give ear-ache to the Year Sevens in the front row. And now I'm going to watch Lizzy Brookes front a rock covers band on her 18th birthday, in front of a massive audience. Why did she never tell me about this stuff? I might've enjoyed History a bit more if she had.

If nothing else, no one can tell me 1987 isn't lit. I still can't help but worry if we've been here too long already, and when we're ever going to get a chance to look for this book, but the urgency to return home is fading fast. Even Jasper is looking excited.

Chapter Nineteen - Wanted Dead Or Alive (Bon Jovi, 1987)

Just under an hour later, we're in Brian's dad's garage. Brian's dad doesn't keep his car in the garage; he parks it on the drive. Brian's dad's garage is full of camping junk, old bits of car and the band equipment.

Rob got through to Lizzy, and apparently, she was way lit about performing at her own party, and she wasn't giving Glenda the chance to say no. Will (Brian's older brother, Kim tells me - he was in the same school year as Paul Brookes and Neil Thorpe, and the bassist in the band) had no plans as he was going to the party anyway, so it's game on. They spend all afternoon practising, and Will even lets Jasper have a go on his bass guitar for one of the tracks. It sounds great. We spend most of the afternoon there. They aren't worried that Lizzy is having afternoon tea in a gazebo on the lawn with her fam. My fam. They say she has a set of pipes. I don't think they're talking about a collection of plastic recorders.

Eventually, it's time to pack up and get ready. No one says anything when Rob comes over and kisses me goodbye. Not even Jasper. Ani's too busy snogging Brian to even notice. She seems to be feeling better. It's all starting to feel like we belong here. I am slowly beginning to stop worrying about the consequences. Surely Ani's right? What harm can kissing do?

We leave Jasper with the boys and go off in search of party

perfection at Claire's. She fits me out in a little black bodice with some skinny black jeans, little lace-up purple suede ankle boots, a short purple jacket and a silk scarf in my hair. Not my usual, but I feel good enough not to be complaining. Ani doesn't look too futuristic in her own jeans and Fitch T-shirt, but she found a little necklace with orange plastic stones that she loved in Claire's dressing table, and Claire insisted she borrowed it.

Trinity's in the centre of town. You can walk it from my estate, but not if you have massive speakers and three kilometres of cabling to carry. By the time me, Claire and Ani arrive, Rob, Jasper, Brian and Will are already there in Will's powder blue Ford with the words Escort in silver italics on the back, and they're setting up. They'd said Rob's kit wasn't going to be needed, but Fallen Angel are on first, so their soundcheck is first. Divine Morrissey are around; it's their drum kit all the bands are using. A few hardcore fans are already in the building. Although it's Lizzy's 18th, the groups have been able to invite their friends and fans. Lizzy turns up with Kim, Elaine and Tracy: three are a picture of '80s-rock-goddess in black, denim and backcombed hair in various colours, Kim is a tribute to Cyndi Lauper.

I feel sick with nerves as I watch Lizzy looking out over this vast space with a mike in her hand, although I can see the woman she will become when she's standing in front of a thousand students. She turns to the back of the stage to see Rob smiling back at her; head bobbing in time with the rhythm he's tapping out on the drums, a turn to the right to see Will; head bowed over his bass like he's in awe of it and beside her, Brian strumming out a basic rhythm on his guitar.

'Bloody hell,' she says into the mike, 'Trinity looks even bigger from up here, I can't see beyond maybe four or five yards out in front of my face.'

Then they're ready. The boys take up the opening bars to a song called "Never", and suddenly Lizzy Brookes is actually a rock goddess, not just somebody wearing her outfit. I'm at the edge of the stage, and it's all I can do to stop myself gawping with pride while she's belting out this song. She can sing! My Mum can really sing!

In the end, there're whistles and cheers from the people milling around on the floor. Neil is beside me suddenly, leaning against the front of the stage.

'Tight sound,' he says to me. 'Tell your fella he can stand in for us if our skins ever bail out.' He grins. 'She's got some pipes, that girl. And some lungs.'

'Yes, she does,' I say proudly, not really knowing what he means but hoping somehow it's a compliment and then without warning, Rob leaps off the front of the stage and kisses me so hard that I think my feet are going to leave the floor, and I'm kissing back just as hard and with just as much need; this isn't the slow warmth I felt last night, this is something else. This is pin and needles, adrenalin rush kissing – this is the stuff that messes with your stomach and sets you on fire. I could pull him to the floor right here and now, and in the instant that we stop dead to breathe, he just stares into my face, not saying a word. That took us both by surprise.

'Well, that went well,' Lizzy says, walking past. 'You want to put each other down and come and get a drink?'

Will's got two crate loads of bottles of Stella and a cider called K in the boot of his car. He's also got a half bottle of Smirnoff vodka, which he's swigging neat. The whole gang of us is standing around drinking.

'Paul's coming down with some of his friends once he's helped Mum with the buffet for tonight,' Lizzy says.

'How did the party go?' Ian asks.

'Too many kisses from rellies without any teeth,' Lizzy says. 'Nah, it was cool. Mum and Dad are happy. They'll have a riot without us tonight. There's more booze in my house than *Unwins*.'

Paul passes her a bottle of tequila. 'They won't miss this one.' She grins up at him, her eyes sparkling.

'Is Patchouli coming?' Tracy asks. Lizzy grins even wider, and Tracy rolls her eyes. 'Bloody Hell, girl, you are asking for trouble.'

As we make our way back into Trinity, I can see people starting to walk through the old lychgate at the front and across the churchyard up to the main entrance. Although there's a fair few dressed in a uniform of straight-leg trousers, and shirts with the thinnest of collars under paisley waistcoats, there's a good many denim-clad. Black Diamond's soundcheck was loud and proud, with a full-on screamy frontman and a lead guitarist who hasn't shaved. If I were Neil, I'd be thinking about rocking up a few of my numbers to keep these crowds happy.

Ani's make up isn't covering the fact that, to be honest, she still looks like crap. In truth, I don't believe she's much better in spite of the brave face she's putting on for everyone, I know her too well and I'm hoping it's just a bug or something. Ian dragged Kim off into one of the darker corners of Trinity a while ago, and Elaine and Jasper just keep muttering to each other. Lizzy keeps vanishing. Will, Claire and Tracy are chatting while Tracy eyes up the talent that's walking through the doors.

When Neil comes over, it's only to wish the band good luck, and Elaine is too busy giggling with Jasper to notice him. 'You'll do fine,' he tells Rob. 'Tell your frontwoman I want a birthday kiss.'

There could be two hundred people in Trinity, some at the bar at the back, some moving forward, waiting to see who's about to perform. And that would be my Mum then.

Paul is on stage, and he's talking about highbrow sounding stuff like nurturing local talent and facilitating opportunities for live music in the area, and then he's telling everybody that his little sister is 18 today, and her band are playing and the whole place cheers and claps. They've been given a four-song slot – "Never", "Highway to Hell", "I Wanna Rock and Roll All Night", and "Edge of Seventeen". I never heard any of these songs before today, but I love them all now.

Rob takes my hand and smiles and puts a gentle kiss on my lips before he walks up onto the stage, and the lights are blinding like the Second Coming, and Lizzy taps the mike and looks down into what must seem like a quilt of upturned faces. Then she grins.

Only 20 minutes later and they're off the stage already, and it sounds as if the whole of Trinity is cheering and whistling at them, and I am so fired up again that I want to run screaming around the car park outside. Paul's here upfront cheering them on, and he's slapping everyone on the back; all the faces around me are grinning and nodding, and there's such an electrifying feeling of life inside me, it's intoxicating. As Paul pushes another small bottle of vodka into my hands, and I pour a few mouthfuls neat down my throat I am fit to burst, and I run straight towards the doors at the front of Trinity, through the crowds, yelling stuff I can't make out above the roaring in my ears that's such a rush I can barely stop myself from screaming.

Out the front doors and the cooling evening air hits my face and slows me up for no more than a second, then I'm sprinting across what used to be the churchyard like it's a matter of life and death that I put as much distance between Trinity and me as I possibly can. It's only when I reach the lychgate that I realise I've not been running alone.

There's a bench, and we sink onto it without speaking. I'm vaguely aware of people passing us, but then we're just another couple making out on the bench, I don't expect anyone's giving us more than a passing glance, and I don't care. We're not just another couple though, and we both know it, but it's not stopping me any more. Right now I don't care if we never find the book, and I don't care if we never make it back to 2019. I want to be here with him. I want this rush every day of my life.

I can feel the silk of his warm skin under my fingers as I run my hands under his T-shirt. We're kissing like we did offstage earlier; it's urgent and it's been somehow inevitable since I first laid eyes on him in the PA Block in 2019. I've been holding onto these feelings. I push my hands up towards his shoulders and feel the toned muscles tensing under my touch, his muscular drummer's arms wrapping around me tightly and pulling me over his legs, so I'm sitting astride him, our lips still moving together, lost in wherever this is taking us.

'Let's go back to the caravan,' I say into his neck, stilling his hands, and it's not a question.

He nods, and we kiss again as he puts me back on the ground.

'Christ! You two! Why'd you run off like that?'

'Got to go, Tracy,' I say, as Rob runs his lips over my neck and my knees threaten to buckle.

'You can't go,' she says. 'Ani's with the First Aiders. She collapsed in the queue for drinks. Brian's with her.'

That gets our attention. 'Collapsed? What, out cold?' Rob asks.

Tracy nods. 'You better come.' She double takes at our faces and smiles a little. 'Sorry. Looks like you had other plans.'

The heat inside Trinity is volcanic now, and someone is playing How Soon Is Now over the sound system (I recognise the theme tune to the reruns of *Charmed*) while the next band gets ready to face the crowds. Tracy disappears as we walk towards First Aid.

We find them in a box room behind an old oak-beamed door with black lacquered barn door hinges. Ani's sitting on a high-backed wooden chair in one corner, and with her, there's a St. John's Ambulance girl in a black uniform with a hi-vis waistcoat over the top. Brian's sitting on the floor next to her. I can just make out a small square white ceramic sink at the far back of the room. Ani's eyes are open, but her face is shiny, and her hair is stuck to her forehead and the edges of her cheeks.

When Rob and me walk in, she gives us a weak smile.

'You are seriously sickening for something,' I kneel in front of her and take a clammy hand.

'She's got a bit hot and bothered is all,' the St. John's girl says. 'Nothing a bit of water and a few minutes' sit-down won't fix.'

Ani's holding a plastic beaker of water that she sips while staring past us, playing with the orange necklace at the base of her neck.

'That necklace suits you,' I say.

'It's pretty, isn't it?' she says softly. 'Could you do me a favour?'

'Sure.'

'Can you all find Jasper for me?'

I frown. 'Of course. Look, if you want to go home; I mean -' I stop short. It has to be a trick of the light. Her eyes have lost all their colour.

'Just get him? Please,' she asks. 'Brian, you go too. Please?'

'But I want to stay with you,' he replies.

She shakes her head no. 'Please?'

'I'm staying,' he says firmly.

Rob and me walk back into the wall of scream. Black Diamond are pretty hardcore.

I spot Tracy running her hands over some guy in full denim, and decide I owe her one. 'Ani's in a bad way; we might have to get her some real help,' I shout at her once we're close enough. 'Where's Jasper?'

'You need to ask me?' she shouts back. 'He'll be with Lizzy.'

Didn't see that one coming. With Lizzy? *Jasper*?

On the way towards the back exit, we see Kim and Ian getting into the band; there's no sign of Jasper but there's no sign of Lizzy either. I'm not sure whether that's a good or bad thing.

Once we're out in the car park again, Rob pulls me against him and makes my ears ring with another world-dissolving kiss. As we come apart, I can hear slow hand clapping.

'Nice work,' Will says, leaning against the Escort, a cigarette burning from the corner of his mouth. 'Not much between you, I have to say.'

I'm about to ask what he means when I see it through the glass of the Escort's back window. Lizzy's leg, foot upwards against the glass.

'Oh!' No. Please, no. She's my mother. I have to say, though, that this turn of events is way unexpected.

'Don't worry, they're not broken through the 15 ratings yet,' Will says, swigging from a bottle. 'We're still at 12A. No nudity, no full sex. You two okay? Lizzy got first dibs on the back seat, sorry.'

'It's Ani. She's ill. She wants Jasper,' I say. 'Is he -'
I walk over to the car, hardly believing what I'm seeing, and I bang on the roof, looking back at Rob, who's got his hands deep in his pockets.

'What?' snaps a pissed off male voice from within.

'Jasper. Ani's really sick. She wants you.'

There's some muttering that I can't quite catch the meaning of, then the door opens, and Lizzy spills slowly backwards onto the tarmac, looking not so much undressed as attempted. 'She better be really bloody sick,' she says, getting to her feet and doing up a few buttons. I'm about to be sick myself. She grabs hold of my arm, and I prop her up against the wing of the Escort.

'Jasper, what the hell are you -?'

A mussed-up blond head and a pair of piercing blue eyes grin at me out of the open car door. 'It's her 18th. She doesn't need a nursemaid. Who's Jasper?'

Relief rushes over me as Rob comes forward, and together we manage to get Lizzy upright. The guy gets out of the back seat with a bit more finesse. He is blond to Rob's darkness, blue eyes to Rob's green, denim waistcoat over a tight white T-Shirt with black jeans. He is absolutely bloody FAF, and he is trouble. Of course it was never going to be Jasper in the car making out with Lizzy.

'Maybe that last swig of tequila was a bad idea,' he says, the sexy smile not leaving his face as he looks at me, head to toe and back again. Okay, FAF, trouble and a creep.

'You think?' Rob says sarcastically.

Blue Eyes rubs Lizzy's back, and we all shoot backwards as she vomits all over the ground.

'We better get her to First Aid for some fluids,' Blue Eyes says, leaning over and kissing the side of her head vacantly, while he still stares at me. He holds the other hand out to Rob. 'Scott Kelly.'

'Rob Simmons,' Rob shakes the offered hand, and a sweet smell wafts across my senses from the patches on his waistcoat. I know that smell.

'You're Patchouli,' I say.

He smiles. 'And you are -?'

'Maisie Wharton.'

'Maisie. Sweet name. You related to Tim Wharton?'

I nearly choke. Patchouli has just asked me if I'm related to my Dad. 'Why d'you ask me that?'

'Not a name you hear all that often,' he says, shrugging. Finally managing to get a shoulder under her arm, Rob takes the other side, and they stagger towards the back entrance of the throbbing building. I'm dying to ask Patchouli how he knows my dad but there doesn't seem to be a spare moment where it wouldn't sound mad.

After she's got her momentum she can move independently, but by the time we get back to First Aid, there's just Brian, sitting on the floor. He looks white.

'Oh, your friend left a few minutes ago,' St John's says, dabbing an antiseptic-soaked cotton wool ball over a wincing guy's split eyebrow. 'I popped up the back for some more water for her, and when I came back, she wasn't here. Told you she just needed a break. I expect she's looking for you.' She smiles benevolently at Brian. 'This one needs a few minutes now. What on earth are you kids drinking out there?'

'It's a big night,' Patchouli says cheerfully.

I see something on the floor by the chair leg.

'Come on then, we better go and find her,' Rob says. 'You okay, Bry?'

'You got me out of the car on purpose, you cow.' Lizzy laughs and flings her arms around Patchouli's neck. 'You're an amazing kisser, you know.'

'Is your friend okay?' St John's asks.

'Wasted. But fine,' I say. 'Brian?'

He just stares at me as if he doesn't know me. Then something catches my eye again, and I can't ignore it. I reach down and pick it up.

'What's that?' Rob asks.

'Claire's necklace. Ani was wearing it.' I hold it out. A pretty necklace with orange plastic stones dangles in front of us. 'The clasp's still shut,' I say.

'Is that important?' he asks.

'Sure it is,' I say. 'How did it fall off if the clasp didn't fail?'

Brian leans forward and hurls chunks all over the flagstone floor.

Chapter Twenty – Little Lies (Fleetwood Mac, 1987)

'Is he 18?' St John's says, snapping plastic gloves over her hands and putting copious amounts of thick blue blotting towel paper over the mess Brian has made, her nose wrinkling at the smell.

I can't remember. 'Probably half the people drinking here tonight aren't 18,' I say. Me included. No one seems to check.

'So he's not 18?'

'I didn't say that.'

'Stand back,' St John's says, and she's turned all serious on us. 'So are any of you lot 18?'

'Thanks for the compliment, babe – I'm 24,' Scott says.

'And I am 18!' Lizzy says, sounding more like she's four. 'Ani's not here, and I want to boogie. It's my birthday, you know.'

St John's makes a sort of clucking noise, passes Brian a plastic orange bucket, pulls up all the mucky paper into another bucket and tips a load of sawdust over the blue paper. She then goes back into the little office and reappears with a tiny cup full of something blue. 'You don't want to be smelling all pukey on your birthday, honey,' she says, handing it to Lizzy, and I see she's probably still young enough to recognise the importance of mouthwash on your birthday.

Lizzy swigs the mouthwash and spits it all out on the sawdust. Scott shrugs at us and leads her out of the little room. Probably just as well, the guy with the cut forehead is looking a bit greener now.

Rob's gone to Brian's side, but Brian looks me straight in the eyes. 'She was there,' he stammers. 'She was right in front of me – and then she was just … gone.'

As I stare from his hollow eyes back down to the necklace, the panic rises in me like an emotional tsunami. 'Where's Jasper?'

'I don't know,' Brian says. 'Maisie, she was here and then she wasn't. How can that be right?'

I look first at Brian and then at Rob. 'We need to go and find Jasper,' I say.

'This one is going nowhere until he's had some fluids, and his cheeks aren't that shade of institution green,' St John's says.

'Bry, you understand, mate?' Rob repeats. 'We'll be right back.'

Brian nods as if the very effort of doing so drains the last sap of energy from his body. He looks broken. But then if I'd just seen someone vanish in front of my eyes, I'd feel a bit broken too.

Rob takes my hand, and we walk through the heaving crowds to the door back to the car park. For the next half hour, we search in all the places we think she might have gone to: the loos, the lychgate, the bar, the dancefloor, even Will's car, but I'm not surprised when we don't find her.

'Is there a sound reason why Ani would've taken that necklace off before she left the First Aid room?' Rob asks. Behind us, the singer with Black Diamond is screaming through the microphone that he wants to put his love into us. Nice. Rob gives his question some thought. 'It was uncomfortable? Made her itch?' he answers his question out loud. 'She dropped it on the floor instead of putting it in her pocket? Maybe she took it off and put it in her pocket, and it fell out.'

'You saw her. She was in no fit state to move when we last saw her; she could barely string a sentence together,' I say. 'Brian said she vanished.'

'So why disappear off when she knew we were coming back? Why send us off to find Jasper and then up and leave? Why leave without taking Brian with her? Where will we find her? Where would she go? We've looked everywhere. She wouldn't leave the site, would she?'

'I don't think we're going to find her,' I say quietly.

He stops and looks down into my face, hand still holding me tightly. 'What's that s'posed to mean?'

'Brian said she vanished. He didn't say she left.' My heart is thundering nearly as loudly as the rock band. 'Rob, I think this is something to do with the portal.'

'Oh, right. You think Ani just faded away like the kids in the photos in that film? She vanished?' He's smiling at me; he's not being unkind or anything, just trying to lighten me up, and the smile slips when he sees that I'm not biting. 'Jesus. You're serious.'

'She's been fading all day, Rob. I kept thinking; she's not just pale, she's colourless. And tonight, in that chair when she asked us to find the others, I could've sworn -' I take a breath to steady myself, 'Her eyes. They were like glass. There was no colour.'

'So what're you saying? You think she faded away to what? Nothing?

'I don't know.'

His eyes are piercing green jewels of colour. 'But the necklace,' he asks. 'Say you're right, and she's gone. Why did she leave the necklace behind? Why didn't it go with her, like her clothes?'

'She was wearing the clothes she wore to the Fundraiser tonight – the original Fundraiser, I mean, the first one, our one. Claire's mum washed them for her.'

'So the necklace was the only thing she was wearing ...'

'That belonged in 1987,' I finish his sentence. 'Claire lent her the necklace.'

Then we're holding onto each other tightly as if we're both expecting me to slip away through his fingers.' We're talking crap here, aren't we?' he says into my hair.

'If we're not, then where is she?'

A crowd of Divine Morrissey fans tumble out of the front entrance, smoking and holding bottles of lager. I guess the music's a bit much for them, and to be honest, I don't blame them.

'What happens now?' he asks.

'If we're right, then maybe everyone who doesn't belong here is at risk,' I say quietly.

'Like you?' he asks. I look at him. I can't even. 'Do you not belong here?' he asks. 'Because I believe you belong here more than I've ever believed anything.'

I stroke his hair, my chin resting against his neck. 'I don't know what I think. Brian probably thought Ani belonged here too. Something must've changed.'

'Something physical?' he asks quietly.

My stomach lurches. 'Maybe we did something. Maybe we

wiped Ani out of existence. Oh My God, no.'

'Not us necessarily,' he says quickly, 'it could've been something she did or something Jasper did.'

'It doesn't matter who did it! We have to warn Jasper,' I say, stepping away from him. 'And we have to find the book. Ani knew it was the best hope we have for finding answers to any of this, and the chances are it's locked up in Copperfield's office.'

'And if we find it?'

'Then we have to find out what's happened here, and put it right.'

He reaches out for me, and my heart is already starting to break, but I move back a little. 'Maisie?'

'I just can't, Rob, not until I know what's going on, what that bloody Old Library is, how it works, and whether I can get my bestie back.'

'Don't push me away, please …'

'Don't make this harder than it already is! I've been here for two days, and I lived my other life for nearly 18! What if we're the reason Ani's gone? What if our next kiss sends *me* off into Never Never Land?' My hands fly across to my mouth. 'What are we going to tell the others?'

'I don't want to finish this, Maisie,' he says quietly. 'We've barely even started out.'

I'm both relieved and maddened when Claire appears out of the front entrance with Tracy and Will because I don't want to stop hearing Rob's voice, but I don't want to have this conversation with him. My head is aching as bad as my heart, and it's nothing to do with the music.

'Did you find Jasper?' Will asks.

'Still looking,' I ram the necklace quickly into my back pocket.

'I gather Ani's in a bad way.'

You. Have. No. Idea. 'She was in First Aid throwing up last time we saw her.'

'Brian got her drunk?' Claire says. 'Why did he get her drunk? He didn't need to; they've been eating each other alive since the Fundraiser.'

'She didn't look as if she was too upset about being drunk,' Rob says. 'Just a bit sick.'

Someone's banging a saucepan against the inside of my skull. 'I need to find Jasper,' I say, and the last word comes out almost like a yell.

'Why, what've I done now?' he asks, walking towards us, arms linked with Elaine.

'I need to speak to you,' I say.

'I'm right here, Maisie.'

'No.' I look around at the other faces: they are surprised, amused, annoyed at me. 'No, I need to speak to you in private.'

'It's okay, Maisie, we all know you're with Rob now,' Elaine says, impatiently. 'Jasper doesn't mind.'

Am I ever going to get through to them on that story?

'Maisie has never been my bae,' Jasper says, but I can see the glittering of anxiety beginning in his eyes, and he starts to walk away from the group. 'Maisie is my blud. Give us five, okay?'

I squeeze Rob's hand as I release it, giving him a hopeful look that he understands. The small smile tells me he does – he may know the secret, but if he comes for the private chat, it will throw up too many questions. Like the ones in their heads about what Jasper just said.

Jasper's reaction is a bit confused, but I guess he's had as much to drink as the rest of us. 'OMG,' he exclaims. 'My God. My God! No. We don't know for sure that she's gone,' he says. 'She might be in the loo. Or here in the gardens. Maybe she went for a walk.'

'If she did, she'll turn up, won't she? And if she doesn't turn up? If we look for her all day and all night, and she doesn't show?'

'If Ani has ... gone,' he says., swallowing hard, 'if she's gone, where has she gone?'

We look at each other.

'I don't want to go back yet. Okay, there it is, I don't want to, I want to stay here with Rob, but I think it's our fault,' I blurt out. I feel the sharp boot of responsibility in my shin. There's a roar back inside Trinity as Black Diamond finish their set into the silence between me and my one remaining BFF.

'You think you and Rob changed something about the past?' he says in awe-touched tones.

'Or Ani did it to herself. With Brian,' I say.

'How is Brian?'

'Oh, he's bloody lit. He just watched his new bae disintegrate in front of his eyes.'

Jasper breathes out slowly. 'We so need to get our hands on that book.'

'If it exists.' I rub my hands over my face. With the heat in the hall, my makeup must be halfway down my neck, or all over Rob's.

'It has to exist, Maisie,' he says, sighing. 'The Portal exists, so the book must exist. It's the only thing that can give us any answers.' He takes my arm. 'I know you're into Rob, and he's into you. I shouldn't have ripped you up this morning, but we can't go on like this, and you know it.'

'It's okay.' I put my hand over his. 'You're right. We must find the book. Do you honestly think it is in that awful Head's office!'

'It's as good a place as any to start hunting. I didn't see it when we were up there, but then I didn't get much of a look around,' he says. 'There has to be a way of getting in there for a proper search. It's summer half term, but teachers will be working at the school so it should be open. There are always teachers working at Drake's during the holidays. Your mum practically lives there.'

'I still have the key to the van,' I say, pulling it out of an inside pocket in my little bolero jacket. 'No one's asked me for it back. So we should be good for another night in the caravan, and then we can go to Drake's in the morning.'

'What are we going to say to the others when they ask about Ani?' he asks.

I shrug. 'It'll come to me. Look, if you start feeling strange or weird,' I look at Jasper sadly, 'you need to tell me.'

'Why?' he asks.

'Because you might be next,' I say, and I'm marching back into Trinity, my head pounding and my heart racing. Torn in two? That idiom doesn't come anywhere close to describing the agony I'm feeling right now.

Eventually, Divine Morrissey play, and they are sound, in spite of their name, and the fact that their lead guitarist is a tool. I can appreciate their talent even if it's not my type of music. Kim runs around at the front of the audience, taking action shots of the band with a huge black camera like a professional, climbing up onto the stage and shooting artistically from the wings, but Neil knows where his audience is. Eventually, Kim runs out of film – whatever that means - and she and Ian are dancing – well, she's dancing and Ian's holding her hand and smiling at her while she dances.

Jasper asks her whether he can see the photographs.

'Of course, once I get them developed,' she smiles. 'I can't afford Same Day Delivery, and Boots aren't open until Tuesday now so I'll probably send them away.'

'Send them? To someone with a dark room?' he squeaks, and I have to elbow him hard before he realises.

'No, to Truprint in a prepaid envelope,' she says and gives him a confused look.

Brian and Claire are in the dark spaces at the side of the hall, leaning against the bare stone walls, deep in conversation. I wish I were a fly on the wall for that one – I hope Brian can keep his head.

Lizzy's with Patchouli, standing without support and she's cleaned up pretty well thanks to St John's, although I think she's probably lucked out on whatever she'd planned to do with him in the back of Will's Ford. They are laughing a lot and kissing more. I wonder if Glenda knows Lizzy's boyfriend is 24, and if it would bother her.

I try to imagine what Elizabeth Wharton would say if I rocked up at home with a 24-year-old man. Patchouli is bare hot, although there's something about how he is with Lizzy that doesn't quite ring right. Something in the way he looks at her, as if what's on his face is different from what's behind his eyes. Will's with Tracy and a gang of guys from FCAB; Jasper's hovering around with Elaine, watching the band nearby.

It's a perfect night, and it's a total nightmare.

Rob hasn't let go of my hand since I came back from talking to Jasper. I keep hoping I'll feel a tap on my shoulder and Ani will be standing there, grinning at us, saying she only went to get some fresh air and telling us how much better she's feeling, but there's a dark emptiness deep in my guts that knows it's not going to happen. She's gone who knows where or when, and all I can do now is hope that she's back safe in our own time with her fam and that her life isn't too different from before, with her best friends all here in 1987.

Rob stands behind me, with his hands clasped gently against the skin of my stomach under my short bodice. My hands rest over his, his chin on my left shoulder, his lips against my ear, occasionally kissing my cheek, sometimes nudging his nose into my hair, every now and then making a comment about a great riff the guitarist plays, or the drum riff Neil follows.

It can't last forever. I was a mong to ever think it could.

Maybe we can reverse the damage that's been done. Perhaps we can find some way of getting the Portal to work for us, as Ani said. But I can't allow myself to believe it, because that way, only madness lies. If I start to plan my future around Rob Simmons, I'm not just likely to break my heart – I'm going to shatter it, and risk a lot more on top.

Chapter Twenty-One – Hymn To Her (The Pretenders, 1987)

'So, she went home. Just like that?' Tracy says irritably. 'She didn't even wait to say goodbye?'

'She did say goodbye,' Rob says firmly, 'but only to a few of us.'

'She was embarrassed,' Jasper looks down, not meeting Tracy's steely gaze. 'She didn't want to act all thirsty, so she told us not to say anything to the rest of you until after the end of the party.'

I guess everyone is used to some of the words we use by now, as no one asks what he means. Rob and me, we searched everywhere for Ani before we left, several times over, but once we were sure she wasn't there, we had to tell some story to the others, and it seemed like the most reasonable solution.

'Well she could've given me back my necklace in person,' Claire huffs, fingers toying with the orange stones I've returned to her. 'Wouldn't have hurt her to thank me. We wouldn't have stopped her going home, would we?'

'She did say goodbye to me,' Brian pipes up helpfully.

'I should bloody hope so!' Ian exclaims. 'You okay, mate?'

Brian looks at him sadly and shrugs.

'It's a pretty necklace,' Kim says, touching the plastic stones.

'It's yours, honey,' Claire says with a sigh, putting it into her hands. Kim squeals with delight. 'Keep it. Never liked it much anyway.'

I can tell Claire's not satisfied with our story, but what else are we supposed to tell her? "We're from a future where you are old, and at worst our friend is somewhere out there, floating in pieces in the atmosphere?" Would she be as quick to believe as Rob or Brian?

'You want a lift home?' Will asks us, as people start to leave Trinity.

'You can take me,' Elaine says, her face all flushed. 'Buggered if I'm going home as the extra wheel.' If Jasper sees the meaningful look I see her give him, he doesn't react.

'I'll walk Kim back to Lizzy's,' Ian says.

'We'll walk too,' Rob says.

Will gives him a nod of understanding. 'Give you blokes a chance to finish what you started,' he says evilly.

I glare at him, but it soon dissolves into a laugh.

'I'd like to walk with them anyway,' Brian says. 'I need some air.'

'My brother the gooseberry,' Will says, but there's no real malice in his voice.

Paul's met some girl who Tracy says left Drake's last year, so I give him a wide berth and hope he doesn't ask for the caravan key back. Takes a few minutes for us all to hug goodnight, and then Will's gone, his ancient blue Escort belching fumes into the air as it staggers back towards the outskirts of town with Elaine, Paul, his girl, Lizzy and Patchouli. We leave Tracy and Claire still reeling a little, waiting for Tracy's mum to collect them. The rest of us walk home.

Kim and Ian walk with us for a while, and then we fall back and let them walk further ahead, giving them privacy and protecting ours. It's a warm night, and the stars are bright against the full moon overhead. The roads out of town are relatively busy with people leaving pubs. There are so many more pubs in town in 1987, but people still seem to go home a lot earlier.

Me, Rob, Jasper and Brian talk about the gig, Elaine and Neil, Lizzy and Patchouli, Paul and Rowena (Brian tells us that's her name) and even Kim and Ian – every subject we can come up with to keep our minds off the one thing we want to discuss. But it breaks out in the end, as I guess we all know it will.

'Do you think Ani's okay? I mean, do you think she's back in your time?' Brian asks, eventually.

'I'm sure she is,' Jasper says, patting him on the shoulder.

'You're not convincing me. You think she's slipped into oblivion, don't you?'

I sigh. This boy needs a hug. I need a hug. 'The truth is, Brian, we don't know where she is, but we're not giving up on her.'

'Well, all I know is that I don't want you going back into your own time or oblivion. Either of you,' Rob says.

'Got a plan?' Brian asks.

'Tomorrow's Sunday. Copperfield won't work on a Sunday,' Rob says.

'Why won't she?' Jasper asks.

'No one much works on a Sunday here,' Rob says. 'Only professionals like nurses and policemen. They just defeated a bill in Parliament about it. The government's too worried about people not turning up for church if they can go shopping instead, and the decline of the great Sunday roast dinner. The only shops open tomorrow will be the two garden centres and the corner shop near to my place.'

'Weird.'

'Useful. My Uncle Frank is the caretaker at Drake's. He lives on the site. If we can find him and I give him some flannel, I might be able to convince him to let me in the building to get something Maisie has forgotten.'

'Something I've forgotten?' I repeat.

'Right now, you're the only one who goes to Drake's, Maisie,' Rob says.

Of course I am. 'Like an important book for revision, you mean,' I say, catching his idea.

'Like the book in the Head's Office,' Jasper says.

I nod. 'Okay.'

'It's not much of a plan,' Jasper says into the silence.

'It's the best we've got,' I say, squeezing the arm Rob has fastened across my shoulders. 'We need that book if we're to have a hope of understanding any of this.'

'I know, but it's just a big risk to take, breaking into that Head's office,' Jasper says.

'Jasper! We need the book! More than ever now? What's the matter with you? Why are you bottling it now?'

He shrugs and turns away from me. 'The trouble is that none of us has seen it,' he says. 'I've realised that we don't know exactly what we're looking for.'

We don't say anything else for at least fifteen metres. I honestly hadn't thought about that.

'How in the name of Sod's knacker bag are you going to know what to look for then?' Brian is the one who comments on the elephant in the street.

'Ani told me the name of the book when we were in the Old Library; I can't remember it right now, but I'm sure I will when I see it,' Jasper says. 'She said it was a purple leather bound hardback book, about the size of a tablet.'

'Well, that's bloody stupid,' Rob says, 'why would anyone bother to print such a small book?'

'A tablet is a small computer,' I explain.

'The book is the size of a computer?' Brian exclaims.

This is not getting any easier. 'It's book-sized,' I say, patiently. 'Did Orla tell Ani anything about what she read?'

'She said it was handwritten.'

'Handwritten?' I look at the local boys. 'Surely that's unusual here too.'

'It's 1987, Maisie, not the Dark Ages,' Brian says, shaking his head.

'Anything else, Jasper?'

'Orla said it mentioned teleportation. That was why Ani was so excited.'

'Sounds like witchcraft,' Rob mutters.

'Teleportation's a recognised phenomenon; there's even a suggestion of it in the Bible,' Brian says.

'Yeah, and Aleister Crowley could bilocate, so the stories say; he could be in two places at once,' Jasper says.

'Ozzy's Mr Crowley?' Rob asks. Jasper nods. 'That bloke got up to all kinds of weird shit.'

'It isn't weird shit,' Brian says solemnly, 'it's science, and if it's science, I can fix it.' If anyone questions the egocentric nature of that last statement, no one's going to confront Brian about it. We're walking into the far edges of my estate now; I can just see Kim and Ian as they stop up ahead and start kissing under the light of a streetlamp. 'Do you think it was something we did?' Brian stops walking, turns and faces us.

Having already had a similar conversation, I'm reluctant to start it all up again.

'It's possible, you know. I kissed her,' Brian goes on. 'And she wasn't supposed to be here. I know you aren't either, Jasper. Nor Maisie.' He pauses. 'I kissed Ani a lot.'

'Detail overload, blud,' Jasper says.

'You've kissed Maisie a lot since she's been here too,' Brian says, looking over at Rob.

'Feels like weeks ago,' Rob says quietly, hugging me closer.

'So would I be right in thinking maybe this has something to do with us kissing girls who come from the future?'

Rob shrugs, looking across the quiet road into the stillness of someone's front garden. There's a light on in a small frosted window upstairs in the house. As I watch, it goes out. The thing is Brian's right. I was deluding myself about kisses. Kisses may not harm, but they change realities. Look at Sleeping Beauty, Snow White, Beauty and the Beast and Shrek. Kisses bring people back to life; they save souls, they make you see people for who they truly are. One kiss can change someone forever. Maybe in the wrong circumstances, that kiss can also make someone disappear as if they never existed.

'Maybe it was us that did this to Ani,' Rob says, 'but how can we be sure?'

'We can't be sure but we have to try to put it right,' I say.

'Maybe, but maybe this isn't about making sure you don't all drop off the edge of this reality. Maybe it's about making sure we all stay here? Because that's what we want,' Rob says. 'Ani too. Obviously,' he adds with a pertinent look at Brian.

'I'm not sure that's possible,' I begin. 'It's not what's right -'

'Fuck what's right!' Rob steps away from me. 'What's right, what's wrong, what's normal, what's weird – they're all just bloody words! How I felt tonight, playing in our band and the way we were after that - I've never felt like that in my entire life!' He turns on me. 'Can you look me in the face now and tell me you didn't feel the same?'

I can feel Brian and Jasper's discomfort, and they walk on ahead – any quicker, and they'd have broken into a run.

I can't. I can't tell Rob I didn't feel the same. FML. He knows it, and after a few seconds, he grabs my hands and holds them between us. Like in Lizzy's bedroom, when he pulled me to my feet to dance with him. Crap, that feels like a lifetime ago. Well, a good couple of decades ago, not yesterday.

'All you have to do,' he says, and his voice is controlled, but I can hear the tremors, 'is tell me if there's another reason you want to go home. You tell me why you want to go back, and I won't hassle you. I'll even help. No hard feelings. Just tell me.' He looks down at the path. 'Is there another bloke back in way back when?'

Kim and Ian are still kissing, but under a new streetlamp now, their bodies silhouetted against the eerie orange light as Jasper and Brian catch up with them. Above us, the full moon glows grey-white against a starry backdrop. A cat gives a single mew pitifully in a nearby garden, and a car crunches up a gear in the distance.

'I'm from the future, not the past,' I say. My voice sounds small and tired in my ears. 'This is Way Back When, and yes there is a … bloke. You.

'And if we wake up tomorrow, and we're back where we

started, and I'm still 17,' I blurt out, all my fears that have been churning in my head, 'how will you feel? If we see each other in the future, you looking at me when you probably have a wife and kids – Jesus, maybe even grandkids? How d'you think that'll make me feel? I don't want to see the regret in your eyes! I don't want to feel that regret!'

'If you vanished right this second, do you think I wouldn't already spend the rest of my life regretting that we didn't get more time together?' he says. 'Do you think I'd only feel sad if we carry on like this, and then you go back after a month or two? If you go back to your time now, and you run into me in the future as an old man, all you'll see in my eyes is -'

Our eyes lock. I'm the first to look away.

'I'd already be sad,' he finishes. 'Because I already care. You don't think you'd look into my eyes and feel those regrets too? You wouldn't regret what we could've had? Don't push me away, please. We'll find your book, and we'll get Ani back, and then we'll sort out a way to make this work.'

Someone closes a window on the night in a nearby house.

'Please say something to me,' he adds gently, after a pause.

'I can't,' I say, my mind in overdrive. 'But I will. Soon.' I squeeze his hand before I let it go. 'I promise. I just need to get my head straight.'

We walk the rest of the streets back to my house in silence, arms around each other, down the back lane to the van, me hoping we're not going to be interrupting any of my relatives.

All the house lights are blaring, and I can hear music coming from the open windows. It looks like the rents are still partying hard. Kim's in no mood for sleep, though, so she comes down to the van with us. It's going to be bare crowded in the caravan tonight. Just as well, since I don't think I trust myself alone with Rob at the moment.

'That was a brilliant night,' Kim whispers.

'Yeah. I saw you and Ian getting down to the indie band. Traitors.'

'Don't be like that.'

'Teasing. Things look good with you two.'

She pauses before she answers. 'He's sweet. I don't think we are like you and Rob though.'

'Why d'you say that?'

'Oh, nothing. It's just when I see you two together; it's like you've been like that for always. Like two halves of the same whole. Like you belong together.' She gives me a small smile. 'I don't think I would see that if I looked at Ian and me.'

She's smacked me in the mouth. She doesn't know it, but I'm stinging badly. Without answering her, I open the caravan door and peer inside. Nothing has changed since last night when we rapidly tidied up the car rugs and cushions. It doesn't look like Glenda's prepared it for proper guests. Kim goes in first, and then everyone clambers in, stifling giggles, and Rob is last. As he steps up, I put a hand on his arm and close the door in front of him.

'I don't have any reason to want to go back,' I say quietly, my breath coming in short gusts. 'I don't want to push you away.'

He takes my hand and turns me back towards the house. 'Too busy in there,' he nods towards the caravan.

'Way too busy up there though!' I say in alarm, looking up at my house and garden, still pumping out music from an open kitchen window, and laughter and voices drifting up from the gazebo in the garden. He looks up, nods, and we turn around.

There's a makeshift fence between the road and the apple orchard, where they eventually build Jasper's house. The fence posts are linked at the top and bottom with wire and stand loosely in the dry dirt. Some of them are skew, propped at an angle and easy to move. We push our way through one of the larger gaps. I can feel the dusty soil breaking up beneath the thin soles of my boots, and smell the scent of the blossom on the trees as we pass further into the orchard. Fresh petals on the ground reflect the light of the full moon over our heads, like pearls under our feet.

Rob takes my hand and leads me deeper into the trees. A fox screeches to my left. When he stops, it's next to an unremarkable tree, like he's decided we've come far enough to wait any longer.

He pulls me down to the ground beside him; it's tinder-dry under us as it hasn't rained in weeks. The jewels of his green eyes are dark in the moonlight, and I wonder if I'm opening my own door to wherever Ani's gone.

'If I'm going to be here for a while, you better talk to me about 1987,' I say.

He smiles. 'Surely it can't be all that different?'

Chapter Twenty-Two – I Get The Sweetest Feeling (Jackie Wilson, 1987 (1968))

It turns out 1987 is all that different, and it's not just the lack of smartphones and tablets or the entire Internet. It's the Sunday closing and four channels on the television which can only be recorded one at a time (if you've got the right equipment, and if you miss the start then you have to wait for a "repeat") although Tracy's getting something called "Cable TV" and it's really cool, though Rob has never seen it. The Government just laid out its plan to dig a channel tunnel to connect England to France. Music comes from a gadget called a Walkman and plays off a black plastic box called a cassette with tape ribbon in it that contains the sound. They have ten brand new Nimbus computers at FCAB, but you can only use them if you are studying Maths 'A' Level, and they use black plastic envelopes called floppy discs to play games and save essays. No one has an email address. Morrissey is fresh and so are mullet hairstyles. Everyone watches *Top of the Pops* on a Thursday, and *Neighbours*, the show from Australia that everyone raves about, is on BBC1 every day. *Blackadder* is excellent for A level History revision, and Hugh Laurie is hysterical in it. All the girls all love Tom Cruise. Apparently, Jasper and me dress like the Jock from *The Breakfast Club*, which is why they thought we were American. It's all so familiar, but it's all so different because it's my history, and it's his nowadays.

He asks me loads of questions as well, but I try not to reply. Or at least I tell him vague stuff. I am trying not to influence the future, even if I've already done it. My stomach lurches for the thousandth time as I wonder when Ani is. As he finishes telling me about the boys are looking forward to a new film called *The Untouchables*, but the girls want to see *The Witches of Eastwick* instead, I blurt out,

'We must find the book tomorrow.'

He smiles, a little sadly. 'It's today,' he says, pulling me gently down, so my head is resting on his lap, 'and we will.'

As the orange glow of daybreak appears over the roofs of the houses along my street, we slowly walk back through the orchard holding hands. I've taken off my boots, but the small stones and pebbles in the soil don't hurt my bare feet. We push back through the gap in the fence, cross the unmade road and tap as loud as we dare on the van door. Takes a while to get an answer: Kim looks as if she's had as much sleep as I have: Brian looks wretched, Jasper pale, Ian is happy.

'We'll be back at nine,' Rob says into my ear as he hugs me goodbye. 'Need to grab a shower and a change of clothes. Meet under the Willow, and then we go up to Drake's. Okay?' He pats Jasper on the shoulder. 'Jasper, you come with us and grab a cleanup, and don't even start with the being concerned you're taking the piss.'

Kim's yawning; she needs to get indoors. As the boys walk up the track and we walk up the garden path, the sun is already filling the garden with light. I see the trestle tables in the gazebo still have the remains of the buffet on them, there are white paper plates, and purple napkins all over the grass and a couple of men and women are still asleep with their heads resting on the backs of the picnic chairs.

'Looks like the olds had a good time,' I say quietly.

'Well?' she whispers.

'Well, what?'

'Did you do it?'

I blush. 'Kim!'

'I know you did, anyway,' she hisses matter-of-factly, 'it was written all over your faces when you came back. Way to go, Maisie, you've only known him for three days!'

'Well, I don't expect you and Ian did Sudoku all night,' I say defensively, walking past the old shed.

She looks confused for about three seconds, and then offended – finally she crumples into a pile of suppressed snorts and giggles. 'It's not very comfortable, that caravan,' she mutters, still stifling the laughter, 'but we *were* in there with Bry and Jasper, you know. Where did you go?'

'The orchard.'

'That's romantic. So was he any good? D'you love him?'

I shake my head at her enthusiasm. 'We didn't do it, Kim.'

'Why not?' she asks as we get to the back door. 'What did you do all night?'

We kissed, and we talked; we kissed some more, and we talked a whole lot more. We talked about his world and I avoided his questions about my world, and then we just fell asleep. When the sun started to rise, and it was time to go back to the caravan, I felt like I had spent the night with my soul mate, but I just tell her, 'We got to know each other better.'

'I wish me and Ian could be a bit more like that,' she says.

'You could've fooled me,' I tease. 'You can't put each other down.'

'Yes, but that's all he ever wants to do,' she sighs.

We walk into the kitchen, and both take a sharp breath. It looks like a tornado passed through here at some point last night. There are glasses, some full, some empty, as far as the eye can see, on the sink drainer, on the round pine dining table, on the pine dresser in the corner, on the cooker, on the fridge freezer. Ashtrays are overflowing with cigarette butts, and there is a blue haze hovering just below the ceiling like a summer cloud. It stinks of smoke and stale beer. A board game lies abandoned.

Kim turns to me, and the playful look from the garden has vanished. 'The stepmonster's going to kill me for staying here tonight, Maisie. I'm s'posed to be somewhere this morning. What if I get grounded all week? What if I don't get to Tracy's barby queue?

'I don't think that's likely, Kim. Glenda will sort it all out.'

'You think?'

We make our way to the stairs to the first floor, avoiding the creaky one that is third down from the top (and it still squeaks now), and then past Lizzy's room and up the next staircase to the second floor where Kim's been staying. It's a guest room, and thankfully, it has a bathroom next door to it. At least I can get a shower, and I plan to, but I'm so exhausted that as soon as I sit on the bed, I'm curling up for a snooze.

We doze off for maybe an hour or two, but I'm so psyched up about finding the book and getting Ani back that I wake as soon as I hear people starting to stir downstairs. Kim is still out cold on her side of the bed, her new necklace glinting like hot coals against her neck in the sunlight that filters through the gap in the curtains. I shower and grab a change of clothes, and she doesn't even roll over.

If Glenda's surprised to see me in her kitchen, or that I'm a teen up before nine on a Sunday; she doesn't say. She asks about the gig, and I give her the bones; she's not interested really, she makes the right sorts of noises, but they mostly sound like grunts. She looks like she partied as hard as Lizzy did.

I fall out the door with a couple of slices of toast in my hands fresh from the grill, out into another warm late May morning, leaving them to their bad heads.

The boys lie in the shade of what Rob now calls 'our tree'; the Willow that will become so big, up near the Park's front gates. Jasper's propped up against the trunk, his mouth slack and his arms loose by his sides, but Rob's curled up on the grass, foetal-like with his hands tucked under his head as if he's diving. Looking vulnerable and frail, he seems the opposite of what he is. I wonder if he's had as much sleep as me, whether he's still as wired as I am.

As I walk up to him, his eyes snap open, and his face transforms as the biggest smile affects every inch of his features and answers my question. He pushes himself up onto his knees, puts his arms around me in an enveloping hug, and kisses me until Jasper coughs loudly. Then we're moving on again, out of the Park and left down to Drake's Bottom Gates.

We take the long walk around though, because Frank's house is just inside the main gates up to Drake's off the bottom road, like the gatekeeper's house to a rolling mansion. Drake's doesn't look like a fortress or a stately home.

Rob says Frank has lived here and looked after the site for over ten years already. He's where Rob hoped he'd be on a warm Sunday morning, watering his prized flowers and weeding the pampas grass beds in the front garden. 'Hiya, Uncle Frank!' he calls out. 'Flowers are looking nice!'

Frank looks up. He's wearing an unflattering pair of baggy blue overalls that look as shiny on the back in the sunlight as his bald head. He wears a checked short-sleeve shirt, and there's an unlit rolled up cigarette behind one ear. 'Hello, Robbie! I was only thinking about your Mum and Dad this morning; haven't seen them down the local this week! Dad still working away, is he?'

Rob nods. 'He's staying somewhere on some conference or other. Mum sends her best.'

'So what're you lot doing hanging around here during the holidays?'

'Well, I came to ask you a favour actually,' he says.

'Me?' Frank puts his watering can down on the lawn.

'This is my new friend, Maisie. She's just started at Drake's. And her brother Jasper's at FCAB with me.'

'Nice to meet you young people,' Frank says, giving Rob a look that I think I translate uncomfortably as approval.

As I start to speak, I can feel my voice changing, sweetening, becoming more feminine to play into this man's baser instincts. 'I've been really silly. School finished on Friday, and with all the excitement of the Leavers' Assembly, and saying goodbye to everyone, I forgot to take an important book out of my locker.'

'Oh.'

'It's so important;' I go on, laying it on with a garden trowel, 'it's for my first exam next Tuesday, and if I don't get it soon, it'll ruin my whole revision schedule for this week!'

Frank looks at me thoughtfully, walks into the house and comes out a few moments later with a set of keys more commonly seen hanging from a prison guard's belt buckle.

'Can't have one of Drake's girls messing up her exams,' he says, closing the front door behind him. 'Where're your lockers?'

'Main building,' I say quickly. 'Upstairs.'

'All right. I'll let you in. But no crazy stuff when you're in there, okay? I'm trusting you three. And don't go anywhere else! More than my job's worth. You can tell your mum that she owes me a pint of light and mild, Robbie.'

I give him my sweetest smile. 'Thank you! You're dope. Fab! Super!' I correct myself helplessly.

Frank opens the doors to the entrance hall, and disables the alarm, says he's going back to his rhododendrons and to let him know when we've finished. We shower him with more sweet talk before we disappear up the stairs. No matter how many years you've lived on the planet, it's not what you know, but who you know. We watch him walk down the driveway back to his house, and take the stairs up to Copperfield's office on the fourth floor two at a time.

There's something creepy about a school during the holidays; it's like the building shuts down without the kids' laughter or the teachers' shouting and the buzzers signalling the end of each class. We storm into Copperfield's waiting room like we're on a raid, but it's not until we're standing in her office that the enormity of what we're about to do kicks in for me. I wouldn't dream of doing this to my mother back in the day, let alone as a random student going through Marguerite Copperfield's desk.

'Where d'you think the book might be?' Rob asks, breathlessly.

'No idea. Check the desk. Bookcases. Don't move anything,' I add hurriedly.

'How can I check the desk and bookcases and not move anything?' he asks, sounding a bit frantic.

'I mean, try to leave the place looking the same as it did before we got here,' I say.

Jasper's already opening filing cabinets and fingering his way through manila folders of confidential material. It suddenly occurs to me that if we get caught, Frank might lose his job. The police might even be called. Technically we are breaking and entering with the intention of stealing school property. So many people could be affected by what we're doing here in the past.

I pull open a few drawers full of stationery and a small half-drunk bottle of Captain Morgan's rum and then open a tall wardrobe-like wooden cupboard hoping it's a bookcase, but it's full of box files and mottled grey lever arch files over spilling with paper with rows of bunches of keys hanging on hooks inside the door. Jasper's flicking through a cabinet labelled "Notifiable Incidents".

Rob finds a locked drawer. 'Anyone found a key to this?' he mutters.

I open another tall cabinet door as wide as it'll go.

'Shit,' he says.

I swear we try every key on every hook in that cabinet, but whatever's locked in that drawer is staying there. I'm hanging the last set of keys back on the inside of the door when Rob holds his hand up; the index finger raised authoritatively; the universal sign for don't-move-a-bloody-inch-I-can hear-something.

I can hear it. The sound of heels clipping across school linoleum.

If we can just get out into the waiting room, we can come up with a reason for being there, as long as we get out of the office, as long as we leave it the way she left it whenever she was last here. We're sliding drawers shut in stealth mode, straightening notepads, and finally, we're in the waiting room and Rob's pulling the door to her office closed behind him with the quietest of clicks just as Copperfield walks in.

She stares at us, and we stare back. Seconds pass that feel like millennia.

'Would you like to explain to me exactly what you're doing in here?' she says.

I want to tell her that you should never discipline using a question because challenging kids will answer with a brief "No, Miss, I wouldn't", but in all honesty, I'm more distracted by what she's wearing. I'd thought of Copperfield as being old: an old school disciplinarian, old fashioned, old aged. But standing in front of me with a pair of pink cowboy boot heels sticking out of the bottom of her wide-leg bleached jeans, a floral open-necked shirt untucked and her tight curly hair loose over her shoulders, I'd be surprised if she was more than 20 years older than me. Or my mother.

'Looking for my earring,' I say lamely.

'Your earring,' she repeats.

'Yes, Miss. I lost one at the Fundraiser, and they were a present from my Grandmother. Real gold. The caretaker very kindly allowed me to come in here to fetch a book I forgot to take home for my revision ...'

'My office is nowhere near the Sixth Form Common Room, Miss Wharton.'

She remembers my name. 'No. I know. I know, but I thought that, while I was here ...'

Copperfield looks at the boys. 'We meet again, Lau. And you are?'

'Robert Simmons, Miss. Upper Sixth at FCAB. We didn't mean any harm,' he says. 'Maisie just wanted to find her school-book, and the earrings are precious to her -'

'How valiant you are,' she says, her eyes flicking across to the now-closed door into her office. 'Defending your girl. Very courteous.'

'It's the truth, Miss,' he says.

'The truth,' she says. 'Yes. It's a fascinating thing, the truth. Shall I tell you what I think?' She walks over to the office door and doesn't wait for us to reply. 'I think that you all came here under false pretences, that you tricked Mr Bennett into believing you had a valid reason to be here because he's your uncle, Simmons, and I have caught you in the act of attempting to search my office - but for what?'

Rob looks defeated. 'He told you.'

'Well, of course he told me, Simmons, since I had to inform him I was entering the building and intended to disable the alarm.' She looks back at us. 'And not least because I am his boss, and I know his family background. Surely this fuss is not about Miss Brookes' marijuana?'

'No, Miss, that's not right at all,' I say, but my voice has gone all croaky.

'It's of little consequence,' she says, unexpectedly. 'What's more important, Miss Wharton, is that your mother or father can spare me ten minutes to discuss whether or not I'm still happy to allow you to take your A-Level examinations in the light of your recent episode, and to formally enter you onto our registers.' She pushes open the door to her office, has a glance around and turns back to us again. 'Lau also concerns me greatly because he doesn't attend Fletcher Clark Academy for Boys, but he wants us all to think he does. Why would that be?'

Okay, she's good even by 21st century standards. This is how my mother would react if she met a strange teen on a Fundraiser night who told her the phone in his house was cut off because the bill wasn't paid. Educational Welfare Officer Amber alert goes off in her head. I can imagine the rest - she rings FCAB to ask if they're aware that there's a student on their books that could be at risk, and they say; Jasper Lau? We don't have anyone by that name on our registers. Educational Welfare Officer alert becomes – what? Social Services? The Police?

Jasper looks like a fox caught in the headlights of a Porsche on a dark lane. 'I do go there, Miss.'

'Please do not insult my intelligence, Lau; you are not registered as a student at FCAB. I checked already. So if you are not a student there, I ask myself, then where are you a student - if you are a student at all - and why are you loitering in my school for the third time in as many days?'

I can feel Jasper's eyes burning into the side of my face. I can't look; I don't know what to say to him. If he's frightened, what can I say to help him that doesn't make matters worse? Is she onto me too?

'Perhaps you would like to go and retrieve your forgotten textbook, Miss Wharton,' Copperfield says slowly, 'and I will have a little chat with Lau and Simmons here.'

She looks at Jasper. Jasper's not just pale; he looks like someone has drained all the blood from his body, and he's lost what little command of the spoken language he had to start with. 'Come in and shut the door, gentlemen, and let's have a little chat about why you're both trespassing in my school today with one of my most attractive sixth-formers,' Copperfield says pleasantly.

I guess she has a sense of humour I never noticed the first time around.

She gives me one of her best half-moon-spectacle looks, without the spectacles. Funny how they make her seem so much more severe than she is. Maybe that's the reason she wears them.

'I believe you have a book to find?'

Chapter Twenty-Three –
Manhattan Skyline (A-Ha, 1987)

The Sixth Form Common Room looks like it was evacuated straight after a bomb scare – everyone seems to have just got up and walked out, leaving a carnage of papers, magazines and books behind them. I look around; there's a little yellow and black version of *York Notes* on *Tess of the d'Urbervilles* on one of the tables, which I grab, hoping it's on the A-Level syllabus. Holding the book firmly in front of me like a tiny shield, I make my way quickly back up to Copperfield's waiting room.

I can still hear voices behind her office door as I step cautiously into the waiting room, and at first, I'm worried that she's talking on the phone, but then I hear Jasper's voice, low but reasonably confident; more so than before, anyway. I sit down on one of the hard, inflexible wooden chairs.

After a few minutes, the door opens, and Copperfield comes out, followed by Jasper and Rob. She's smiling. I look at them in disbelief.

'There you are, Miss Wharton. I see you have found your book. It seems that, like our Tess, you have arguably been responsible for your own suffering.'

Smiling; she's almost cracking jokes! I steal a glance at Rob. He winks quickly. What the hell has he done to her? 'Losing an earring and a book can't really be considered as suffering, Miss.'

'Though irritating in its own right, but at least we have

righted one wrong. Now I've sorted the enigma that is Mr Lau out, perhaps we can all get on with the rest of our day. And Maisie?'

It startles me to hear her use my name. 'Miss?'

'If your mother wishes to speak to me regarding your examinations, I shall be working here for the rest of today and all day tomorrow.'

'Yes, Miss. Thank you, Miss,' I say.

'Goodbye, Simmons. Lau,' she says, and she closes herself in her office.

Back outside the main block in the increasing heat of the day, the three of us stand in a square, staring at each other, speechless for a few moments.

'What the hell did you do to Copperfield?' I ask. 'She was nearly human!'

'Nothing!' Jasper looks all innocence, but he's suddenly laughing, and I know there's something more.

'I told her he only just started at FCAB last week, and she rang them up there and then to check,' Rob says. ' Miss Potts on Admissions said we'd had several new students starting last week, but they hadn't had all the paperwork through, so the chances are we were telling the truth 'cos I knew the layout. Bit of luck really.'

'He brown-nosed,' Jasper says. 'It was classic. Then I got a bit lucky. I said we'd come over from Manhattan because I went to New York for a holiday a couple of years ago, remember?' Jasper says. I nod. 'Turns out it's somewhere she's always wanted to visit.

'Anyway, then I explained that Mum was ill, but I was staying with my Aunty Valerie for the time being until she got better, and I'd panicked the other night when she asked about the phone, and I didn't know Aunt Valerie's number anyway. Then we talked about Latin, and I made a couple of funnies.'

'He brown-nosed,' Rob says. "He was great.'

'Okay, I brown-nosed,' Jasper admits, 'but I watched a master in action getting the school keys off the caretaker earlier, and I picked up a few tips.'

'You had a good teacher,' I say, smiling at them. 'But we still don't have the book.'

We make our way back to Lizzy's house, and I know I'm in a funk, hardly speaking a word, squeezing Rob's hand to reassure him I'm good when I'm not. It occurs to me that if I were in my own time, I'd be drowning in timetabled online revision sessions now, so I should be happy I've got some extension to my freedom but somehow, with Ani gone, it seems all we can do is wait until Lizzy and her friends decide to travel through the portal.

How long will that be? Days? Months? How does Lizzy even find out it's a portal? Does she come through it by accident like we did? How long can we survive here without a proper place to stay? Without money? Because it's clear to me now - as much as I want to see how things turn out with Rob, it isn't going to happen. Nothing good can come of this. I feel like I'm lost in another country. Walking in Manhattan like Jasper did and enjoying the view, but with no way of getting home.

Rob squeezes my hand as we walk through the plastic windbreaker into Glenda's kitchen. It feels weird just walking in, even now. The blue fog has gone, but the room still stinks of cigarettes. There are several people slumped over the circular pine table in the diner part of the kitchen. Glenda is leaning against the sink unit, hugging a large mug of something steaming. I guess these guys really hit the juice last night. A messy head of red hair lifts slowly from the table, and Lizzy's bloodshot eyes meet mine.

'How is it that I'm dead and you're alive?' she moans and puts her head back onto her folded arms.

'The difference between us having a couple of shots and you having a pint of tequila maybe?' Jasper says, grinning.

I'm not sure from Glenda's expression that she's as amused as he is; I turn to give him a glare, but then I see his face, and it's changed dramatically, as if someone's punched him in the goods.

'You did go for it last night, Lizzy,' Rob says, 'but you are only 18 once.'

'I may not make it to 19,' she wails through her arms.

I try to attract Jasper's attention, but he won't look at me. 'What's wrong?' I mutter lightly. Still getting no response, I follow his line of sight to the pine dresser at the back of the dining area. 'Jasper?'

'I think he needs a cuppa,' Glenda says, turning sluggishly to reboil the kettle.

'Jasper, you're freaking me out!' I hiss a little more urgently, and finally, he seems to wake up, but when he turns towards me, his eyes are wide like he's smoked all the weed Lizzy had in her pocket at the Fundraiser.

'I need some air!' he declares, turning a perfect netballer's pivot and walking straight out the back door again.

I make apologetic faces at the people who are looking at me

and follow him out the door, down the steps past the old shed and onto the multi-coloured patio. 'What's wrong with you?' I snap. 'It's hard enough being normal here without you acting all thirsty!'

'The book,' he says, and his face is drained of all colour. 'It's here.'

I look at him for a few seconds. 'Don't be a tool.'

'I'm not a tool! I saw it!'

'Where?'

'Lying on that big wooden dresser in the kitchen.'

'*What?*' I put my hands on my hips. 'That's not possible. Don't be stupid -'

'It's not stupid! Ani said it was a purple leather book, and I saw one lying on the shelf, so I was trying to read the title out of interest, and I could see the words printed on the front, and then I remembered what Ani had called it! *The Trewthe of the Weyfarere!* It's there on the dresser in your fucking Nan's kitchen!' he squeaks all in a rush.

'Shut up,' I say, feeling unsure.

'How the hell is it in your Nan's kitchen?' he yells, and I'm dragging him further down the garden, away from the open window and Glenda's sudden interested looks.

'I ... I don't know,' I say, confusion muddling my speech processes. 'I don't – what in hell even does that mean? Trewthe?'

'Did you want this cuppa or not?' Glenda calls out of the window.

'We have to get that book,' Jasper gives me an urgent look.

'And exactly how do you think we're going to manage that?'

'Ask her if we can have a look at it?' he shrugs.

I rub a hand down my hot, sweaty cheek. It's going to be another scorcher of a day. 'If that book is really a historical document containing the truth behind the legend of a mysterious time portal stuck in the middle of Drake's School, do you really think she's going to hand it over to us with a chocolate Hobnob?'

'Have Hobnobs even been invented?' Jasper asks.

'Do I look like I know?' I hiss. Glenda is giving us some severe watching now. 'We have to go back in. Now.'

Rob asks me the inevitable silent questions with his eyes as we walk back into the kitchen, but I shake my head lightly and accept the cup of tea from Glenda. The biscuit she gives me looks like dead flies have been baked into it. 'Have a garibaldi,' she says inexplicably. I take a polite bite; to my relief, it's currants.

'So what are your plans for today?' Glenda says brightly as if she's trying hard to be cheerful, but, apart from the fact that her family have wrecked the house, I can't see any reason for her to be worried.

'Dying,' Lizzy mutters into her folded arms. She hasn't moved since I followed Jasper into the garden. I risk a glance over her shoulder at the pine dresser.

I remember this piece of furniture although we don't have it now, pine's way out of fashion. It's got two big old cupboards at the base where I remember Nan keeping board games and playing cards, and then perched on top is a four-shelf bookcase. Two of the shelves have plates on them with chintzy patterns, and the other two are full of books.

Not that I ever doubted him, but Jasper's right, there is a

book there. The cover is the deep purple of Cadbury chocolate wrappers, but the leather is cracked and worn as if it's been used as a scoring pad for a blade in DT. It's similar in size to my *iPad Mini* and not very thick, but on the front are thick, golden letters embossed deeply into the leather covering. The letters aren't familiar, although you can make out the strange words Jasper repeated. The letters look like runes. I've seen all the *Lord of the Rings* and *The Hobbit* films. Uncle Paul made me watch them all when I was staying over while my mother and Dad were having their final meltdown before Dad left. The leather looks delicate. Whether it's the book we've been searching for or not, I can't think why it would've been pulled off the shelf and left there. It looks precious, as if it ought to be in a safe. Or locked up in a headteacher's office at the very least.

'You'll be fine in a few hours, Liz,' Paul says without lifting his head.

The person sitting next to Lizzy scraps the chair across the lino flooring and pulls herself unsteadily to her feet.

'More tea, Rowena?' Glenda asks, holding a shiny brown teapot out like a waitress.

'No, thanks. I best be going. Thanks for the tea and toast, and again, sorry about earlier. I honestly meant no harm.'

'No point crying over split milk,' Glenda says, her words clipped like the angry teacher her daughter will become. 'No harm done. Just keep the door shut … next time.'

Rowena drops a kiss onto the top of Paul's head. 'Give me a call when they resurrect you.' She sends a smile around the room to anyone looking and disappears out through the windbreaker into the back garden.

'Will you have another cuppa, Scott?'

Scott Kelly lifts his head from the table and looks as divine in broad daylight after a bender as he looked in the twilight of a drunken stupor. 'No, you're fine, Glenda, thanks.'

Such piercing blue eyes he has. I know Tracy for one thought he was too old for Lizzy – and he is a bit – but he's totally buff. Even the way he's sitting now; sprawled back all casual on the wooden dining chair with one hand placed possessively over the top of one of Lizzy's arms, watching me. Tracy is right, though. He is trouble, but he's the kind of trouble I'd find hard to resist. I shake my head. I can't believe I'm thinking like this. Things are complicated enough with Rob.

I suddenly remember Scott asking me about my Dad – at least, asking about my Dad's name. In all the drama with Ani at Trinity last night, it went out of my head to ask him about it. I fight the urge to ask him now, but Glenda puts a side plate with more buttered toast on the table (real, yellow, creamy butter), and I'm starving, and suddenly I can't face another scene right now. I shuffle over, take a slice and return to Rob and Jasper. Paul seems to react to the presence of the plate, and he sits up, his eyes gluey and bloodshot.

'So if you've got no plans for today, Lizzy, then maybe we can spend some time together?' Glenda asks into the void. 'I don't have to start the deep clean at school until Tuesday.'

'Mum I am much too ill to wander around boring castles looking at pretty flower beds today,' Lizzy mutters without taking a breath.

'Oh, we don't need to be doing anything like that.' There's that unnaturally bright voice again - like she's forcing herself to be smiley. 'I just thought I might tell you the story behind that key I gave you for your birthday.'

'It's a beautiful piece, Glenda,' Scott says, rocking the back of his chair so that it hits the dresser.

Everyone jumps as if we are all on edge.

Even Lizzy's not such a tool that she doesn't notice that this is important, as much as we do. 'It is pretty. I know it's an heirloom. Thank you. I love it, Mum.'

Glenda smiles. 'That's good because it's the most precious thing you will ever own.'

There's a white clock on the wall with a tick like a road jackhammer that can drown out a quiet television, but I hadn't noticed it until now.

Lizzy finally lifts her head. 'Tell me more about my precious.'

Glenda looks around at me, Jasper, Scott and Rob. Paul is picking something from his fingernails with a penknife, and Scott looks like a dog that doesn't understand the command. She stands up and walks unsteadily over to the kettle. 'I'm sorry everyone – you can come back later to see Lizzy, but right now we need some family time.'

Chapter Twenty-Four – Behind The Mask (Eric Clapton, 1987)

We all look at each other, and Lizzy catches my eye. 'Mum! That's bang out of order! You can't just send them away,' she says. 'I need to talk to you about them, anyway.'

'Yes, I've been wondering if that was coming,' Glenda says, putting the kettle down and leaning against the sink. Suddenly she's looking bleak, in spite of the high-heeled pink fluffy slippers. 'They aren't new kids at all, are they?'

Lizzy glares at Paul. 'You talked to her about them. You promised you wouldn't. Don't think I'm doing one bloody saucer of your washing up.'

'Back off, sis,' he says mildly. 'I kept your secrets. Maybe you should listen to Mum for a change?'

'I'll listen to Mum when she listens to me.' Lizzy slurps a great mouthful of tea and swallows hard. Her eyes are still bloodshot and shrunken into her face as she faces Glenda. 'Mum, these two – they're like Kim. They've got nowhere to go. I said we'd give them a place to stay until they can get themselves sorted.' No one says anything. 'Mum? We always take in people who've lost their way! You told me that when I was tiny.' She sounds less sure of herself now. I can hardly swallow, and Rob has a hand on my shoulder as he stands behind me. Jasper is leaning against the dresser behind Scott. 'You've always sorted them out. I'm 18 now. I get to have a say in helping, you said.'

'We do take people in, Lizzy,' Glenda sighs. 'We take people in, and we sent them on their Wey again.' She looks at us, and there's a deep sadness in her eyes. 'Kim's one of us, and we do our best for her, but these two are nothing like Kim, love. I had my suspicions the minute I laid eyes on them. Normally I deal with them straight away, but I think they are for you.'

'You're not making any sense,' Lizzy says.

Glenda shakes her head and looks around at us all, her eyes pleading. 'This isn't fair. She needs to be told in the safety of her family. Please give us some space and let her have time to deal with it.'

'You know, don't you?' Jasper says, too quietly. 'You know about the portal.'

Glenda gives him a look that would melt most metals.

'Jasper!' I snap. 'That isn't going to help anyone, and we still don't know what we're dealing with!'

'She obviously knows about the portal, Maisie!' Jasper cries. 'She's got the book! What more proof do you need that she knows what we're dealing with? No one gave us any time to deal with it! Where was our cosy chat?' He turns back to Glenda and adds bitterly, 'We were with the safety of our families in our own time, and now we're stuck here and you want to send us out of the room while you talk about us?'

'I will not discuss any of what's happened with you until my daughter has been acquainted with the facts, bystander,' Glenda says, her voice strained.

'Bystander?' he says, confused. 'What kind of word is that? Are you dissing me?'

Where have I heard that word before?

'Sorry, but what the hell?' Rob says into the silence. 'Are you saying you know about this stuff happening, Glenda? People appearing through doors from the future or the past?'

'So she told you as well then,' Glenda's drink-flushed face pales.

'Maisie told me how she got here. Brian knows as well,' he says grimly.

'It looks like I'm the only one left who has no fucking idea what the rest of you are jabbering on about!' Lizzy shouts and then holds her head.

'Not strictly true, baby,' Scott says quietly. 'What's all this about a portal?'

'I'm not sure of the details if it's any consolation, sis,' Paul puts a silver tin on the table and starts to roll a cigarette. 'It's women's stuff, according to Dad.'

Glenda looks shrunken like someone sucked all the fight out of her, like she's frail, even though she can be no more than 30 years older than us. 'We need time as a family to discuss this; then I promise you there will be answers. To *all* your questions.' She makes a point of the qualifier and looks meaningfully at Jasper.

'Well, bloody good job too, because if someone doesn't start talking English, I'm going to spew all over the carpet tiles,' Lizzy says, and she does look green.

It's Paul who stands up, and he somehow manages to get across the fact that we need to leave the kitchen without being threatening or sarcastic.

'I'm sorry. You need to go,' he says. He stares down at the man still holding the arm of his little sister. 'You too, Scott. Sorry, man.'

'It's not going to do any good losing our shit over this, Jasper,' I say. 'We have to trust them that they can get us home.'

But before he can reply, I find myself falling forwards towards the tiled carpet of the kitchen floor. The force of the back door slamming open onto me and the people launching themselves into the room is so great that I lose my footing entirely and would definitely tumble to a concussion if it isn't for Rob, who (if he wasn't such a shit hot drummer) should definitely consider signing as a goalie for a local league.

I spin around, ready to give my attacker some well-aimed verbal but I'm silenced by what I see.

I watch the tall woman scan the room like a sniper: Rob with a protective arm still across my shoulders, both of us sprawled on the floor, Paul next to Jasper with his back to the larder door, Glenda by the sink, Lizzy sitting slumped over the round pine dining table, Scott standing with his back to the dresser. The woman's face is a garish blotchy pink, and she's wringing her hands, like Lady Macbeth washing away the stains. On closer inspection, she's a lot younger than I first thought, from the way she rants.

'Where are you hiding my stepdaughter?' she says, her voice just slightly left of sane.

'How dare you just storm into my house!' Glenda begins, but she has seen the same as me; there's now a man storming in from the garden to join the attack. They must have parked on the road at the front of the house. We would've seen someone leaving a car by the caravan.

'Tell me where you are keeping my stepdaughter, and I'll go,' the Woman says to Glenda, and on hearing her a second time, I'd say we were quite a long way from sane.

'Out!' Glenda points at the door. 'Or I'll call the police! Henry!'

Paul steps forward and stands up in front of her. 'I don't think my mother is pleased about you being in here,' he says firmly. 'She's asked you to leave.'

'Don't you threaten me, you delinquent!' the Woman screeches unexpectedly and points at the floor to where I am tangled up in Rob but thankfully not broken. 'You see, Nigel! This woman lets her daughter lay on her floor with boys in full view of the breakfast table!'

Suddenly my brain swipes right. There is considerable padding in the shiny suit jacket she's wearing, over the drop-waisted flowery skirt and high necked blue nylon blouse. He looks as if he's just walked out of a high street store, with his perfectly ironed shiny suit and tie drawn right up against his collar.

Glenda clears her throat. 'Mrs Fox? Mary?'

Of course it is, and although I don't believe Kim was ever short on sympathy from the Brookes household, that support has now tripled from the extended fam.

'Don't you act like we are friends, Glenda Brookes. Where is my stepdaughter? You made me a promise on the telephone that my stepdaughter would be home for Services today, and she wasn't on the early bus.' She pulled her rigid body even straighter. 'We know. We waited for it.'

'It was a big night last night, Mrs Fox,' Lizzy says, her voice suddenly light and cheerful. 'I was 18 yesterday. Kim had a lie-in.'

'Kimberley doesn't sleep in on Sundays. There are chores to do before Services,' Mrs Fox says, and her tight lips are getting thinner.

Mr Fox gives us a look of disgust. 'Kim is being led astray by your wicked ways. Look at you all. Sitting in each other's squalor, stinking of alcohol, allowing yourselves to wallow in your own disgrace.'

He is certifiable. She was probably there first.

'Don't talk to us like that,' Rob says.

'I'll talk to you how I choose, young man,' Mr Fox says, towering over the two of them as he prowls around the dining room.

'I can go and get Kim for you, but I'm not doing anything unless you stop insulting my children and their friends,' Glenda says, standing tall herself now, no longer slumped over the sink with her mug of tea. Paul, Scott, Rob and Jasper are all now standing in defensive mode. I decide I'm not going to stay on the floor like some out-dated stereotype. Lizzy clearly has the same idea as we both stand as equals with the guys.

'You'll get her now,' Mrs Fox snaps.

Glenda's arms remain tightly folded. 'No, I don't think I will. Perhaps you'll just leave my home, and perhaps I won't call the police. Henry!'

'Perhaps you should call them anyway,' Mr Fox says. 'Are you aware of the demonic reading material on your Welsh dresser, Mrs Brookes?'

We've been watching Kim's stepmum so intently; I hadn't noticed Mr Fox picking up the purple leather book until he's waving it above his head like a flag. *Demonic reading material?*

'That's just silly teenagers' stuff,' Glenda says coolly. 'They like to experiment.'

'And this is how you have kept our daughter safe!' Mr Fox

yells. 'Exposing her to the darkness of sexual deviancy, allowing her to shirk her responsibility? What atrocities lie within these pages?' He flicks across the pages of the book, and a small cellophane packet falls onto the carpet at his feet.

Mrs Fox stares at the book as if it's ignited in her husband's hands.

Several things happen all at once then. Mr Fox drops the book, picks up the little packet of marijuana and starts yelling as if he's trying to contact the police on the other side of town without a smartphone. Paul tries to grab the packet from him but isn't quite tall enough to reach, so he hits Mr Fox in the stomach; Rob grabs the packet as the older man folds, and they all start shouting at each other.

Henry appears in the door, moaning about the noise, twisting his silver bracelet round and round, his face flushed with hangover and anger. He starts yelling too when he sees what's going on, and when no one seems to hear, he moves in on the shouting match with the guys.

I realise a split second before she moves what she's going to do, so I'm too late to stop Mrs Fox as she dives through the door to the hallway. She's over the squeaky third stair from the top before me, Glenda, Jasper and Lizzy have even started the chase up the stairs, leaving the fight in the dining area.

We catch up with her as she flings open the doors to Lizzy's bedroom, but Kim isn't there. Glenda grabs hold of her shoulder pads but can't stop her from opening Paul's door. Me and Lizzy stand on the bottom of the second flight of stairs, trying to prevent her from getting up to the second floor because we know that's where she will find Kim, but we're thrown aside and Lizzy yelps as she crashes to the floor of the landing, her exposed leg scraping against over a forgotten nail in the rough wooden skirting boards. Jasper stays back to help Lizzy to her feet as Mrs Fox runs up the staircase and Glenda and me follow as she throws open the room that Kim always uses.

She's just about awake, and I watch in horror as she goes from sleepy wake-up to Def Con Five in three seconds.

'Stepmother?'

'Get your bag, child,' Mrs Fox snaps. 'You disgust me, mixing with these people. Don't expect to be seeing them again.'

'She's 18 in a few weeks,' Lizzy shouts from the doorway, propped up on Rob's arm, a big red weal on her ankle. 'Then she can do what the fuck she likes.'

'Do not attempt to cloud my judgement with your profanity. 18 is an arbitrary number used to create policies for sexuality and responsibility. We do not agree with them.' Mrs Fox glares back at her cowering stepdaughter. 'You will be an adult when we believe you can accept the responsibilities required of an adult. Right now, you aren't even capable of doing the simplest chores without being chased down like a rat in the gutter. Get your bag!' She shouts the last three words so loudly that I swear the glass in the windowpanes rattles.

'I'll be speaking to Social Services about you people,' Glenda says, her horrified voice little more than a whisper.

'Do as you please. As you say, Kimberley is 18 in a few weeks. See if they care after that,' Mrs Fox says, her mouth distorted in a final rictus, and I realise I am looking into the eyes of my first sociopath.

When they leave ten minutes later, Mr Fox is threatening to press assault charges against Rob, Paul and Henry, and only relents when he hears that his wife pushed Lizzy to the ground upstairs. Kim is ashen in the clothes we found her sleeping in, as he shoves her out of the kitchen. Mrs Fox is jubilant as she slams the door on our silence.

Glenda is rummaging through the drawers next to the sink unit for ointment and bandages for Lizzy's ankle, as it's bleeding quite badly. No one says anything. I try to give Rob a reassuring hug, and he doesn't push me away, but his green eyes are dark with anger and frustration. Henry is puce in the face and looks about set for a coronary. Jasper sits at the dining table, nibbling on the stone-cold piece of toast that someone left.

'Lizzy, you did have your tetanus jab at school, didn't you?' Glenda says resentfully, wiping the blood from Lizzy's ankle, and dabbing Savlon on it.

'Years ago,' she winces.

'You should've let me call the Old Bill, Henry.'

'Kim's 17. We have no grounds to keep her here without their permission,' Henry says slowly. 'Besides, there's a packet of weed on the dining room table. God, my head hurts. What did we drink last night?'

'Mum? That book where I hid my stash, that you got out to show Lizzy?' Paul says. 'It's gone. Was it important?'

Chapter Twenty-Five – Running In The Family (Level 42, 1987)

Glenda drops Lizzy's bandaged foot onto the floor. Lizzy yelps. 'That's not possible,' she whispers. 'It must be there.'

'It was on the third shelf down, and it's gone,' Paul says.

I look over at the dresser. So does Jasper. Our eyes meet. Paul's not wrong. The purple book has gone.

'Where did Scott go?' Lizzy asks, massaging her swollen ankle.

No one replies. To be honest, I hadn't even noticed he left. It looks like he did a runner as soon as things kicked off, from where I'm standing, but I'm not going to say that out loud. Tracy was convinced he wasn't right for Lizzy. Surely he'd have stuck around just now if he was sound?

'Looks like he got out of the kitchen, sis,' Paul says. 'Couldn't stand the heat. You know.'

'I'm sure he just had somewhere he needed to be,' she says, but her voice is smaller.

'It's not there, Mum, I looked,' Paul says. I realise that Glenda is actually losing her cool; she's on the floor on her hands and knees, picking up bits of paper that clearly don't have a purple book hidden underneath. 'Mum?'

'We have to find it!' she says, and I'm uncomfortable that she sounds close to tears.

'I didn't mean to hide my stash in it,' Paul says into the silence. 'I didn't realise it was that important.'

'Without it, we are all doomed!' Glenda says dramatically, and she pulls a chair away from the dining table and sits down heavily with her head in her hands.

The clock jackhammers a few more ticks into the silence.

'Doomed is a bit Aunt Ada, Mum,' Lizzy says.

'Mum?' Paul pulls a cigarette out of the black packet we're used to seeing. 'Can you tell us what's going on? Please?' Glenda looks at him as if he's asked her to take a bullet for him. 'All my life you've told me the women in this family are the important ones, the women are the ones with the burden, and when Lizzy turned 18, it would be her burden too. I think we should all know. She's my sister.'

Lizzy looks up from rubbing her bandaged ankle. 'Burden?'

'It is a burden,' Glenda says.

Slowly, those of us standing find seats at the dining table: Paul passes Henry and Lizzy cigarettes. I almost wish I smoked. Lizzy props her bandaged ankle onto Jasper's lap. We look at Glenda.

'You don't come from around here,' Glenda says, looking at Jasper. 'Neither you nor your friend.'

'Go on,' Jasper says quietly. 'Spill the tea.'

Glenda reaches across and unexpectedly takes a cigarette from Paul's black packet. 'This isn't how it should be,' she says sadly.

'But it's how it is,' I say, suddenly frustrated, 'so can't you just explain things to us?'

She stares at me, and I feel uneasy – does she know I'm her granddaughter? Then she looks down at the burning cigarette, and finally, up at Lizzy. ' Women in our family are Weyfarere.'

If she expected a round of applause or fanfare, she must've been disappointed. 'Weyfarere?' Lizzy repeated.

'Weyfarere are the Guardians of the Weys,' Glenda says.

'I'm a Weyfarere?' Lizzy asks.

'Weyfare. A Guardian of the Weys,' Glenda took a deep drag of her cigarette. 'The Weys are ancient tracks made by the Earth's energy. They channel the fourth dimension. By-standers call them the ley lines.'

'Sounds like one of Brian's essays,' Rob says.

'Sounds a bit too mystic for Brian,' Lizzy says.

'Isn't the fourth dimension Time?' Jasper asks.

'It is,' Glenda says. 'The Weys are as old as the Earth itself, channelling part of its ancient energies. There are rifts in the Weys like the faults in the Earth's physical crust - we call them Weydoors - and these rifts allow people to slip through and travel across the time dimension.' She takes another deep drag and looks at Jasper and me. 'Which is what has happened to you two. Am I wrong?'

'There's this place at school,' I hear myself saying slowly. After days of keeping this secret from most of the people I've met, it feels odd to be telling my family. Even if they don't know I'm their family. And hearing what Glenda is saying, I don't think they ever can.

'The Old Library,' Glenda draws deeply on the cigarette and coughs. 'The Weydoor is now inside it. Our ancestors built a Folly to protect it in the 1600s when it became part of a big house called Drake's Manor. Once the manor was converted to a school, the Folly was made into a library for the students.'

'Why doesn't anyone know about it?' Jasper asks.

'It's hidden at the back,' I say. 'You can't see it unless you go right to the back of the room.'

'It. Glows. Purple.' Jasper shakes his head. 'You're trying to tell me that generations of students have been inside that library and haven't noticed that one of the bookcases looks like something out of a *Doctor Who* episode?'

'He has a point,' I say. 'How have we all missed that?'

'It only glows in the presence of a Weyfare's key.' Glenda taps the ash into the re-overflowing green glass ashtray. 'Or if someone has just come through. The rest of the time it's a false impression. A master illusionist created it to mask the actual Weydoor when the Old Library was built. My family have always worked on the site to protect it and try to keep it secret. The oldest ancestor I can trace was a maid to the first Lady of Drake's Manor in 1717.' She takes a deep breath. 'It's her copy of the book that I've lost.'

Crap. That book is 300 years old. No wonder Glenda is crawling up the walls.

'Nobody ever never noticed that people went missing?' Paul asks.

'There are no records until very recently. Drake's became a girls' school in the late 1800s, and there's a section in *The Truth* written by my great grandmother Ada of a load of schoolgirls going missing after using the Library. The Headmistress at the time decided reading was too dangerous for young ladies, and so they were only allowed inside with supervision after that.' Glenda stubs out the cigarette and immediately lights another. 'After the school was bombed in the Second World War, it was even easier to keep people out. Most of my family have worked at Drake's one way or another.' She gives her daughter a meaningful look. 'We're hoping for something a bit grander for

Lizzy.'

'She could be a teacher,' I mutter.

Lizzy splutters tea all over the lace tablecloth. 'Sod that for a game of soldiers!'

'I was thinking maybe one of the office staff,' Glenda almost smiles. 'I can't see Lizzy behaving for long enough to be a teacher.' She sighs and pushes her fingers through her heavy fringe. 'I can remember everything I need to tell you, Lizzy, but we must find the book. It contains knowledge and history that can only be known by Weyfarere. It mustn't get into the wrong hands.'

'We've been looking for that book,' Jasper says, out of nowhere.

'You know about *The Truth*?' Glenda asks suspiciously.

'That's how we found out about the Portal ... the Weydoor. A friend of Ani's said she saw the book, and Ani wanted to find out about it.' It seems like such a long time ago, and it was a matter of hours, really, and now everything has changed. 'What is the book?' I ask.

'It's called 'The Truth of the Weyfarere'. The original was written in Middle English. There have been translations down through the years, but they are becoming nearly as faded as the book itself. The book contains everything a Weyfare needs to know.'

'Like a handbook,' Jasper says. 'So Orla was being straight with Ani.'

'A handbook? Yes and no,' Glenda says. 'Look, the less you know about all this, the better.'

'Bit late for that,' Jasper says.

'Is this a big secret then? Are you like spies?' Rob asks.

'Not secret so much as non-existent.' Glenda looks at her hands. 'To my knowledge, we are the last remaining family left that actively protect a Weydoor,' Glenda says. 'It's just the two of us now, Lizzy, since Mum went senile.'

'So the other Weydoors aren't protected?'

'The records of the existence of other Weydoors has been lost over time, as the families gave up their traditions,' she says, sadly. 'I read about some strange happenings down in Devon that might've been evidence of one, but I wasn't able to get out of work to go and investigate.'

'So what do you do? Stop other people from passing through this door?' Rob asks, looking at me.

'No, anyone can pass through. They just can't get back again.'

'I'm sorry? Did you just say we can't get back?' Jasper asks faintly.

'No, no,' Glenda says kindly, 'let me finish. You are a by-stander. It just means you can't get back on your own. You need Weyfarere to help you get home.'

'And I'm a Weyfare - rere,' Lizzy says again.

'Weyfare. Once, the eldest girl in every Weyfarere family was expected to do her duty.' Glenda stubs the half-smoked cigarette out violently in the cut-glass ashtray that is already overflowing with ends as if it disgusts her. 'Look, I'm not saying anything else until we are alone as a family. I'm sorry!' she says, turning to Jasper and me. 'I've already said too much. We need to talk to Lizzy alone, and then she can help you to get back to -'

'2019,' Jasper says stonily.

Glenda looks even paler, if that's possible. 'The future?' She looks at me then; a fearful look that I've not really seen. You don't need a magnifying glass to see the similarities between Lizzy and me. Has she worked out who I am?

Because I have.

I'm Lizzy Brookes' eldest daughter. Only daughter.

That makes me Weyfare too.

'No, you tell all of us everything,' Lizzy says firmly, 'because if you don't, I will tell them. Let's go back to the beginning, please.' She leans forward over her damaged ankle and peers into Jasper's eyes. 'You're from the fucking future?'

Jasper shrugs and gives a little smile as if she's just told him he's FAF.

'Here? In Stoneford? In 2019?'

'That's right.'

Lizzy laughs and claps her hands. 'That's insane!'

'Pretty much,' I manage to squeak out. Jasper glances at me, but I'm not sure he's realised the implications of all this for me at the moment.

'How do Weyfarere help people to find their way back to their own time?' Rob asks.

'*The Truth* tells us that the energies of each time attach themselves to objects that belong. So long as the bystander has a Token Object that was given to them in their time, the Weyfare can use her key to boost the grounding nature of that object to get them back onto their timeline.'

'This key?' Lizzy pulls out her silver birthday key. Glenda nods.

'How do they do that?' Jasper asks.

'Weyfare keys have homing skills. *The Truth* says that if the Weyfare transfers some of the key's power to the token object, it will be attracted back to its home ten-fold.' Glenda looks back at Lizzy. 'But the Weyfare will always return to her original timeline. Because of their keys, they are the only ones who can safely travel the Weys and return to their original timelines.'

'This is freaky,' Lizzy says. 'Is this why we always had weird people turning up at the house and then disappearing again when I was a kid?'

'I tried to protect you from it until you were ready,' Glenda says quietly. Henry puts a hand on her arm, and she gives him a grateful smile. 'It's been a burden. At least hardly anyone comes through now; the place is locked down all the time.'

'How did the other bystanders know where to find you?' Rob asks.

'It was more a case of me keeping an eye out for them,' Glenda says. 'If I found them, I helped them. I'd take them back through the tunnels.'

'The tunnels?'

'There's a tunnel from the back of the Old Library to a trapdoor in the Old Shed in our garden. It was built to get by-standers back to the Weydoor when it became school property, and Ada's husband built this house. She was the first headmis-tress of Drake's.'

Well, no wonder my mother didn't want me messing about in the Old Shed. I guess it had nothing to do with power tools after all. 'And if they didn't find you?' I ask. 'The bystanders?'

Glenda shrugs. 'We were not obliged to help bystanders that we know nothing about.'

'So they'd try and go back through the ... Weydoor and what?' I ask, my mind suddenly very much on the ether that may or may not contain Ani.

'Some probably stayed in the time they find. Some may have tried to travel back through the Weydoor. Either outcome, without the help of the Weyfarere, wouldn't have a good success rate.'

'That's a bit harsh, isn't it?' Jasper says grimly.

'Life is hard, and it isn't always fair,' Glenda replies, her fingers twisting together, 'but we all have to do our best.'

'Glenda?' I ask into the short silence that follows. 'We have a friend. Ani? She was with us when we came through the Weydoor. Then at Lizzy's party last night, she vanished.' Jesus. Was it really only last night? 'Where did she go?'

For the first time in telling all these muddled and confusing stories, Glenda looks properly horrified. 'She just vanished?'

'Everything apart from a necklace Claire lent to her.'

Glenda puts her head in her hands. 'I knew I should have acted on my instincts, but it's been such a long time since anyone came through to me, and I've been so busy with your birthday, Lizzy, and preparing how to tell you - I've failed.' She bursts into noisy sobs then, and Henry instantly wraps his arms around her. The sight makes my eyes water too. It's awful, watching an adult cry. It must mean something catastrophic.

'So - our friend?' Jasper whispers.

Glenda lifts her head from Henry's arms and wipes a hand across her nose as if she were a child. 'I'm afraid it's likely that your friend has been extinguished.'

Chapter Twenty-Six – With Or Without You (U2, 1987)

I'm beginning to see why Glenda keeps saying it's a burden.

Henry hugs her tightly and strokes her hair. 'I told you years ago love -when you first told me about your birthright – you can't be held responsible for every time one of them doesn't make it back.'

'Extinguished sounds very final.' Rob has become the voice of reason when neither me nor Jasper can find any words to say.

'But I thought you said she went home,' Lizzy says. 'Oh. You aren't runaways, are you? Well, looking on the bright side,' she reaches across and grabs another cigarette from her brother's pack, 'she might just have gone back to where you were when you started. 2019. 2019? I'll be 50!' she exclaims, with a look of familiar disgust.

'No, she didn't go through the Weydoor.' Glenda takes the piece of kitchen roll that Paul is offering her and dabs her eyes. 'You said she just disappeared. That means that something happened to prevent her existence in the future, so she was extinguished from our time. We call it extinction.'

'You were right,' I said to Rob. 'Films are always based on some kind of truth.' Thanks, Marty McFly. My heart is heavy. Ani's extinguished.

'Something happened while you were here in 1987 that

affected Ani's original timeline. Maybe her parents didn't meet, so they didn't conceive her. I need my book!' Glenda exclaims, fresh tears pouring down her face. 'I need my book because we need to read it all together, Lizzy! That's how it was for your Grandma Joan and me. It must be here somewhere.'

'It isn't here, Mum,' Paul says.

'Then it's gone with someone who's left,' I say. 'Kim's parents, or Scott.'

Lizzy snorts. 'What would Scott want with an old history book? I bet Kim's dad took it. He was banging on about pagan runes or something like that when he picked it up. Probably wants to burn it.'

'We must get it back!' Glenda cries. 'It must not be damaged, and it must not fall into the wrong hands!'

'So are we going to Kim's house to get it back, if it's that critical?' Rob asks. 'If we get it back, does it tell you a way of getting Ani back?' He rubs my shoulders, and they feel like stone beneath his touch.

'There might be a way of getting your friend back, but it is probably really complicated, and I don't remember the details because I don't have my book!'

'Mum, you're so embarrassing,' Lizzy says. 'Stop with the pink fits already. I get it. It's fine. I'm a superhuman time travel gatekeeper, and the book tells me all about my history, and if for no other reason than that it's ours, we need it back. So let's all go over to see Kim and ask her nightmarish parents nicely to return our history book, and we won't get them done for theft.'

'You don't understand the half of it,' Glenda whispers. 'You don't know how this changes you, Lizzy. It changes everything. I've made such a mess of things, and I planned it so well. Now I've got bystanders who know more than is healthy about the Weys, and *The Truth* is missing.'

Paul gets up abruptly, scraping the wooden chair across the floor. 'I don't know about you lot,' he says, 'but I need a break. I'm going up to the garage to get some more smokes since you lot seem dead set on smoking all of mine.'

I catch Jasper's eye, and now they are like saucers. I guess he's finally noticed the elephant in the dining room.

Rob sighs behind me. 'Maybe I should leave you guys to it,' he says. 'I think I need to tell Brian what's going on and ...' he stares fixedly at the bookcase, 'tell him what's likely happened to his girlfriend.'

'Girlfriend?' Glenda's pitch lifts another few notes again. 'He was involved with Ani? But you've only been here a couple of days!'

'Days feel like months, feel like years,' he says flatly. 'You can't control it when it happens.' I look up at him then, and he's looking at me finally, and a tear leaks out onto my cheek. I wipe it away roughly. I don't have time for this.

Glenda looks at us both. 'This is even more of a disaster than I thought,' she whimpers.

Henry stands up. 'Right,' he says authoritatively. 'Let's have a breather. Rob, you take the time travellers with you to Brian's and fill him in, since he clearly knows about what's going on.'

'Shouldn't we stay here with you, though?' Jasper asks.

'I don't see why you need to, as long as you stay close enough so that when one of my girls is ready, they can see you back on your Wey. Paul, go get some fags from the garage.' Henry pulls some paper money out of his pocket and gives it to his son. 'Forty Bensons please, those JPS taste like monkey scrotum. Glenda, you need a proper drink. Hair of the dog and restorative. Lizzy, go see if there's any of your mother's ginger wine left.'

I can feel Jasper's eyes burning into the side of my face as we walk towards Brian's house. I know he wants to talk to me about Weyfarere. I know he's worked out what I worked out, as I sat there watching my Nan cry and my mother receive the news. I am Elizabeth Wharton's only daughter. If I get back to 2019, I am 18 in a few days, and she will present me with a golden key like her own, and tell me that I'm a Weyfare, and that means I can travel the Weys and always come home. But if Jasper starts asking me about all this, then Rob will know that I'm Lizzy's daughter and I can't ask him to keep such a massive secret from her. So I don't look at Jasper, and I will him to keep his silence. The clouds that have gathered over our heads break, and it starts to rain.

In the garage later, Brian doesn't speak for at least a minute. His face goes ashen, and then very red as if he's going to cry, but finally he gathers himself together enough to say, 'Gone for good?'

'Not for good we hope,' Jasper says kindly, picking at the rubber on the pile of old tyres he's sitting on. 'Glenda did seem to think there might be a way to help Ani, but without her book, she can't remember how.'

'And Glenda thinks it happened because we kissed?'

'No,' I reach over from the carpet on the floor to pat him on the shoulder. 'Truly, Brian. She thinks something must have happened to stop Ani even being born.'

'Heavy. And the Brookes girls are in charge of the Portal. No, what did you call it? The Weydoor. This is huge!' Suddenly Brian is his old window-licking self. 'If Lizzy can open the Weydoor, then we can go forth and sort it all out!' He plays his usual imaginary trumpet. 'So they're going to get this Truth book back from Kim's dad? Good luck with that, the bloke's a whacko.'

'Glenda acted like it was a massive deal.'

'You think there are more secrets in there?'

'Can't see any other reason why she'd be so twisted up about losing it,' Rob says, playing with my hair from behind, his legs in a protective spot around me.

'Once they've got it back, then I guess it's goodbye,' Jasper says. 'Glenda or Lizzy will send Maisie and me back through the Weydoor.'

This time, not one of us has anything to say.

We are sitting there, lost in our own thoughts when Brian's Mum pokes her head around the door of the garage. 'I've got Tracy on the phone, love,' she says. 'She doesn't sound pleased. Something about a barby queue?'

In all the drama, we've forgotten about Tracy's barbeque, and when she's finished with Brian, he has an earache. Armed to the teeth with excuses for Lizzy and Paul not being there, an adapted version of events and a box of frozen burgers from Brian's Mum's chest freezer, we're about to make our way to Tracy's house when Will beeps at us from the ancient Ford parked on the road. Tracy invited him, too.

So we're sailing down the bottom road into town, taking

the sharp left down towards the railway line with the silver birch lined avenues past Neil Thorpe's flat, under the railway arches and then roaring up the hill past the Railway Gardens to where the big townhouses stand like guardians looking down over Stoneford.

I can hear the voices in the garden from this side of the house. Rob rings the doorbell. When it opens they all fall on us like they have known us for years and haven't seen us in weeks, and I'm awash with hugs. Tracy's pushing a bottle of 1080 into my hands as she's relieving Brian of his box of frozen offerings, Claire's mothering me like I've been recently hospitalised, Ian is punching Rob and Jasper on the arm and Elaine is already moaning about the trauma Jasper put her through because she was so worried about where we all were, and where are Kim and Lizzy?

'We've been calling Lizzy's house since 12:30, and no one's answering the phone,' Tracy explains crossly, as she returns from depositing the burgers at a tall man's sandaled feet. 'We did quite clearly say twelve. Dad was starting to worry that the hamburgers would go to waste. Paul's not here either. Rowena's tried calling for him too. She's out the back. With Patchouli.'

'Scott's here? ' All three of us say at once.

Claire laughs, but Elaine and Tracy are more curious. 'Yes, Patchouli. Obviously. Lizzy's new squeeze?' Tracy says.

'We know who he is. Didn't he say anything?' Jasper asks.

'Anything about what?' Elaine asks.

'About this morning?' I say. 'There's been a bit of a bitch-fest at Lizzy's.'

'You with your weird phrases,' Tracy says. 'But I think I can translate that one. Argument? Who with? Not him and Liz already? I told her it would never work out. That bloke cannot be trusted, I'm telling you.'

Rob, Jasper, Brian and me take turns in bringing them up to speed. With notable omissions, of course. We don't mention *The Truth*, and we don't mention the Weys, and we definitely don't mention the fact that Lizzy and I are descended from a long line of female time travelling gatekeepers.

Even so, by the time we've finished, Ian's eyes look like he's drunk a vat of coffee. 'Kim's dad really said all that about debauchery and stuff?'

'Just as well I got Dad to buy a couple of crates of this stuff –sounds like we're all going to need it.' Tracy tosses her fluffy blonde locks and throws back a mouthful of 1080. 'So I'm guessing neither Kim, Lizzy nor Paul will be joining us because of their family crisis over Kim's family crisis. Fine,' she adds, underlining the fact that it really isn't fine, crisis or no crisis. She marches off into the house, and we follow through the dining room, with its grand clock on the mantelpiece in a golden case with balls rotating at the bottom. It chimes twice as we walk out through the patio doors, to where the whiff of paraffin and burning coal attacks my nose.

There's a tall, chrome and black music centre in the lounge, and it's blasting out what I'm pretty sure is Bryan Adams telling us that it's no secret he's a victim of love. The vast expanse of their lawn ends with views down to the outskirts of town, the pool across from the patio twinkles in the sunlight, Tracy's dad is cooking on the barbeque, a blue and white striped butchers apron strapped around his hips, lemon yellow polo shirt, bright green shorts with surfers and bikini-clad girls all over them, sock and sandals on his feet. Brian and Jasper both dive for the grill – I think I should be hungry really, but I feel too sick in my stomach with all these revelations to eat. Tracy's mum is talking to some friends of hers and dishing ladles of drink out of a big silver bowl. I remember lots of the other people vaguely from the gig at Trinity; Tracy's obviously invited people on the back of Fallen Angel's newfound minor local success.

Rowena is sitting by the pool, bare feet dangling in the water, chatting to Dave, Neil Thorpe and Scott and some other guys I don't recognise. When Scott sees us though, he gets to his feet quicker than I think I've ever seen him move.

I feel Rob's hand tense in mine. 'Go easy,' he whispers. 'The guy may be a coward, but it doesn't make him a thief.'

Scott's lazy smile hasn't changed. 'Sorry about earlier,' he says as he approaches us, 'I realised I had to be somewhere, and you fellas looked like you had the situation in hand.' And that, it seems, is to be his sole explanation for not hanging around to make sure his girlfriend's family were okay after their house was invaded.

'One of their books has gone missing,' I say. 'They think it disappeared during the fight. Know anything about that?'

Scott's face doesn't register the slightest recognition. 'Why would I know anything about a book? I work in the hippy shop, baby, not Ottakers.' There doesn't seem to be much we can add to that comment. An unexpected shiver tumbles down my back. 'Is Lizzy coming here?' he adds.

Rob shakes his head. 'Too much to deal with at home.'

Scott looks over my shoulder, and the lazy smile broadens into a dazzling grin. 'Obviously not as much as you thought.'

Me and Rob turn as if we're joined, and to our surprises, Paul is walking through the patio doors into Tracy's garden.

Chapter Twenty-Seven – Take My Breath Away (Berlin, 1987)

Paul makes straight for us, his face a mask of forced indifference. 'You're wanted out front,' he says, and I'm about to reply when he adds quietly, 'Brian and Jasper too. Don't make a big deal about it. She wants to talk to you. Away from all this lot.'

'Not sure that's going to be possible,' Rob says just as Elaine and Claire saunter over, and Tracy holds out a beer, which he takes. Brian and Jasper return with a burger in a bun. Some things never change.

'So much for your family drama,' she says.

'Family drama?' Paul looks at Rob and me.

'We just told her you had some stuff to work out with your rents,' Jasper explains, and then, seeing the blank expressions, adds, 'Parents.'

'Oh.' Paul takes the black box from the inside of his denim jacket and pulls a cigarette out with the tips of his teeth, the other hand taking the offered bottle of cider. 'Well, we got that sorted.' He looks across at Ian. 'Kim won't be here, mate. Her mum and dad came to collect her.'

Ian shrugs and, to be honest, looks fairly uninterested. 'Nothing that I wasn't expecting,' he says. Maybe Kim is right, and the two of them aren't that good a match.

'Well, whatever the crisis was I'm glad it's over, and we can concentrate on some more serious drinking,' Tracy says. 'Rowena can give it a rest with looking like a constipated horse, and you lot can come and help me drink my weight in 1080.'

'I'd like to go there as well,' Elaine says, trotting off after her, with a sideways glance back at Jasper.

'I think we all need a drink.' I realise Scott is now standing on the other side of Jasper.

'Don't draw attention to yourselves,' Paul mutters. 'Liz just wants to talk to the people who were up at our house when the shit hit the fan. Ian, you come and get a burger with me, mate.' Ian starts to protest, but Paul's arm across his shoulders must be firm, and they wander across the lawn to the barbeque and join the line of people all standing politely in the queue for a burnt sausage and a piece of salmonella chicken.

Lizzy is sitting on the low grey stone wall at the front of Tracy's garden, scraping bits of loose cement out from between the bricks with her fingers. As we emerge from Tracy's front door – me, Rob, Jasper, Brian and Scott – her eyes narrow as she sees her boyfriend and they darken in the sunlight. 'So where did you get to earlier when we were trying to evict Mary Whitehouse and her husband?' she snaps.

'I'm sorry, baby. I had to nip back to the shop. Tim ordered another batch of essential oils for this morning. I had to be there to take delivery.' He sits down beside her.

Tim. *Tim* ordered the oils? Tim works with Scott at the shop? My dad works at a New Age shop in town? Is this how Mum and Dad met? Through Scott Kelly?

'This morning? It's a Sunday.' She shakes her head. 'Like I believe you. Maisie, you look like you're about to be sick. I don't see what you've got to worry about now. Look, Scott, I don't actually give a toss why you left, but the fact is, everything's gone arse over apex.'

'Explain?' Jasper asks, sitting on the other side of the wall beside her.

'My mother is trying to ruin my life,' Lizzy says dolefully,' and I've only just turned 18.'

'Looks like I left yesterday at the crucial moment,' Scott says. 'What are you saying, baby?'

'I'm in charge of a hole in Time, and these two are from the future,' she says, waving dismissively at Jasper and me.

'Blimey,' Scott says. 'The Portal lets you travel through Time?

'Keep up, blud,' Jasper says.

'So why is it going to ruin your life?' Rob asks.

'It's all to do with a bloody stupid family tradition.' She looks up at Brian. 'I take it they filled you in on what happened at my place?'

'They did.' Brian sits down on the pavement in front of her. 'It's actually fascinating. Well, it was fascinating until I remembered my girlfriend vanished. What did you call it?'

'Glenda said Ani had been extinguished,' I say, my voice sounding hollow. 'She called it extinction.'

'Like the dodo,' Brian says solemnly.

I'd have found it funny if it wasn't all so tragic.

'It gets worse.' Lizzy reaches into her back pocket and pulls out a golden packet of cigarettes. She only offers them to Scott, and he takes two and lights them both, returning one to her. 'Well, not worse. That's pretty mean of me to say that.'

'Has Glenda told you some other stuff then?' I ask, sitting on the pavement next to Brian.

'Oh, you bet she has,' Lizzy says.

'Care to share?' Jasper asks.

Lizzy sighs, draws on the cigarette and exhales. 'I have to carry on the family business.'

'I don't understand,' Rob says, standing behind me with his arms crossed.

'I'm a Weyfare.' Lizzy sighs the word into the air between us. 'We are the only family left, so far as Mum knows, so she says I can't let another family's legacy die out. She says;' she sighs again, as if trying to keep control of her voice; 'she says I can never leave town. I have to stay here for the rest of my life in the family house and protect the Weydoor.'

'Protect it from what?' Scott asks.

'I have to help people who travel on the Weys from changing their timelines. Either accidentally or on purpose.'

No one else comments. Maybe they are thinking of Ani, like me. I can only imagine what they are all thinking, but it's like dustsheets are being slowly lifted on the room of my life, to reveal what's really been happening underneath.

'What about Uni?' Brian asks. 'Are you allowed to go to Uni?'

'I'm allowed to go, but I have to come home afterwards and find a job in town, and live in our house.' She puts her forehead in the heel of her hands, the cigarette threatening to spill the filthy ash all over her clothes. 'Mum says the oldest girl in the family is always the Weyfare because traditionally women stay at home and raise families and don't have ambition. I told her, "Mum, this is the 20th century for God's sake, haven't you heard of equal rights?" Then she yelled at me and said she'd been protecting the Weydoor all by herself since Grandma lost her marbles and died, and I have to help her now I'm of age.' She looks wildly around at us all. 'I don't want to be stuck in this fucking dive my whole life!'

I hang my head. I wanted to get out of Stoneford as well, and now I don't even know if I'll get back to the Stoneford I knew.

Scott strokes her hair, his face crumpled with concern. 'Did she say anything else about this Weydoor?' he murmurs, running his mouth gently over the top of her ear and staring unnervingly at me.

'She told me a lot of bollocks about some ancient fella called Wayland the Smith and how we're descended from him. Something else about brothers that went over to the dark side -' She shakes her head. 'I don't remember. Anyway, the main thing she said was that I have to get you lot home. She's gone over to Kim's place to get the book back. Apparently, I have to read the book. It has loads of history in it, names of all the Weyfarere in my family, that kind of thing. Mum says it can't get into the wrong hands, but she didn't tell me what that meant or why not.' Abruptly she stands, and Scott's arm slaps down against the top of the stone wall. She looks straight at me. 'Have either of you got something from your time?'

'I've still got my smartphone,' I say. 'My m ... I was given it on the day we came through the Weydoor.'

'Perfect. That'll do, I think.'

Rob takes a step forward. 'Hey, hang on a minute,' he says, 'you're going to send them back *right now*?'

'Mum says they have to get back as soon as possible or they run more of a risk of changing their original timelines.'

'Yes, but they don't need to go right this minute. You've got to give me some time here, Lizzy, come on.' I can't look at him; I can hear the desperation in his voice. Everything is breaking up.

'They're not supposed to be here, Rob, and I have to get them home. We don't want them vanishing like Ani did.'

'How about you both stop talking about us as if we aren't here?' I cry out.

A car drives past.

'I'm sorry, Maisie. I really am,' Lizzy says.

I shake my head; my hair covers my face.

'How are you getting them back?' Scott asks.

'This key Mum gave me,' Lizzy says, pulling it out from under her T-shirt, 'Mum wasn't clear, but I think I use it to get people back to where they started, and get home again.'

'This is all getting really heavy,' Brian says, manically playing his little imaginary trumpet over and over.

'If you send Maisie back now, I'm going with her!' Rob mutters, which is enough to silence all of us.

But not for long. 'If you're going back, I'm coming too,' Brian says. 'I want to see the future. I can write about it for my application for Cambridge after my gap year.' The imaginary trumpet is suddenly still. 'I want to see if Ani made it back.'

'Neither of you can come with us because you already exist in 2019 as two middle-aged men,' Jasper points out.

'To be fair, we don't know that,' I hear myself saying.

'Maisie! Yes, we bloody do!'

'Yes, well, maybe they don't live in town any more, maybe I changed my mind because lots of things are changing, aren't they, and I have to get my head around all of it! All of it, Jasper!' My voice is getting louder now. If we don't calm down, we're going to have Tracy and the others out the front here wondering what the hell is going on with us all.

'Yes, I realise that,' he snaps, with a heavy emphasis on the realising.

'Rob,' Lizzy says, and there is a real pain for him in her eyes, 'they can't stay here.' She looks at me then, and I see the apology. 'Maisie knows this. Don't you? So does Jasper. I can see it now. I can see why she's been so reluctant to make out with you. They've always known this was going to happen. They've known a lot longer than I have.'

My head is a mess of *what-ifs* and *yes-buts* and *can't-I-justs*, not to mention the *how-do-Is* and the *there-must-be-a-ways*. I'm a Weyfare. I'm a Guardian of the Weys. I need my mum to sit down and explain all this to me, but she's sitting here in front of me, and she hasn't got a Scooby. What's going to happen if she gets Jasper and me back to 2019? Aside from the fact that my heart will be splintering into tiny pieces, will she remember me? Will she remember the faces of the first girl and boy she sent back on their Wey, and suddenly realise that they are the faces of her teenage daughter and one of her best friends?

'Maisie?' I turn to look at Rob, and he's standing there like a little boy who cant believe some bully has broken his brand new toy truck – he can't accept the cruelty of separation, he doesn't see a reason for the destruction of something that could be so special.

'She's right, Rob,' I reach out, and touch his hand. 'We have to go back. We always knew I'd have to go back. You have to stay here. This is where you belong.'

He looks so bleak and lost, and I am suddenly desperately afraid that he's going to cry because I know if he starts, I won't stop.

'This is garbage,' Scott says suddenly. 'Sounds to me like you've been told the most amazing piece of news ever, and you're all here howling like it's the end of the world! You can travel through time Lizzy, for Christ's sake! You can ferry these two blokes backwards and forwards to see their girls. You can use that key and travel through time and always come back to the right place! It's incredible! Why are you mewling about being stuck here when you can bloody well go wherever the hell you want, whenever you want?'

A few cars pass by on the road out of town.

'Mum said we don't travel on the Weys. It's too dangerous. I just have to stop the bystanders coming through the Weydoor, and if they get through, I have to send them back through it,' Lizzy says quietly.

'And since when have you ever done what you were told to do, Brookes?' he says, equally as quietly, and there is a glimmer in his eyes I haven't seen before.

She turns to look at him then, and as the seconds pass and I watch her, it's like an iron mask of misery and responsibility is falling away from her face, and suddenly, like the sun coming up, the most wicked of smiles dawns across her lips, and the roses come back into her cheeks.

'He's right.' She looks at Jasper and me. 'Shit, he's right! Okay, Rob. Tell you what. Let's all go party at their place for a bit.' She pats Brian on the shoulder. 'See if we can't find your future girlie and if she's not there, we'll find you another one.'

Jasper opens his mouth, but I shake my head, and he silently agrees and closes it again. We both know he was going to tell her she couldn't do that, but the thing is, we already know that she did. Turns out that it's Scott's fault that we all get to go back home.

Chapter Twenty-Eight
– The Great Pretender
(Freddie Mercury, 1987)

'We have to go through the tunnel from the house because I don't have a key to the Old Library door,' Lizzy says, as we wander back through town. 'Mum has keys to everywhere at school because she's the lead cleaner, but I don't know where she keeps them.'

It's a mixed party. There is excitement here, and pain and regret and anticipation all muddled up in the six of us: Lizzy and Scott, me and Rob, Brian and Jasper. As we trudge up the steep Town Hill road back towards The Park, a bus travels past and stops just before the junction. We all watch as a girl falls out, stumbling under what must be the weight of a huge bag, and then she sits down at the edge of the road and puts her head in her hands. We are all running towards her without needing to say a word.

'Kim, are you all right?' Jasper, always a decent sprinter at any Sports Day, is on the scene first. We can make her out more clearly now; Kim is a mess. Her hair isn't brushed, there are mascara tracks down both cheeks, the bag isn't done up correctly and it's threatening to spew the crumpled clothes all over the pavement. Saving her dignity, I start to push the underwear back deeper into the bag, which on second glance isn't suited to carrying an entire wardrobe of clothing – which is what I think is in there.

'Kim, talk to me sweetie,' Lizzy is saying, holding her friend's head in her arms like a baby. 'What's happened here? Did they hurt you?'

'Have they chucked you out?' Rob asks, rubbing at Kim's arm.

'No,' we hear her mumble, 'no, they haven't.' She pulls herself up straight, and we all look at something we've not seen before in Kim's eyes – anger. 'I left.'

'You left?' Brian says, and there's a hint of a smile on his lips. 'You walked out?'

Kim nods, returning the small smile. 'I did. I told them I was done with the systematic abuse and the total lack of privacy, and they said as long as I lived under their roof I had to follow their rules, so I told them;' she stops to catch her breath, fingers playing nervously with the necklace Claire gave her last night; 'I told them they could pay for a slave if that's what they wanted and I threw a few of my things in a bag and I caught the last bus over here.' She gives us a defiant look. 'They told me if I walked out the front door just then, I didn't ever need to come back. Suits me just fine. I'm not putting up with any more of their crap.'

'How did you manage not to get locked into your bedroom this time?' Jasper asks.

Kim looks proud. 'I stuffed the keyhole up with random shit earlier this week. Bits of paper, cotton wool, Blu Tack. By the time she came upstairs to lock me in, the hole was jammed just enough that by the time she managed to get all the crap out, I was well out of there.' She pauses. 'I pushed Dad hard as he tried to stop me opening the front door and he fell, but I don't care. I ran out of the door, and I didn't look back. I had just enough coppers saved in the bottom of this school bag to buy a one-way Half into town, and the bus driver didn't question it.'

'Half-price ticket,' Rob says to me. 'You have to be under 16.'

'Kids ride half in our time too,' I tell him, 'not everything's changed.'

Kim frowns. 'Don't you travel on the bus?' She then takes us all in. 'Why aren't you all up at Tracy's burger party? I was going to come to find you; this is the closest my bus stops to Tracy's place.' She looks around. 'Where's Ian?'

Now it's our turn to tell the stories, but I'm not sure how Lizzy wants to perform them. A passerby has to step over us and makes some comment about the youth of today.

'Something came up,' Jasper says ineffectually.

Lizzy laughs. It's a full-bodied belly rasp that I don't hear very much in my days. 'Talk about understatement of the century, Jay! Kim's one of my best mates. She needs to know what's going on. She's been told enough lies by her bastard excuses for parents over the years.' She looks at Kim. 'There's a hole in Time in the Old Library, and I have to stop time travellers coming through it and messing up the future.'

Kim looks at her, and now she bursts out with the laughter. 'I take it Tracy got her dad to buy that crate of 1080 then,' she says through the giggles. 'And you drank the lot by the sounds of it.'

'Seriously, Kim,' Brian pulls her to her feet as another passerby steps around us all, huffing about delinquents. 'Listen. She's being straight with you.'

We go and sit on the wooden bench in the bus stop, all in

a row like unwise monkeys: Brian, me, Rob, Jasper, Kim, Lizzy and Scott. Lizzy gives a potted history of the day: how she found out she was a Weyfare; how the Weyfarere guard the Weys; how me, Ani and Jasper were from the future, and Lizzy had to help us get home because Ani disappeared; how Glenda told her she could travel anywhere in Time and always return, and then told her she'd have to spend her whole life in Stoneford protecting the Weydoor after all.

Kim is very still while Lizzy's talking and no one else speaks. Eventually, she says, 'You're not runaways then?' Me and Jasper shake our heads. 'And you think my dad stole your Truth book?'

'Mum and Dad were driving over to yours to have it out with them about it,' Lizzy says, 'but it looks like you left before they got there.'

'Pity,' Kim says, 'they could've saved me the bus fare.' She sits up, stretching out her back and taking a deep breath, stroking a few crumbs of road dust from her orange leggings. 'Well, this all sounds crazy to me, but you all seem to believe it, and if Brian believes it, it must be true. Brian's too clever to believe nonsense.' Brian plays his imaginary trumpet and nods like the Churchill dog on the adverts. She turns to Jasper, who is sitting at her side, and smiles. 'So you're from the future. It explains the clothes and funny sayings. Well, if we're all having an adventure, count me in. My new life starts today.' Jasper shakes his head with a wry smile. 'I take it you're going with them, Rob?'

Rob, sitting next to me, holding my hand, looks at me, but he says nothing. We haven't discussed it. There's been no time, ironically, or maybe there has, and we just haven't been able to face it. I know we both know the right answer. No, he's not coming with me. He belongs here, and I belong there. I've even said it out loud. But we can't bring ourselves to say goodbye out loud, because out loud makes it real, and I don't think either of us is ready for that.

'Maybe just a visit to see what the future looks like,' he says, and I hurt on so many levels, because our futures are without each other, whether he comes through or not. Whether he comes through and plays the drums again in the PA Block like he did the first time we met. Days ago. Lifetimes ago.

'Same here,' Brian says. 'I'm using this experience in my application to Cambridge next year. Not the real experience, of course, just the theory. Lizzy's identity has to be protected.'

'And you want to see if Ani made it back?' Kim said, entirely on point. Some of the colour leaves Brian's cheeks, and he says nothing. She gets up, goes over and hugs him.

'Well, now we're all finally on the same page, I say we get going with this adventure?' Scott says brightly.

When we get back to Lizzy's house, the sun is lower in the sky. The place is quiet finally. Glenda and Henry are trying to get *The Truth* back at Kim's place, and Paul is at Tracy's barbeque. The gazebo is still up, the paper plates are where they were when me and Rob walked up the garden this morning, but the people inside have left. If there are still relatives about, they aren't disturbed by the footfalls of seven teenagers, padding down the steps and opening the Old Shed door with Lizzy's golden key.

Inside the Shed, it is dark, cramped and full of bikes, lawnmowers and gardening tools, but they are scattered along the walls, and in the middle of the Shed there is an old rug, like a magic carpet from the stories of Aladdin, and when Lizzy lifts the rug, there is a trap door.

The trap door is heavy and takes a while to lift, but eventually, it creaks open, and the light catches the dust mites dancing as it shines down on a set of stone steps, descending steeply into the ground. Lizzy grabs a massive black plastic torch from the rack of tools on the wall, and as we follow her down, Jasper looks back at me, and I shake my head, no, I had no fucking clue there was a secret passage to the Old Library in my garden shed.

The tunnel is narrow, and we have to bend slightly to fit in. Lizzy's torch gives just enough light to see the walls are shored up with the same stone as the walls of the Old Library, and for the first time I realise that my house is also built from the same stone. How have I never noticed this before? I know I was never into History, but I'm not a total tard. I feel like everything I took for granted in my life has somehow been a lie. At least I know the truth now, but at what cost?

We walk for at least 15 minutes, under The Park I'm guessing, and under the road, until the tunnel floor begins to steepen, and I'm suddenly worried that we've come all this way and what if Lizzy can't open the other end of the tunnel? Then she's pushing against something in front of her rather than a hatch above her head, and a door swings open, and I can see past everyone to the fading light and onto the high dark wooden bookshelves of the Old Library.

We move into the space like moles, blinking as our eyes adjust to the light. The door seems to be hidden behind a bookshelf and Lizzy, Scott and Jasper push the whole bookcase back in place to protect the entrance to the secret passage.

'Mum said the key on this side was in the spine of a book, but I can't remember the name,' Lizzy says. 'She told me so much, and I can't remember half of it.'

'You remember what's important,' Scott says. 'You know the key opens the doors, and you know you can travel the Weys.'

He looks around and takes a deep breath. We all do.

Last time I saw it, it was 2019, and I heard my mum and her teenage friends talking before they vanished. Brian ran through seconds later, and knocked us down; me, Ani and Jasper, having no idea what was ahead of us, and what would happen if we fell through the light. It's like the bookcase is framed in indigo light that waves and flickers to the beat of a heart. A hole in the fourth dimension tucked away out of sight at the back of the Old Library at Drake's School. A Weydoor. The Weydoor my family is dedicated to protecting. If Lizzy remembers, she'll think it's glowing in her presence as a Weyfare.

Of course, it's glowing for us both.

'Is that it?' Brian says, his voice all breathy.

'The door to the future,' Rob says.

'And the past,' Lizzy says.

'Isn't it pretty though?' Kim says.

'Do we just walk through?' Jasper asks.

'We just fell through it before,' I say. He shrugs and nods.

'An actual Weydoor,' Scott says.

'Give me your thingy,' Lizzy says to me.

We all look at her. 'My thingy?' I repeat.

She shakes her head in annoyance and holds out her hand. 'Your thingy! Your object from 2019.'

I pull my smartphone, completely dead and useless now, out of my back pocket. Everyone looks at it, although now it doesn't work it's not nearly as impressive to people living 32 years in the past.

'You say you got given this on the day you came through the Weydoor?' Lizzy asks, looking down at it.

By you. 'Yes,' I say out loud. 'I'm 18 in a few days. In my time. It was … is an early birthday present.'

'Nice. Happy birthday,' Lizzy says. 'Now Mum said I had to give the object my power, which I guess is in this.' She pulls the silver key out from under her T-shirt and holds it flat on my smartphone.

Nothing happens.

'Should something happen?' Brian asks.

'I'm not sure,' Lizzy says.

'What is this supposed to do?' Jasper asks.

'It makes sure we go back to your time,' Lizzy says.

'And if it doesn't work?' Rob asks.

'Will you lot quit with the Spanish Inquisition?' Lizzy snaps.

'If it doesn't work, we're in for one hell of an adventure,' Kim says. 'We could end up anywhere.'

'Sounds like a plan,' Scott says.

I look at Rob, and I shrug. He smiles, and grabs hold of my hand.

'So then,' Jasper says, and his voice breaks a little, and I know he's scared, but he's never going to admit it. 'Are we going to do this?'

'Too bloody right we are,' Lizzy says. 'Hold hands.' She pushes my smartphone against the bookcase, and her arm just seems to slip through the books as if they are a kind of projection, and the next thing I know we're falling against the bookshelves, and there's white heat, purple light, black - nothing.

I'm lying on my back when I open my eyes. I move my hands, and then I move my feet. It takes a few moments to register that everything is still working, and I don't seem to be bleeding, or broken the way I thought I might be.

Jasper is lying beside me. He looks peaceful. He doesn't look ill or hurt, but something is different.

I sit up and look around the Old Library. There's the long wooden table in the middle of the room and the same smell of age as usual. Moonlight filtering in through the high windows. A few textbooks scattered over the peeling varnish ...

A cold finger strokes the line of my spine.

Moonlight.

The posters on the wall are dark with dust. Rob has sprawled on the floor a few metres away, and Brian is under a table beside Kim. They seem to be out cold. Lizzy and Scott are sitting against a cabinet, both of them shaking their heads as they get their bearings. The same eerie purple light is framing the bookcase at the back of the room.

I stand up, and I know instinctively I'm home, and I am filled with euphoria and devastation at the same time. I can see it's dark through the high windows, and the stars are twinkling in the bright May sky. 'Lizzy,' I say. 'I think you did it.'

She steps into a beam of moonlight, her red hair vibrant and big, like hair is in 1987. 'I did?'

'Yeah, you did,' I say. 'You really did.'

As the rest of them wake up, I notice more and more that is

familiar for my time. I'm sure we are back in 2019 when I try the main door, and it's unlocked – because we opened it in 2019 before we left.

It's May 24th 2019, and it's the night of our Fundraiser. Outside the Old Library, The DJ in the Main Hall breaks into the unmistakable opening notes of Ed Sheeran's latest.

So here we are then; Home Sweet Home. Game over. Curtains down, turn the lights off on your way out. This is what me and Jasper knew we had to do from the moment we knew we had travelled back in Time, but even Jasper isn't looking as lit as I expected.

It was never going to be a happy ending, was it?

Rob takes hold of my hand. 'Is there a Music Block here in your time?' he asks. 'I could do with some skins to beat the shit out of, or I may just sit down here and scream like a girl.'

Brian says, 'I think I'm going up to the fields to have a look at FCAB then.'

Kim takes a deep breath. 'I'm not sure of this music. Is this really what you listen to? Sounds a bit like the Carpenters.'

Lizzy looks up at the stars, and she smiles at me. 'My first bystanders,' she says, and I can hear the pride in her voice. 'I'm not going to waste this gift. I'm going to travel. Travel properly. Not like most people do. I'm not interested in inter-railing. I want to see what town was like when Queen Victoria was on the throne. I want to see what it was like here in the Second World War. I want to travel through history, not the world.'

Does she do that before she meets my dad and has my brothers and me? I don't know. But I'm a Weyfare too. Can I travel? Can I wait a few days until I'm 18 and she gives me my silver key, and then can I travel the Weys? Can I travel back to

Rob? Can I choose to grow older with him instead of her? Can I leave her behind and go back to her past and the boy I love?

'But you won't, will you?' a voice breaks through my thoughts, and it's harsh and unfamiliar. Lizzy and I both turn to face him. 'You won't do anything with it.' His face is grey and shadowed with anger. ' You won't travel, and you won't change the world. You're all mouth and no trousers. You like to think you're a rebel but you're still in school, doing your exams, off to University like Mummy's good little girl and you'll spend your whole life spoiling people's opportunities to make a difference to their futures and make something of themselves because that's what you've been told to do. You'll send people back when they want to go forward. You don't deserve your gift. It's wasted on you.'

Talk about coming out of left field.

'Scott?' Lizzy says, but even as she's reaching out to him for some reassurance, he's grabbing hold of her, and then one of his hands is on the silver key, and he's pulling on it, his beautiful face twisted and ugly. I hear myself yelling, Rob is only just turning back to see what's going on, Brian and Kim seem to be frozen to the spot, and Jasper looks like he's been struck by lightning. Lizzy screams, and then Scott has pulled the chain of the silver key so hard that he's broken it, and he has run back into the Old Library.

Me and Rob run to the back of the room, watching in dismay as Lizzy runs ahead of us, down between the ancient bookcases and around the end of the last bookcase where the Weydoor is still flickering its secrets at us, and we all skid to a halt and watch in horror as she catches him up and they struggle in front of the ominous glowing purple light, two shadowy figures yelling at each other; Rob's reaching out to grab hold of Scott, and I'm trying to help, when Lizzy grabs hold of Scott's arm and hauls on it so hard that they both lose their footing, and instinctively, I pull Rob away as Lizzy tumbles back towards the Weydoor, catching my eye grief-stricken as she pulls Scott through it with her, probably back to 1987 and the day that she was given her key, and her arm just seems to slip through the books as if they are a kind of projection, and the next thing I know they're falling against the bookshelves, and there's a flash of white heat, another of purple light, then black - nothing.

When my eyes adjust to the darkness again, the Weydoor glows at us in the awful silence of their leaving. Behind me and Rob, I can hear them finally catching up.

'Where did they go?' Jasper asks, breathing hard.

'1987, at a guess,' Rob says. I can't read his expression; the light in here is too faint.

'Holy mother of Sod, they've gone back through the Weydoor, haven't they?' Brian exclaims, staring at the glowing frame.

'But how are we all going to get home again without Lizzy and her key?' Kim asks. She knows what we all know now; if they travel on the Weys again without Lizzy's key to guide them, they could end up anywhere in Time.

Rob, Brian and Kim have been abandoned in 2019, and there's only one person left here who can get them all home.

Chapter Twenty-Nine – Bad Guy (Billie Eilish, 2019)

The music in the Main Hall is pounding through open fire doors as we walk out of the Old Library. I close the door to avoid drawing people's attention and video footage. It looks like Lizzy has brought us back to the exact moment that me, Ani and Jasper left 2019. Where there was quiet when Scott turned on Lizzy, now there are kids are milling all around on the place where the three paths meet, giving us weird looks as we stand there outside the Old Library, staring at each other like freeze frames against the videos that they are starting to take on their tiny screens as they mutter at each other.

'Nothing to see here, move on!' Jasper says uber-brightly. Reading his mind, I grab Kim with one hand, and with the other, I take Rob's hand, and Jasper grips onto Brian's arm.

'What were all those little screens?' Kim asks once we are inside the Music Room. 'Why did they keep pointing them at us?'

'Cameras,' I say, trying to keep it simple and not give too much away.

'I suppose people film everything they do now instead of keeping a diary,' Brian says. 'Very practical. Is paper rationed now the rainforests have all been cut down?'

'We're not quite there yet, Brian,' I tell him.

'Not all that far away either,' Jasper says solemnly.

Rob goes and sits on the black stool behind the drum kit. 'So are we stuck here now?' he asks quietly. 'Forever, I mean?'

'I don't know.'

'So where is here exactly?' Brian asks, finding a seat next to Kim on a prominent black guitar speaker.

'It's about nine o'clock on May 24th, 2019. It's just a few minutes after we came through the Weydoor the first time,' Jasper says, now pacing the room. 'There's about another hour of music to play.'

'I can't believe Scott would do that,' Kim says tearfully. 'Poor Lizzy.'

'I always thought he was shifty,' Brian remarks.

'I'm guessing he took Glenda's book earlier as well then,' Rob says. 'It wasn't your folk, Kim. Looks like Tracy was right about him.'

'Not for the right reasons though,' I say. 'Listen, this situation isn't like when we came through the Weydoor to you. We weren't already there.' I took a deep breath and prepared to lie. 'You are all already here somewhere, much older, and I don't know where. I don't know what will happen if we run into the other versions of you.'

'We must be really old,' Kim says.

'I think there might be someone here I can ask for help,' I tell them.

'You know one of us here, don't you?' Rob says, after a pause.

I nod slowly. 'Don't ask me which one. It's easier if you don't know.'

He nods, leaves the drum kit and comes over to me, wrapping his arms around me in a colossal bear hug and holding me there. I could sleep in his arms right now. I could stay in his arms forever right now.

'It's obvious,' Brian says. 'It's Lizzy.'

I glance sharply across at Jasper. 'Why do you say that?' I ask, looking back as casually as I can manage at Brian.

'Because she's the Weyfare, so she might be able to help us get back,' he says as if it's that simple. 'Does she work here now, like her Mum used to?'

'Don't ask me things about the future,' I say more brightly than I feel. 'I bet that book says it's dangerous and you've already seen too much. We have to get you all back to 1987 so that you can come through to this time naturally.'

'And if we can't get back?' Rob asks, heart hammering against my own.

'Then, we stay. That suits me fine. Let my stepmonster try and find me here,' Kim says.

But none of the rest seems too sure. I remember how muddled me, Jasper and Ani all felt when we first went through the Weydoor.

I pull gently away from Rob and place a soft kiss on the side of his mouth. 'I'll be back.' I look over at Jasper and hope my BFF can read my mind. 'Don't go anywhere, any of you,' I say. He nods quickly, his usually lively face still and solemn. I hope he can convince them to wait for me because Brian is right. I'm going to find my mother.

I walk out of the Music Room and open the PA Block door onto the pathway down to the Main Hall, wishing I could lock them in. The music is full of bass that makes my stomach pound as I push through the fire doors into the Hall, and fight my way through the crowds staring at small screens, out towards the back, and the Entrance Hall. I thought I'd be lit to be back here, with everything normal, information screen scrolling motivational memes in Reception, up towards the Computing Centre on the third floor planning on going up to my mother's office, but suddenly she is standing there, on the staircase as if she's been waiting for me.

She's dressed differently from before I left, in faded blue denim jeans and a black vest top. Her hair is still short and greying though, and there's recognition in her eyes. Does she recognise me from over 30 years ago?

'You've come back, haven't you?' she says, only just loudly enough for me to here. 'Tonight. You went through the Wey-door tonight, and you've come back. Quick, in here. We don't have much time,' she says, pushing me down the stairs to the third floor and into a stock cupboard next door to an office.

I say that was a yes, then.

'Mother, I -' I stop speaking as she turns on the electric strip light and turns back to face me. This isn't my mother any more. She is Mum, and all the questions I have for her: all the accusations, the years of animosity, the endless arguing, the tears - they all vanish, and I throw myself into her arms, and she holds me close. Not for long enough, though. Not for nearly long enough.

'Are you okay? Lucas, Blake – Dad? Is everyone okay?'

'Don't speak, sweetness. Just listen, please. Everyone's fine. I know they are all here somewhere. Rob and the others. Have you left them somewhere safe? You've worked out who you are, haven't you?' I nod in answer to all her questions. 'I watched you leave tonight. I've been waiting for you to leave a Fund-raiser for a couple of years now. I couldn't remember which year you said it was, or exactly how old you were. I couldn't even remember which birthday present we used as your token. I couldn't watch to see if you came back in case I saw myself.'

She stops speaking, and she pulls a silver key out of her back pocket and holds it in her hands in front of me. We both look down at the key. In all my blurry thoughts about how and where this would happen, the last place I expected was here in a stock cupboard on the third floor at Drake's. The key looks heavy and solid, and I realise with a shock that it is solid silver, the top inlaid with black and purple stones. I can feel the energy coming off the metal, and my fingertips are tingling.

'You know you are Weyfare now. You know you would have been given your key on your 18th birthday. It's your grounding key, and it also unlocks the tunnel that connects the Old Library to the Shed in the back garden of Travellers' Rest.'

I'm about to tell her I know about the key, that we only came through the tunnel a few minutes ago, but I already have too many questions. 'Travellers' Rest? What is that?'

'The house on the edge of the Park. Your grandparents' old house.'

'You mean our house?' I say, frowning at her.

My stomach swoops in fear as she shakes her head. 'No, it's not our house. I used to live there with your Nan and Grandad, before -'

'What's happened?' I reach out for her hand. 'Why are you dressed like that? Why are we talking in here instead of in your office?'

'My office?'

'The Head's Office?' I say, thinking she's all cray since I've been travelling in Time.

'Why would you think that was my office?' Her eyes widen. 'Please don't tell me any more. Please. Don't tell me things about a life I haven't known and never will know.'

Like a hard smack in the face, it hits me. All my memories are of a different timeline. A timeline that has gone. None of my memories exists in reality. Her memories are different from mine. The enormity of this makes me sink down to the concrete floor and sit like a little girl, cross-legged in the dust while Mum tells me what I need to know.

'Listen to me now, sweetness, because I don't think we have much time. Scott stole my key today on your timeline, didn't he? It's so hard to remember that far back – it's been over 30 years.' I nod. I can't take all this in. 'Maisie, you have to go back to 1987 and get my key back because - well, it seems to set off a chain of events.' She swallows, and I realise she's trying not to cry.

'Did Scott go back there?' I ask.

She nods. 'Yes, my key took us both back to the moment we left 1987. Token Objects are special, they carry the energy of their Time, and the Weyfarere keys are ten times as powerful.'

'Token Objects?'

'Objects that are gifted to people,' she explains.

'Did he steal *The Truth*?' I ask.

She shrugs. 'I never found out. All I know about being a Weyfare is what we found out together back then. We never got the book back, and Nan didn't have time to tell me much more about being a Weyfare than you heard that morning.' Her voice breaks.

'Why not?' My voice sounds hollow in the tiny space. Surrounded by dusty plastic folders, printer paper and old computer hard drives, Mum sits down hard on a footstool. 'Why didn't Nan have time to tell you more?'

She is properly crying now, and now I am crying because she doesn't have to tell me what has happened; I just know it: in my bones, and my soul and my heart.

'No,' I whisper. 'No, you can't be telling me that.'

She shakes her head. 'I don't know what I'm telling you,' she tells me, her voice little more than a whisper. 'Nothing was ever proved, and they never found a body. She just vanished later that day. She said she had to go somewhere. She left the house, and we never saw her again. It was too much of a coincidence. It broke my dad into pieces and he never recovered.'

I crouch down beside her, tears still wet on my face. 'You think Glenda was extinguished? Like Ani? But that can't be right – you wouldn't exist – and neither would I, or my brothers.'

'I know, and it gives me hope that it wasn't extinction, but she did disappear; she never came back, and she would never have left your granddad, Maisie.' She holds out the key toward me. 'This was Joan's key. Joan was your great grandmother. She had dementia, though we didn't call it that back then, and she died young. When your grandad sold the house, we had to leave the safe behind, but he opened it before we left and took Joan's key from inside. Obviously, Nan's key disappeared when she did, and you know what happened to mine.'

Did Henry sell the house? I want to ask her why, but it is too important a moment.

'I am giving Joan's key to you, so now it should always anchor you to your natural timeline,' Mum takes it and places it around my neck. 'This is your key now,' she says, brightly.

'There wasn't a Weyfare left to give it to me, so I could never use it to go back, because it would have grounded me back to the time it was given to Joan. Now it is yours. Can you think of anything you can use as a token to get you back to 1987?'

'I think Kim is wearing the necklace Claire gave her over the weekend of your 18th.' I say, remembering her playing with it on the road as she told us of her escape.

'Use the key to boost the power of the necklace, and you should go back to that day. Find Scott. Stop him from stealing my key. Find our book. Find your Nan, and then come home to me.' She stops talking, and as she does so, I hear it. There's a slight shuffling sound outside the door as if someone is adjusting their position and a tiny metallic scrape.

Without warning, Mum springs to her feet, grabs a single metal file rack and throws herself against the store cupboard door. Instinctively, I leap out of the room after her and we tumble to the ground, me scraping my hands on the unswept floor, to be confronted by a man also sprawled on the floor behind the door, his smart gun-metal grey suit dusty and crumpled, a bunch of keys next to his knees.

Was he trying to lock us in?

'Run!' Mum yells, and I run as fast as I can down the staircase, not because I was ever particularly good at doing what my Mum says but because I have just looked into the dazed blue eyes of the man on the floor, and as I scramble to my feet, I see the nameplate across the door of the office next door.

Scott Kelly, School Business Manager.

Chapter Thirty – Don't Dream It's Over (Crowded House, 1987)

I'm running down the stairs two at a time, back into the Entrance Hall where the noise hits me again like a wall of sound after the quiet shattering revelations upstairs. I slide to a halt, as people are looking at me as if they're waiting for me to do something *Snapchat*-worthy, so I try hard to look casual, with my chest heaving and my hair a mess. They are starting to lose interest, until Mum cannons into the back of me and sends us both flying across the floor.

'Don't they give you mops to clean the floor any more, Mrs Wharton?' one of the girls quips. 'Got to use your kids to sweep up our crap?' Her friends laugh, everyone snaps a shot, and they walk away.

'Get up and keep moving,' Mum hisses into my ear, 'I didn't wallop him hard. He could be coming round now.'

'You hit him?' I get up and face her, her hair all sticking up all spiky like Rob's in 1987. Like Rob's in 2019. 'Mum. *Scott Kelly* is the Business Manager at Drake's?'

'Yes. I don't know who was here when you were here before, and I don't want to know now,' Mum says, leaning forward on her thighs as she gets her breath back. 'When Nan disappeared, Granddad went to pieces and lost his job. We couldn't afford to keep the house, and there seemed little point since we didn't have a key I could use to help bystanders.' She stands up straighter and gives me a sad smile. 'Scott bought the house. We need to move. Follow me.'

What?

She pushes through the crowds in the Main Hall, all the way back to the fire doors, and pulls me outside, where we can just about hear ourselves speaking. 'Truth is, Dad wanted to be free of it all, and then Scott offered Dad a stupid amount of money for our house. Dad didn't want to sell to him, but he couldn't turn down that sum, not having any work. Scott came into a lot of money when he turned 25 – a trust fund apparently, from his family business. We rented a few places until I met your Dad. He managed the Hippy shop in town.' The memory brightens her face. 'I got a job as a cleaner here to supplement the money the shop makes, and to be near the Weydoor for the day you came back through it. When Scott became the SBM here a couple of years ago, I thought he would try to sack me, but he cornered me once in his office and just laughed at me for still being here. He said he knew I'd never go through the Weydoor again because I'm too much of a coward to risk it without my key.' She looks at her black gym shoes and shakes her head. 'And he's right, I am, but I knew roughly when you were coming, and I don't think he did, and now you're here, and you can take everyone back through the Weydoor, and get my key back. And if you can stop your Nan disappearing, that would be beyond anything.'

'You've been waiting all this time?' I say slowly, thinking of the years behind her.

'Wondering, rather than waiting. Wondering who you would turn out to be,' she smiles, and it's almost shy. 'Wondering if you would even turn up. When I finally had a baby girl, I called her Maisie because I always liked your name, and then as you grew up I became more and more sure that you were actually the Maisie from that weekend. You're the image of me, at that age. You got your Dad's hair though.' She reaches out and lets a lock of my messy dark hair tumble through her fingers. 'I got the job as a cleaner here like your Nan, but I sent you to FCA in Year Twelve when Scott turned up and took up a post as a senior teacher, in case he recognised you as well. I'm pretty sure he doesn't realise that you are my daughter, but I'm sure he came to work here because he knew you were coming sometime and I don't know what he wants, Maisie, but I don't believe it can be good.'

My heart sinks into my dusty trainers. There's every chance Scott would know who I am, if he remembers meeting me at Trinity when I told him my surname was the same as the guy he worked with in the shop. Would he remember that over 30 years later?

'I knew I just had to wait until you came to find me during a Fundraiser.' She clasps my hands. Hers are cold and bony. She's had years of wanting to tell me, of wanting to solve the mystery, knowing she had to wait until I came back to her. Not being able to tell me my future. Her memories of my past are completely different from mine.

'This is actually my third Fundraiser this week,' I say, trying to bring a bit of humour into the situation. 'I'm a bit over Fundraisers now.'

'You might have to get used to them. I gave you your key today. On Fundraiser day,' she says. I sigh heavily, and then she pulls me to her and hugs me so tightly that I think my ribs will snap and pierce my breaking heart. 'Go now, quickly. I've kept you long enough. I'll deal with Scott here. You get the others back to 2019.' She plants a firm kiss on my hair before she pushes me away. 'Give my love to everyone. I never see them now.'

'Why don't you come with us?' I exclaim, the idea bursting into my head. 'You gave me the key, and if we stay together and always go through the Weydoor together, we'll always anchored here to my timeline!'

But she's shaking her head sadly, and I know what she's going to say before the words leave her lips. 'I'm 50 years old, Maisie. I can't go back to 1987. I'm already there as a teenager, like you and my friends. How would you explain me to any of them? How would I avoid my teenage self?' She looks down. 'I'm too old to take risks. I'm too scared. I guess I'm a coward when all is said and done.'

'I don't want to leave you here!' My eyes are smarting, and I'm trying to be strong, but I don't want to leave her here in this weirdsville that isn't her real home, even if she doesn't know any different.

'You have to,' she says gently. 'Please. I'll see you real soon. Now go.'

I wish I had time to think this through, but I know she's right. I wish I had time to look to see if Ani is here, but I don't. But I do have time for one thing. There should always be time for this. I throw my arms around her neck and bury my head, breathing in the warmth of security and love that I always knew I had, but pretty much had forgotten to appreciate.

'I will sort this out. It'll be like it was before. I love you,' I whisper. 'And don't call yourself a coward. Fuck, you're the bravest person I've ever met.'

'Language!' she yells after me as I run up the path to the PA block, and I know I hear her voice break.

They are waiting for me in the PA Block exactly where I left them: Rob is leaning against a large black speaker next to the drums; Kim and Brian are sitting on another lower speaker; Jasper is pacing the room. As I run in, they are all on their feet, and as I show them the silver key, they all step back.

'Lizzy gave you her key?' Rob asks in surprise. 'But I thought -'

'It's not her key. It's a long story,' I say, 'and we have no time for this now, we have to leave here before he finds us.'

'Before who finds us?' Kim asks, her voice shaky.

'Scott Kelly,' Jasper says. They all look at him in shock. 'I'm right though, aren't I?'

I look at my best friend. Finally, he's got his wish, and we've come home at last, and now I have to tell him that he can't stay. 'He's changed everything here, Jasper.'

'I know.' He points at a poster on the wall, and I see a framed recent colour newspaper cutting of Scott and two other olds surrounded by adoring Year Elevens with their GCSE passes under the headline, "A record year for school's new senior management". I nod.

'Scott is a teacher?' Kim asks, her eyes wide.

'We have to get you guys back home. Kim, do you have the necklace Claire gave you after the party at Trinity?' I ask.

She pulls it out from under her T-Shirt. 'I haven't taken it off since. It's here.'

'Thank whoever's listening,' I say. 'Can you let me have it?'

She undoes the clasp at the back and pours the orange plastic stones into my cupped hands. I feel Rob's eyes boring into me, but I can't meet the look. There is no time. I take the key, and I rub it gently over the necklace, the way we watched Lizzy do it little more than an hour ago.

It's quieter outside now, and there are fewer people as we slip down to where the paths join and then up again to the Old Library. But when we get there, the door is not only shut. Someone has locked it.

'I've been wondering whether or not you lot would make an appearance at this Fundraiser,' he says, appearing like a spectre from the darkness at the side of the building. 'I remember the music, but not the year. It's been a long time. Details become blurred.'

'Not for us, it hasn't been a long time,' I say more bravely than I feel, hoping the wobble in my voice isn't too noticeable. 'You stole Lizzy Brookes' key about an hour ago.'

'Isn't time travel fascinating?' he says, and smiles the same lazy grin as he had in 1987, except there are deep lines around Scott's twinkling blue eyes now, eyes that seem to me to twinkle with malevolence rather than fun, and the blond hair is cropped and mostly white, a goatee on his chin and receding from his head. His voice is clipped and different like he's been educated somewhere expensive. 'Here we are, what is it – 30 something years on and you don't look a day older, any of you!'

He gives a little laugh, and I sense rather than watch the others as they move around to defend me. 'Speak for yourself, you're a crumbly old man,' I say.

'You still fancy the pants off me,' he says smoothly.

'You're totally ratchet,' I say, my cheeks glowing. 'Disgusting old perv.'

'And yet I am living such a very fulfilling life! What a charming coincidence it was when lovely Lizzy came into the shop that day. There was me, thinking I was simply having a bit of fun with a fiery sixth-former when out of the blue, she starts bleating on about time travel. And I've waited all these years to make sure you didn't stop me getting my hands on that key. I needn't have worried. What a difference it's made to my life.' He takes a step closer to me, and Rob takes a step forward to match it. 'Still defending your lovely girl, Rob. Cute. Your mother would be so proud.' He chuckles again and stares at my chest, and I am totally grossed out until I realise he's looking at my key. 'I'm looking out of the window of my very plush and luxurious office when what do I see but darling little Maisie, walking down the path to the Main Hall as bright and shiny as she looked when I met her all those years ago. And here you are now, with yet another one of those delightful shiny keys! I confess I didn't see that one coming. I wonder where this one will take us. Perhaps you should hand it over to me.' He turns sharply to stare at me, and his tone turns sour and cold so quickly that it's like a spirit has passed in the breeze.

'That's so never going to happen,' I say, tucking it back inside my T-Shirt.

'I'll tell you what, Maisie. I'll do you a swap,' he says lightly as if he's trying to make himself sound like he used to. 'I'll give you the key that I just used to lock this door. You go through to the Weydoor and send your friends back to their timeline. I'm sure they've got something on them that will ground them;

you can power it up, and I'll have your key in return for their safe passage home.' He pulls his hand out of his suit jacket pocket, and a bunch of keys of all shapes and sizes dangle down from his fingers. 'You can't say fairer than that.'

Jasper nudges me from behind. I know what he's thinking, but I can't tell him out loud that no, I don't have the key I stole from Mum's office the first time we were here, investigating the possibility of a door through Time. I don't even know where that key is; after I failed to open the Old Library door in 1987, I probably just dropped it somewhere.

'You stole Lizzy's key. You're not having another one,' Kim says. 'Why would you want even another one?'

'Why, indeed? Interestingly, where did Maisie get that key? From Lizzy, I'm guessing. More interestingly is why Lizzy would give it to you,' he says, thoughtfully, stroking his silvery beard, still holding out the bunch of keys, 'after all, I thought it was only Weyfarere that were allowed to own the keys. Unless you're Weyfare as well, pretty little Maisie? Wouldn't that be a turn up for the books?'

'You've got a key as well, *Mister* Kelly, 'I snap back at him, hoping the others will miss the fact that he has a valid point. 'Maybe even two of them. Are you a woman? Because the last I heard, only women can be Weyfarere. Not arrogant thieving bastards like you.'

His face twists into a comic-book rictus, and there is a loud noise behind me. I spin around as a surge of teenage girls and boys come flooding out of the Main Hall, cheering and shouting and laughing and they push past ignoring us, power in their numbers as they grab hold of their senior manager.

'Mr Kelly! Mr Kelly! You've got to come and dance a slow

with Mrs Wharton!' one of the girls shrieks. I recognise her from my English Lit. group but she's having way too much fun to notice me having yet another life-changing moment.

'She said she'd donate 100 quid to the Fundraiser if you dance with her!' another boy shouts.

They all start at him then and grab onto him, and they start pulling him away from the Old Library door, amidst many cries of 'Oh come on, Sir; don't be all boring about it; it's for a good cause,' and so on.

We stand to the side as he is virtually carried past us, trending on everybody's *Snapchat*. I see the moment it dawns on him: when he understands he is a senior member of staff here, that he can't be seen to do the wrong thing by refusing this dance, and the light goes out in his eyes as he knows he's lost us. I risk a smile, but we're not safe yet.

As they manhandle him through the fire doors into the Main Hall, something metallic flies above the crowd's heads and lands with a tinkle on the pathway between them and us. It is a set of keys. Scott's collection of keys.

'Leave them on the table!' I hear her scream above the rabble, but I can't see her, and I know we're not supposed to. I run forward and pick up the keys, and quickly unlock the Old Library door.

'Mrs Wharton?' Rob says behind me as I open the door. 'That's your name, isn't it?'

'No relation. Just one of the staff here,' The lie comes easily out of my mouth.

'And the keys?' Brian asks.

'Lizzy,' I say, telling the truth this time.

We run down the length of the old, crumbling building,

and face the purple light framing the Weydoor again. I chuck Scott's school keys onto the nearest table. I hold Kim's necklace and my key against the Weydoor, make sure we are all holding hands, and then my arm just seems to slip through the books as if they are a kind of projection, and the next thing I know we're falling against the bookshelves, and there's white heat, purple light, black – nothing.

It is quiet in the Old Library as I open my eyes, and I see the moonlight coming through the high windows that line the old stone walls. Rob is behind me, his arm over my waist. Brian is crumpled under the nearest table, and Kim and Jasper are propped up against a bookcase. Moonlight. I wonder for a second if we are back.

Then the alarm goes off.

We are all sluggish and hardly thinking straight, but I know it'll take the caretaker a few minutes to come across from his house and investigate why the alarm has gone off in the Old Library. Pulling the key out on its chain while the others stagger to their feet, I look frantically for the book Lizzy couldn't remember the name of. Luck is finally with us as I see a spine covered in purple leather that says 'Resten of Weyfarere' because I know where I have seen those runes before, and sure enough when I push hard against the spine, it slides out to reveal a keyhole embedded in the front of what is a fake book. I use my key, turn it once, and the whole bookcase swings forward to reveal the tunnel behind.

We manage to get into the narrow stone tunnel and close the door on the Old Library before Frank comes to investigate, but without Lizzy's torchlight, it is a lengthy and challenging journey along in the darkness to Lizzy's house. At least, I hope it is still her house. I have no idea whether Kim's necklace worked. We could have come back to any day in any year. I'm suddenly scared about what I might find now at the other end of the tunnel.

As I push up the trapdoor, with Kim and Rob's help, I emerge like a little mole into the darkness of the wooden room and peer through the window at the row I can hear outside. I realise the reality of our situation is less dangerous but no less complicated than I thought. There are loud bouts of laughter and raucous voices coming from outside the Old Shed.

'Kim, when did Claire give you that necklace?' I ask.

'After the party at Trinity,' she says, climbing up the stone steps from the tunnel below.

'So it should have brought us back to that point in Time,' I say. 'Lizzy's 18th. May 23rd. We're a day early.'

'It's Saturday night then,' Rob says, wiping the dirt from his eyes as he emerges into the little room. 'It's the day of Lizzy's party. All her rellies are still here.'

'That's awkward,' Kim says.

'So where are we?' Jasper asks.

'In the Old Shed,' I tell him.

'No, crazyfool,' he snaps. 'Where are the other we's?'

'Shit,' I exclaim. 'There's two of all of us! We must still be up at Trinity!'

'Well, that's going to be a massive cock-up then because we can't meet our other selves. I need to do some research into this time-travelling lark, but I can't see how two of me in the past can be any better than two of me in the future,' Brian says, pushing the trapdoor closed.

'No. We have to stay out of the way until we've - they've gone back to 2019,' I say. 'Then it'll just be us again.'

'You mean forward,' Jasper says.

'Have we got to stay in here until tomorrow afternoon then?' Kim asks.

By now we are all standing in the dirty little wooden room, looking at each other in the light of the enormous lamps coming through the window from the garden and reflecting on the metal of the hanging tools; the trapdoor in the floor closed and locked by my key.

Rob takes my hands in both of his, and the atmosphere in the Shed is instantly dry and airless. 'I guess this is goodbye then,' he says, his voice gravelly with emotion. 'You've done what Lizzy asked. You brought us back here. Now I suppose you have to go back.'

The others turn away, clearly not wanting to be present at such a painful moment for us both but not knowing where to go. Suddenly, the shed is claustrophobically small.

I sigh. 'I said all along it would have to end like this. You knew that.' He nods and leans forward to kiss me, and I can see the streak of a single tear like a rivulet running down the tunnel dirt on his pale cheek, and I can't bear it. I stop him, my hand gently against his chest. 'But I had a long chat with Lizzy.' He looks down, confused. 'It doesn't end like this for us. Not now, anyway.'

'What exactly did she tell you?' Jasper asks.

'She wanted me to come back to 1987 with you all. That's why she … lent me the key. It's the only one she had. But Scott Kelly has done something to the future of … her family and she wants me,' I hesitate, 'she wants us to stop him.' I turn and face Jasper. 'I know how much you wanted to go home,' I say, 'but you saw the poster on the wall. You saw him. That place that we've just come from, it isn't ours. I'm not even sure it's safe there any more. You have to be here. For now.'

'I saw enough,' he says. 'I get it,' and of course, out of all of them he does get it the most because he's still the only one that knows I'm Lizzy's daughter, he's the only one who knows I'm Weyfare, and it has to stay a secret. Rubbing the skin on his fingers as if he wants to pull it off, he adds, 'I get it, but what about extinction? What if one of us vanishes like Ani did?'

'I'm pretty sure I have to prevent it from happening to Lizzy's Mum first,' I say, and his mouth falls open, as everyone else gawps. 'We have to help her.'

'Glenda's going to become extinct too?' Brian says. 'Because of Scott?'

'Are you sure?' Jasper asks. 'Was Lizzy sure?'

'No.' I rub my dirty hands over my face and hope that I don't look like I'm wearing a mudpack. 'She wanted us to find *The Truth* and her key. She wanted us to make sure her mum is safe.'

Jasper looks so distressed that I step forward to comfort him, but Kim is there first. 'Don't be sad,' she chirps. 'We'll sort it all out. If you are staying here for a while, we'll get a chance to get to know you better.' The most wicked grin I think I've ever seen crosses her face. Leaving home suits Kim.

Jasper manages a wry smile.

'And Ani?' Brian asks.

'If I can get this sorted out for Lizzy, I promise I will help you look for her myself,' I say. 'Is that good enough?'

He shrugs and looks around. 'It'll have to do. Sounds like we're going to be busy chasing after scumbag thieves for the time being. And we've all got exams to cram for.'

'Why cram? We can come back here as often as you like with Kim's necklace, and you can have as much time as you like to revise,' I say.

Brian plays the tune on his imaginary trumpet. 'Hadn't thought of that. Major result.'

I turn back to Rob, who is waiting patiently for me to re-assure him, my lovely fit boy from the past with his green eyes glistening with tears he's hoping he no longer has to shed. 'So you see, I can't go back yet. Do you think you can put up with me being around for a little more time?' He grabs me in reply and hugs me to him so hard, I swear my ribs crack as he buries his lips against my hair. 'Totes Amazeballs then,' I wheeze.

He holds me away so that he can look at me. 'Have I ever told you how bizarre you speak?' he says, laughing.

'Yes, but we're not the tards around here. It's you guys who talk weird. Here, in way back when,' I tell him.

Way back when, where I've made friends with my teenage Mum and all her wild and whacko friends. Where I've started to fall for one of them, where one of my best friends vanished, and where I'm still determined to find out what happened to her. Where I found out my Mum and my Nan were Weyfarere, and where I discovered that I was born a Weyfare too, des-cended from a family of ancient Guardians born to protect the hidden doors that cross Time itself. Where whoever Scott Kelly is, and whatever he has stolen from my family - Lizzy's Key, maybe *The Truth* and even perhaps my Nan - I'm here to find out, and I'm going to make him give them back.

'So there's a party out there, full of pissed old people,' I say, smiling in spite of everything. 'We're going to go outside, and just act normal.'

'Normal? Here?' Jasper says.

'I've never been normal not one day of my life,' Brian says.

'Won't they think it's weird that we're not with Lizzy?' Kim asks.

Rob squeezes my hand. 'Are you sure this is going to work?'

I squeeze his hand back. 'We'll just blend in,' I say. 'Worked fine for us before.'

We all step out of the Old Shed one by one, and I'm ready to gatecrash my mum's 18th birthday party. Again.

So, how did Lizzy end up in 2019?

To receive your FREE short story, *The Wey We Were*, all you have to do is tell me where to send it.

I'll also send you details of other events, such as book deals, new launches, and other freebies, but I promise I won't overload your mailbox!

Grab your free story today!

Did you enjoy this book?

Do you want to make an author happy today?

Reviews are one of the most effective ways for me to attract new readers for my books.

Honest reviews help other readers to make the decision to give the Weys a try.

If you enjoyed this book, I would be forever grateful if you could leave a review. It doesn't have to be long, but it might make all the difference.

You can review by clicking on the links below:

UK

US

Thank you.

ABOUT THE AUTHOR

S. J. Blackwell

I'm a British indie author with a love of adventure, romance and nostalgia. I've been a teacher, a strawberry picker, a costing clerk, a research assistant and a frozen fruit packer, but I'm happiest as a writer and reader of books.

When I escape to the past, I'm usually curled up writing in my magical den at the bottom of the garden with the foxes and the pixies. Occasionally, you can find me adventuring in my vintage camper van or playing with my two very soppy greyhounds.

READY FOR THE NEXT PART OF THE JOURNEY?

Wey Back in Time ... where 20th Century time travel meets enduring love and English folklore.

Wey Back When - Book 1

Meet Maisie Wharton. She's invited to a party this weekend, but it's in 1987, and it's her mother's 18th birthday ...

No Wey Of Knowing - Book 2

It's 1987 - Maisie's got a secret now and it changes everything ...

Long Wey Round - Book 3

It's New Year's Eve 1971 and, like 1972, Maisie's journey through time is just beginning ...

Works Both Weys - Book 4

More problems, more choices - now Maisie's back in time, dancing with the Mermaid in 1979 ...

Any Which Wey - Book 5

The past, present and future are catching up with her, but 1987 hasn't finished with Maisie yet ...

Jingle All The Wey - Book 5.5

A seasonal standalone novella that sits between Seasons One and Two. When a cherished family keepsake goes missing, Lizzy and Kim take a new recruit back to 1973 to find it. But it's Christmas, and maybe a few other wishes will be coming true ...

One Wey Or Another - Book 6

She thought she was safe and sound, time travelling days all done, Now trouble's chasing Maisie down in 1981 ...

Look The Other Wey - Book 7

Is returning to 1981 worth the cost, when Maisie's future is bleak and so much remains lost?

Wey Past Caring - Book 8

Will love still prevail in 1974, and will Maisie get to settle the score?

Weys And Means - Book 9

Expected summer 2022!

Printed in Great Britain
by Amazon

84028396R00192